MYSTERY IN FORT RICHFIELD

Raspberry Press

CRYSTAL TAMBOLINE

Mystery In Fort Richfield by Crystal Tamboline

Copyright © 2025 Crystal Tamboline

Published by Raspberry Press

Raspberry
Press
www.raspberrypress.ca

For more information, or to book an event, contact:
crystalbill@telus.net
Paperback: ISBN: 978-1-0698909-0-0
Ebook ISBN: 978-1-0698909-1-7

This book is dedicated to my family and friends, former teachers, colleagues and students, all of whom have inspired me and supported me in my writing endeavours.

Thank you for being a never-ending source of encouragement.

CHAPTER ONE

Saturday, April 27th, 2024

It seemed like your average quiet spring evening where the soft breeze scented the air with the sweet, fragrant smell of fresh-cut grass. Yet tonight, something felt different. There was a heaviness in the air as though the atmosphere had been blanketed in a thick fog. I forced myself to rise from the comfort of the soft, velvety sofa and the knitted blanket that wrapped around me, encompassing me in warmth. Carefully, I pulled open the middle slat of the blinds with my forefinger and thumb and peeked out ever so slightly, my eyes darting about like a laser. Deep in the dark, foreboding brush directly behind my backyard, I caught a glimpse of glowing amber eyes peering back at me, eyes that were headlights in the vastness of the night. I gasped and fell backward towards the sofa, falling in a mangled heap on the velvet cushion. I could not come to grips with what I had just witnessed. Was my mind playing tricks on me? It wasn't unusual for my mind to imprint atypical images into my head, to allow my imagination to manifest dark and foreboding threats. In perfect synchronicity, I would try to talk myself down and convince myself that what I thought I had seen was all part of my overly active imagination. But this time, I wasn't so sure.

Things haven't been normal, or at least my kind of normal, since Ellie Mason had mysteriously vanished one spring night two years ago. She was one of the popular girls, a junior at Richfield High. She was a cheerleader with perfect hair and body, the type all the boys fantasized about. Me, not so much. I wasn't the type a maniacal serial killer would typically target, but I still had lingering fears since no trace of Ellie had ever been found. No one knows what happened to her, but the rumours were rampant. Some say that she went crazy and took her own life; others claim that she was kidnapped and tortured by an unknown assailant. Still, others argue that a mysterious creature lurks in the woods, waiting with hungry eyes and a voracious appetite for flesh. I have to admit, after this unconventional sighting in the brush, I'm starting to lean heavily toward that theory.

I sat on the sofa quietly, trying to free my mind from the terrorizing thoughts lingering in my head. Naturally, as an anxious person, this wasn't an effortless task. I grabbed a novel from the bookshelf beside the sofa and tried to engross myself in someone else's trials and tribulations. I hoped that the distraction of fiction and fantasy would quell my fears: no such luck, none, nada. I grabbed the remote from the side table, hoping that the drama-filled lives of teenage socialites would fill my imagination with nonsensical images of love, hate, and passion-fueled romance. Nope, that wasn't going to work either. I couldn't get the gears inside my brain to stop churning with these dreadful images of fear and murder.

I begrudgingly decided to pick up the phone and call Jenny. Jenny was my closest friend. We had been friends since Kindergarten, and our friendship was more akin to twin sisters. We could read each other's thoughts and finish one another's sentences. We even dressed alike on occasion, although not on purpose. These were only a few examples of the quirks we shared and one of many ways we communicate our thoughts and dreams, as if almost telepathically.

Although Jenny and I were close, I always hesitated to share these types of thoughts with her. Unlike myself, Jenny didn't share in the same kind of anxiety-fueled drivel that I often engrossed myself in. She was the more level-headed one who grounded me and made me question my sanity. I feared that Jenny would question me again for believing I had seen eerie glowing eyes peering straight into my soul from the dark backyard brush. It's not that I didn't appreciate her efforts to try to calm my mind; it was more about my anxieties about her not believing me.

I slowly dialled each number as if it pained me to touch them with my fingertips. The phone's ring echoed endlessly as if I were in an infinite time loop. Suddenly, I heard the familiar "Hello" as Jenny picked up to greet me.

"Hey Jenn… It's Kacey. Can we talk for a bit?" My voice wavered in anticipation of her response. I was sure she could hear the dread in my voice.

"Sure," she responded with a questioning tone.

"Jenn… I think I saw something."

"Saw what?" she asked.

"I'm not sure," I said with quivering lips.

"Kacey, I'm going to come over, okay?"

"Okay," I replied as she hung up the phone.

I waited in deafening silence for the familiar knock-knock on the door. We had our secret knock, so I always knew when it was Jenny. When the familiar knock echoed loudly in the vast entryway of my home, I quickly got up with anticipation and opened the door. Jenny stood with stoic grace and looked at me with concern.

"Tell me all about what happened," she said, almost demandingly.

I hesitated to tell her at first. I could feel that same old self-questioning doubt creeping in. I had to remind myself that I decided to call Jenny. I couldn't call her and let her waste her time coming over to soothe me. What kind of a friend would that make me?

"So," Jenny said, "You gonna tell me what's going on or what?"

As I delineated the details of what I had witnessed in the brush behind my house, Jenny looked at me with wide blue eyes. Her facial expression was blank, but her eyes always gave her genuine emotions away.

"Kacey..." she said with a voice as calm as a soft summer breeze. "I think I saw the same thing."

CHAPTER TWO

Two Years Earlier: Friday, April 29th, 2022

Jenny and I were both anxious, but in a favourable way, for the upcoming Spring Fling Dance. We had never been to a school dance before or had dates. As a Sophomore in high school, the experience felt fresh and exhilarating. Jenny and I revelled in the joy of our newly acquired dresses when the mood suddenly shifted from light and carefree to dark and pessimistic. It was as though the entire student body powered down like an electric generator. Jenny and I ceased our conversation and snapped our heads back like a whip to see what caused this dramatic shift. Ellie Mason was parading down the hall like a model, silken hair flowing like a river. Her usual clique of friends surrounded her, following on her heels like lost puppy dogs looking for approval. It wouldn't be an exaggeration if I told you that you could hear a pin drop. The entire student body stopped in their tracks, almost as if they had witnessed the second coming of Christ. The shrill laugh from Ellie's rose-coloured lips broke the deafening silence. As Ellie and her band of merry misfits strolled closer to Jenny and me, I felt my body tense like a guitar string ready to release from tightened fingers. I inhaled deeply, and Jenny looked over at me with apprehension.

"What's going on, ladies?" Ellie snickered mockingly.

I hesitated for a split second, and just like she always did, Jenny read my mind and retorted sarcastically, "Why do you even care? It's not like we're friends."

I looked over at Jenny with gratitude and relief. I always had difficulty speaking up for myself, and Jenny knew this too well. It paid to have a friend with so much confidence and gusto.

"Wee bit snippy today, huh?" Ellie replied bluntly.

Jenny smirked. "I follow by example," she replied matter-of-factly.

Ellie huffed, nettled by Jenny's response, and stormed off with a look of sheer annoyance, her minions following close behind.

"What a bitch," Jenny said mockingly. "I wonder if she ever wakes up in the morning and asks herself how she can be even more of a bitch today than yesterday?"

I laughed softly, and we continued down the hall just as the warning bell for the first period rang out obnoxiously.

"I'll catch up with you later, Kace. Have a great morning."

"You too, Jenn," I hastily replied as I raced down the hall.

I arrived at my English class and sauntered my way to my desk. Ellie was sitting in the front row, trying to inconspicuously use her cell phone camera to check her makeup and hair. I couldn't help but smirk as I walked past.

She briefly looked up from her beauty consultation, and our eyes met. Her eyes were bright blue icicles penetrating me like an X-ray.

"Anything I can help you with?" she hissed.

My gaze shifted expeditiously, and without uttering a word, I brushed past her and settled into my desk at the back of the classroom. I did not have the prowess or desire to hash it out with Ellie.

Mr. Jenkins was sitting at his desk, rifling through a stack of papers a mile high. He looked up with wire-rimmed glasses over the top of the mountainous heap obstructing his view.

"We will be starting shortly," he murmured, almost unintelligibly. "Please get out your novel and your notes package."

I fumbled clumsily in my backpack, desperately looking for my materials. I'm typically quite organized; however, today, in my endeavour to get out the door and arrive at school post-haste, I was less than prepared for English class. In the kerfuffle of my organized chaos, I managed to find my novel and notes package. It came at a price as my phone slipped out of my pocket and thudded tumultuously onto the cold, hard, tiled floor. At that moment, it was as if time stood still. I looked around sheepishly, hoping that my fumble had gone unnoticed. All eyes were affixed elsewhere except, of course, Ellie, who stared at me in amusement. Her eyes, like daggers, burned through my soul, and I could suddenly feel the heat creeping into my cheekbones.

"What's the matter, Kacey?" she sneered. "You got butter fingers or something?"

She laughed shrilly, and then I noticed the other students

staring at me with pure hilarity in their eyes. I loathed the fact that Ellie had that type of power over people. It was as though her mere presence commanded attention. I hesitated to admit that I often dreamed of the day she would just up and disappear, never to be seen again. I scorned myself for having such thoughts. No matter how loathsome my thoughts of Ellie were, it wasn't acceptable to wish someone harm.

"Settle down," Mr. Jenkins commanded with more authority. "If you're not here to learn, I suggest you leave. Now, let's open our novels to Chapter Six. Ellie, I want you to start reading."

Ellie heaved a sigh of angst and reluctantly began to read out loud. I smiled smugly to myself. It was nice knowing Mr. Jenkins was on my side, even if he remained oblivious.

Time seemed to trickle slowly like a faucet. The scenario with Ellie played on repeat like a skipping record. No matter how hard I tried, I could not fathom how someone could be so vicious, feared, and yet simultaneously revered. Suddenly, I was jolted out of my thoughts by the loud dismissal bell ringing. Had I spent the entire period daydreaming? I couldn't recall anything, not even the melodramatic production of Ellie's Chapter Six reading. I rose ever so slowly from my desk and grabbed my backpack in maladroit fashion, lumbering clumsily to the door. Mr. Jensen called out faintly.

"Kacey, could you come here for a minute? I want to discuss something with you quickly."

"Uhmmm… sure, Mr. Jenkins," I replied, somewhat bewildered.

"Look, it's obvious that there is some sort of opposition

between you and Ellie, and I can tell that it's affecting your performance in class. Please let me know what I can do to help. I'm also planning on conversing with Ellie and possibly her parents."

"Thanks, Mr. Jenkins," I replied, "I think it might help if Ellie could sit closer to your desk. That way, I don't have to walk past her, and with you right there beside her, maybe she won't bother talking to me."

"I think that can be arranged," Mr. Jenkins responded. "Perhaps I'll change the entire seating plan. That way, it won't appear I'm targeting anyone in particular."

"I appreciate it, Mr. Jenkins. Thank you. See you tomorrow."

"See you tomorrow, Kacey."

I rushed out with a sense of urgency. I was already late for period two, but I knew Mr. Jenkins would call to let Ms. Chalice know I was on my way. There was no question about it; Mr. Jenkins had my back. Perhaps he wasn't so oblivious after all.

Endless as a marathon with no finish line, the day dragged on, stretching like shadows reluctant to leave at sunset. When the dismissal bell finally rang out triumphantly at the end of the day, to say I felt a sense of reprieve was no exaggeration. I waited eagerly for Jenny at her locker. I couldn't wait to recount the events of the day with her. While I might have occasionally danced around revealing specific details to her, this particular moment demanded immediate attention. When I finally saw her gallantly trotting down the hall, I couldn't help but smile, teeth sparkling like diamonds. She smiled back with gleaming eyes.

"What's with the smile?" Jenny asked with intense fascination.

"Mr. Jenkins agreed to change the seating plan in English class. No more Ellie drama, or at least I hope," I grinned impishly.

Jenny stared at me with stone-cold eyes. I momentarily questioned why I had been so excited to share this tidbit of information with her. Her piercing gaze etched a hole into my heart. A lump crept into my throat, and I swallowed hard, my eyes shimmering like dewdrops. Although Jenny's eyes were usually the window into her soul, I had difficulty deciphering this chilly stare. She suddenly cracked a smile and began to laugh hysterically.

"Kacey, you're so gullible. I can't believe you would think I don't care about your Ellie drama." She gave me a wink, followed by a big, warm hug. "I've got you. You never have to doubt that."

I smiled foolishly, trying to gain back some dignity. How could I ever doubt Jenny's intentions? She had done nothing but back me up in every drama-filled situation and every anxiety attack, regardless of how absurd.

"I know, I know," I said sheepishly. "I'm sorry, Jenny. I never should have questioned your sincerity. Can you ever forgive me for my decrepitly doubtful mind?"

Jenny grinned warmly, her smile emitting rays of sunshine. "Of course, silly. Now, let's go to Finnegan's Diner and get a milkshake. We can talk about our plans for Spring Fling over some appetizers."

"Sure," I said. "But I want to order the chocolate marshmallow milkshake and split an order of chilli cheese fries and wings."

"Done and done," Jenny replied, smiling.

The two of us promenaded down the street arm in arm, laughing at the most trivial interactions we had encountered with the queen shrew herself, Ellie.

CHAPTER THREE

Saturday, April 27th, 2024

I met Jenny's eyes with incredulous wonder. Did she admit to observing the same glowing amber eyes, the same amber eyes that illuminated like headlights in the vastness of the night? So much relief washed over me that my eyes trickled with tears. I wasn't crazy, I thought, Jenny had just validated my observation.

"Wait, what? You saw the same thing," I gasped in astonishment. "When? Why didn't you say anything?" The words came tumbling out of my mouth rapidly like a waterfall. I was surprised that Jenny could even comprehend what I was saying.

"Honestly, Kacey, I wasn't sure what I had seen. It was late, and it was dark and foggy. I had just left work, and I was super tired. I know some wildlife venture into town occasionally, so I likened my observation to that. You know how some animals have eyes that give off a shine? I thought it might have been a deer, a coyote, or a raccoon. I never really gave it much thought. The colour of the eyes was a wee bit unusual, but it wasn't enough to make me question things any further. This occurred maybe three or four nights ago."

I stared at Jenny in disbelief. How could she brush this whole thing off as though it were simply some random animal encounter? How could she possibly believe this wasn't a symbol of something more dark and sinister? How? Especially considering that other residents of Fort Richfield had reported the same amber-coloured eyes on the very night Ellie had vanished. I was dumbstruck. I was livid. I was confused. But mostly, I was disappointed. I couldn't wrap my head around her complacency.

"Jenny," I questioned curiously, "what would make you think this was the work of a random animal? Don't you think it's peculiar that other town residents reported this same thing on the night Ellie disappeared?"

Jenny paused briefly, her eyes reflecting deep thoughts of contemplation. Then, as she awoke from the reverie, she shattered the enchantment of contemplation with a decisive burst of clarity.

"Kace, you're right. It never occurred to me that the town's residents had observed those same amber eyes on that chilling night. How could I have overlooked the obvious connection? I'm deeply sorry if my failure to acknowledge this caused you distress."

Jenny's face portrayed every single word sincerely. I knew she wasn't bluffing. As usual, her eyes revealed her thoughts with clarity. And why would she bluff? We were friends, after all, best friends. If I could genuinely trust anyone, it would be her.

"No need to apologize, Jenn. I'm just glad you made the connection between these seemingly random events. Besides, we're friends, and friends forgive friends, right?"

"Right," Jenny chuckled with a sigh of relief.

A few hours passed in the blink of an eye. Jenny and I delved into the archives of our past, recalling the days when we painted vibrant pictures of liberated life beyond the confines of teenagehood. Briefly soaring beyond the confines of reality's shackles was a welcome respite. Swiftly, the weighty embrace of real-life descended upon us, shattering our fleeting reprieve, crunching like dry brown leaves crushing into the earth under heavy foot. Then, a bellowing growl, like a hungry wolf, threatened our brief escape from reality.

"What on earth was that?" I cried out nervously.

I had to summon my inner detective and pry open the blinds to unveil the source of the alarming noise outside. I squinted, my eyes struggling to adjust to the darkness. I scanned the brush beyond my yard, looking left, right, up, and down. Nothing. There was no sign of any threat. I was perplexed.

"You heard that, right?" I asked Jenny in terror.

She looked over at me, equally as terrified, and nodded her head. Her eyes, like saucers holding back tears, scanned the brush. Her mouth suddenly gaped, and a gasp of horror escaped. My eyes followed the path of her index finger, which pointed straight like an arrow. Amber eyes glowing with a threatening gaze. I tried to scream, but the deafening silence swallowed the sound. Time stood still, or so it felt. I grabbed Jenny's arm and pulled her upstairs into the safety of my bedroom. I wasn't taking any chances. We locked the door and skillfully barricaded ourselves into my bedroom closet. We remained ensconced within our haven, hesitating to venture out until the comforting rumble of my parents' car echoed in the driveway.

"Kacey, where are you?" my mother called out.

She sounded concerned. Usually, I would sit on the sofa, remote in hand, drink nearby, and have snacks ready for immediate consumption. My absence seemingly had her baffled. Jenny and I dashed down the staircase with spirited haste. My Mom's face broke out into a slight grin.

"Oh, there you are," she said. "I was wondering where you had gone off to. Hi Jenny, how are you? How are your parents?"

Jenny and I exchanged a quick and subtle glance. We knew we couldn't tell my Mom what we had just seen. I didn't want to rehash tonight's events, and I certainly didn't want to reopen old wounds. The town and its people had been through enough and didn't need to be dragged down the rabbit hole again.

"Hey, Mrs. Lundgren," Jenny greeted my mother casually. "How are you and Mr. Lundgren?"

"We're doing great, Jenny, thank you for asking. We will be getting ready for dinner soon. Did you want to join us?" my mother inquired.

"Uhmmm…sure, that sounds great."

"Hey, Mom," I asked, "Is it alright if Jenny spends the night? It's getting late, and Jenny's parents are out of town. I don't want her to spend the night alone."

"I don't see why not. It's a Saturday night, and we don't have anything planned for Sunday. Jenny, did you want to borrow a pair of Kacey's pajamas? I've also got a couple of brand-new toothbrushes in the drawer of the upstairs bathroom. Feel free to take one."

"Thanks, Mrs. Lundgren, I sure appreciate it."

"Anytime, sweetheart, you're family."

Dinner was your typical family gathering, with small talk and a regaling celebration of the day's events. Everyone seemed to have some boisterous story except for Jenny and me. The two of us sat quietly, chewing with such determination that you'd be wise to believe our teeth had rotted and fallen out. A few anxious glances were exchanged occasionally, but nobody appeared to catch wind of it. It wasn't long before we gathered the dishes and cleaned the table.

"Hey, Mom," I said softly, "Is it okay if Jenny and I go upstairs? We need to go over a project for Science class."

"Of course," she replied merrily, "You two go and get some work done. I'll see you both in the morning. Good night."

"Good night," we both replied in unison.

Like twin rockets propelled into orbit, we skyrocketed up the stairs, fueled by an eagerness to dissect and discuss every detail we had witnessed and heard. We puzzled for hours, coming up with every wild scenario one could imagine before Jenny's eyes became heavy with exhaustion. It wasn't long before I heard her snoring faintly in peaceful slumber.

"Good night, Jenn," I whispered before I tucked myself snugly under the blanket and prepared myself for my nightly rest.

CHAPTER FOUR

Friday, May 6th, 2022

The week had fast-forwarded, and Friday gracefully took center stage. Time had raced so swiftly that Friday's arrival felt like a dream's fleeting embrace. Jenny and I were bubbling with excitement, eagerly anticipating the dance tonight. Our gowns gracefully awaited their moment, suspended on our closet doors like eager performers ready for their dazzling entrance. We envisioned our rendezvous, anticipating a Cinderella moment when our dates would herald the grand ball's arrival. Jenny and I dedicated weeks to orchestrating the perfect symphony of hair and makeup for tonight's grand reveal. We giggled like middle schoolers, daydreaming of our high school dance debut. It was refreshing to feel that whimsy once again. Jenny and I had spent many nights planning the perfect dance scenario and envisioning our definition of the ideal guy. I'm not entirely confident that our dates fit the predetermined definition, but ultimately, it didn't matter. We were ecstatic nonetheless. The bell for the first period rang with a resounding echo and awakened us from our daydream.

"I guess we'd better get going, huh?" I said to Jenny somewhat sarcastically.

"I suppose," Jenny sighed.

We both hesitantly parted ways, glancing back at each other with sad eyes. It wasn't so much the separation from Jenny that bothered me; instead, it was grappling with the anticipation for the evening ahead throughout the day. I shuffled my way to Mr. Jenkins' class. The new seating arrangement had been effective thus far, and I felt relieved knowing I did not have to interact with Ellie. Upon arriving, Ellie caught my attention as she sat near the classroom entrance. Was she intentionally lingering, anticipating my arrival? I was taken aback. I hadn't intended to have any association with her today, especially right before the dance. My enthusiasm and self-assurance began to wane. Ellie had that sort of effect on people. She didn't have to speak to make her presence known. I continued to brush past her with imagined gusto. My backpack unintentionally made contact with her shoulder, and I winced. This wasn't going to have a good result.

"Watch where you're going, loser," she growled threateningly. "I can't believe you haven't learned to walk yet."

I tried to ignore Ellie. Typically, I wasn't one to fight battles. Jenny was always the one with grit and passion. I continued past Ellie hurriedly, making my way to my seat.

"You deaf or something?" she yelled after me.

With curious eyes, I could feel the entire class staring at me, burning holes into the back of my head. I twisted around to look at Ellie, arching my body so peculiarly that it felt unnatural. I could feel myself tensing, my knuckles turning white from the tightened fists at my side. With gritted teeth and twisted lips, I opened my mouth. The words came tumbling out like rocks in a rock slide.

"You are a real bitch, you know that? Nobody even likes you. They just pretend to be your friend because they're terrified of you. Is that the legacy you want to leave behind?"

She looked at me with widened eyes. My sudden eruption seemed to have left her utterly thunderstruck. Wow, I thought to myself, did I render the queen bitch speechless? In the realm of disbelief, I struggled to fathom my interaction with Ellie, leaving me to ponder the collective astonishment of both her and my peers. My disbelief was short-lived as I was abruptly snapped back into the realm of reality by the booming voice of Mr. Jenkins.

"Kacey, that's enough. Stop it right now. You know this isn't appropriate classroom behaviour."

Ellie snickered ever so slightly. Mr. Jenkins snapped his neck back so hard I heard a loud crack.

"And you…" he stared at Ellie with cold eyes, "what on earth makes you think you have the authority to sit wherever you desire? There's a seating plan for a reason. I suggest you become familiar with it."

"But Mr. Jenkins…" Ellie started defensively.

"I don't want to hear it. I think you should go to Mrs. Laughlin's office now."

Mr. Jenkins pointed at the door with his slim, yet threatening index finger and commanded us with his irate gaze to vacate the room. I forced myself to get up from my seat, red from embarrassment. Ellie, appearing more composed, got up with a dash of flair and flicked her hair over her shoulders. With a quick wink, she turned to me and dashed down the hall like nothing had happened. Typical princess, I thought. I battled the urge to unleash my frustration on her again, recognizing that I was already treading precarious ground. Within moments, we arrived at the office. Ms. Lythe, the secretary, raised her eyes from the glow of her monitor. She motioned for Ellie and me to follow her. We strolled in unison until Ms. Lythe stopped at Mrs. Laughlin's office.

"Mrs. Laughlin," Ms. Lythe said softly, "Ellie and Kacey are here to see you."

"Come in and have a seat," she replied, motioning to a couple of chairs in front of her desk. "I understand there was some sort of outburst or disagreement between you. Who wants to start? Ellie, how about you?"

"Firstly, Mrs. Laughlin," Ellie started, "Kacey is a bit of a drama queen. I've done absolutely nothing to her. This whole scenario here is all in her head. She's schizophrenic or something."

I stared at Ellie in disbelief. Did she really try to pin this all on me? Seriously? Are you kidding me? What a nerve this girl had. I gritted my teeth once again, but then quickly remembered that my newfound temper got me sent here in the first place. I took a deep breath and gathered my thoughts. I always found the advice to think before I speak to be invaluable.

"Mrs. Laughlin," I started calmly, "I'm not schizophrenic, as I'm sure you can see. The problem here is with Ellie, not me. Every day, she sets out to make somebody's life miserable. For some reason or another, I've become her target of choice. Why? I don't know. But I assure you, my only goal at school is to do my work and get good grades. I have no desire to entertain this type of drama with Ellie or anyone at all, really. Today, she pushed me over the edge, and I could no longer hold back and do nothing. I don't normally speak up, but enough was enough."

"You lying bitch," Ellie cried out dramatically. "Always trying to play the victim."

"Ellie!" Mrs. Laughlin shouted. "Language! Look," Mrs. Laughlin continued, "I've seen and heard things around here, and I'm inclined to believe that Kacey is being truthful. I'm sorry, Ellie, but you're not exactly easy to get along with. It's been known for quite some time that you are extremely standoffish to people you don't normally associate with. Attitudes will have to change, or I'm afraid that if this continues, I will have to suspend you."

"What!" Ellie exclaimed. "How is that fair? Why is she getting off scot free? I can't believe you're taking her side. She called me a bitch first."

"Ellie, get a hold of yourself," Mrs. Laughlin calmly replied. "It's this type of attitude that is going to get you deeper into trouble. You need to learn to control these types of outbursts. And Kacey, while I know you usually don't get confrontational, talk to me or one of your teachers next time before you decide to push back. We cannot, under any circumstances, have these types of disruptions during class time. Is that understood?"

"Absolutely," I replied. "Thank you, Mrs. Laughlin.

She looked at us both seriously and motioned for us to return to class. I left Mrs. Laughlin's office first, trying my best to outpace Ellie. The last thing I needed was for her to instigate more drama in the hallway. Besides, tonight was the night of the dance, and I didn't particularly feel like being down in a funk. I was excited. I had been waiting in anticipation for this night for months, and I wasn't about to let Ellie ruin it for me. This night was all about me and Jenny.

The day stretched out like an infinite highway with no exit in sight. How does that saying go? A watched pot never boils. Truer words have not been spoken. I willed myself to avoid checking the clock, but navigating this challenge was like dancing through a storm – graceful, yet far from easy. When the dismissal bell finally rang, I sprang out of my seat like a leopard pouncing on its prey and headed straight to my locker to look for Jenny. This was the night we had been anxiously waiting for. This was the night we would make our school dance debut. It wasn't long before I spotted Jenny sprinting down the hall, dripping with enthusiasm. Her smile sparkled like stars in the night sky.

"I can't believe it's finally here," she squealed. "Kace, I'm going to come over to your place around 5. We can get ready together, okay? I told Jordan and Chase to pick us up at your place around 6:30 tonight."

Jordan Bally and Chase Dreiger were our dates. Jenny and I had met the boys on our first day at Richfield High. Jordan was your typical tall, dark and handsome stereotype. He was smart and funny, too. His offbeat sense of humour always had Jenny and me in stitches. Chase was the more studious of the two. He, too, was tall but had light hair and emerald green eyes. Jenny was head over heels the minute she laid eyes on him. It wasn't like that for Jordan and me. We started as friends, but one night at the movie theatre, we simultaneously reached for a handful of popcorn, and our fingers gently brushed against each other. I felt a rush of electricity pulsing throughout my body at that moment. He must have felt it too because he leaned over, brushed my hair from my cheek and kissed me. I had goosebumps all over. From that moment on, we had been inseparable.

"That sounds great, Jenn," I replied. " I'm so freaking excited for the dance. Could you please help me with my makeup? I suck so bad at doing my eyes. I can never get the eyeshadow to blend properly or the eyeliner quite right."

"Kace, you don't even need to ask. I've got you, babe." She giggled. "I just realized that I made a Sonny and Cher reference." We both laughed.

It was 6 pm, and the boys would be here in a matter of time. The clock continued to tick rapidly like a bomb ready to explode. It was quite the opposite of earlier in the day at school. I suppose when you're anxious and excited, time just flies. Jenny was rushing to do her nails. She chose a deep purple shade, one that matched her dress perfectly. I was frantically searching my makeup bag for my favourite strawberry-flavoured lip gloss.

"You're probably not going to even need that, Kace," Jenny teased.

I smiled coyly. Before we knew it, 6:30 had arrived. Like clockwork, the doorbell rang. Jenny and I rapidly descended the stairs, nearly bowling over my dad and little brother.

"Slow down there, girls," my dad called out. "I don't want to have to make a trip to the emergency room."

"Sorry, Dad," I apologized hastily.

With a less-than-elegant arrival, we reached the door and simultaneously indulged in two hearty breaths. We both looked at each other nervously and together reached for the door knob.

"You ready for the best night of our lives?" Jenny grinned from ear to ear.

"You bet I am," I replied gleefully. "Wild horses couldn't keep me away."

We unlocked the door hand in hand, our grins transforming us into delightfully goofy jesters.

CHAPTER FIVE

Friday, May 3rd, 2024

It had been nearly a week since I first encountered the mysterious glowing amber eyes. Time's embrace failed to quell the lingering unease, an unsettling companion persisting through the ticking seconds. My stomach retained its queasy churn, a relentless reminder whenever the image manifested within the recesses of my mind. Only Jenny knew about my sighting, and I had to admit, I felt guilty that I hadn't confided in Jordan. Jordan and I were still a thing. We, of course, had our ups and downs, but the emotions we exchanged remained unwavering. Skeptical of the towns' tales about amber-eyed beings, I hesitated to confess my encounter to Jordan. I placed my faith in Jordan without hesitation, yet the real issue surfaced from my internal struggle with self-assurance. Someday, maybe, I'd overcome this internal struggle. Little did I realize that the day would arrive much sooner than expected.

Jenny came over after school today to work on our

science project. This one was a doozy, and we worked on it for nearly 3 weeks. We were tasked with designing a vehicle made from ordinary household materials that could propel at least one meter. Jenny and I had designed multiple vehicles, but only one was able to reach the stated parameters. Our mission was to create at least one that propelled beyond those parameters. Mr. Newhope, our science teacher, motivated us by announcing that the top 3 teams would compete nationwide, with the winning team earning a $5000 scholarship. We rode the waves of unwavering concentration until an abrupt knock on the door sent ripples through the sea of our focused minds. Lifting my gaze from the tapestry of strategic contemplation, I moved briskly, fueled by curiosity that sparked like a comet, toward the enigmatic call of the door. I opened it with cautious optimism, hoping that the visitor on the other side would bring some welcome distraction from the monotony of school. I was pleasantly surprised.

"Jordan," I called out with confusion and a touch of joy. "What are you doing here?"

"I thought you ladies could use a little downtime, you know, because you've both been working so hard on this project. Chase is here, too. He's waiting outside."

He smiled devilishly. His grin cast a spell, melting my heart as I felt a fluttering dance within my chest.

"Yeah, absolutely," I replied enthusiastically. Jenn, whaddya think? Should we take a break?"

"Uhmmm, yeah, like I'd say no to two handsome boys," she giggled.

"Well, okay then, let's go," he replied.

"Where might our adventure lead?" I inquired with a

curious spark in my voice.

"You'll see," he said. "I don't want to ruin the surprise."

Exhilarated to spend time with the boys, Jenny and I hastily put on our jackets and shoes and raced out the door. The smell of adventure was in the air. This break turned out to be a hidden necessity, unveiling its importance in ways I hadn't initially grasped. As the tension melted away, I found myself instantly able to unwind and fully embrace the present moment.

Jordan drove for what seemed like an eternity. We went from one end of town to another, eventually ending up on the freeway. The vibrant hustle in the city gradually transformed into a majestic panorama of trees, lakes, and mountains, unveiling nature's serene grandeur. Jenny and I both exchanged curious glances. Where on earth were the boys taking us? I wasn't complaining by any means. I loved nature; any opportunity to get out and explore, breathe in the fragrant smell of pine, and enjoy nature's portrait was a welcome reprieve.

"We're almost there," Jordan exclaimed. "We just have to park the car and hike a little ways up the trail."

We pulled into the parking lot and prepared ourselves for the arduous task of hiking up the steep trail. I'm grateful that Jenny and I chose to wear sensible shoes. Jordan hadn't given us any inclination that we would be hiking today.

"Alright, my ladies, Chase and I will lead the way."

Jordan and Chase ascended the steep staircase leading to the trailhead's beginning. Jenny and I followed closely behind, gingerly stepping over some overgrown roots from the billowing trees. During my previous hiking trip with Jordan, I came close to breaking my leg after stumbling over random rocks and branches. From then on, I was cautious and more aware of my surroundings. We continued to hike for what felt like hours. I glanced at my watch and was somewhat startled that we had only been walking for 35 minutes. I turned to find Jenny, her face flushed and a profound exhaustion evident in her expression. I, too, was exhausted, having great difficulty catching my breath. Meanwhile, the boys exuded boundless energy and composure, ascending with such fervour that I struggled to comprehend their seemingly boundless stamina.

''Jordan," I called out breathlessly, "can we please take a break? I don't think Jenny and I are going to make it."

"Just a few more minutes, I promise," he replied endearingly. "Trust me, it'll be worth it."

We continued the ascent, finally reaching a clearing. I could hear the rushing water, crashing into what sounded like a valley below. A waterfall? Did we have waterfalls out this way? This would be my first experience observing the grandeur of a waterfall. My excitement surged as we turned the corner atop the clearing, revealing the breathtaking waterfall in majestic splendour. With eyes as wide as constellations, I absorbed every detail of the magnificent spectacle. Jenny stared in disbelief and was left speechless.

"Beautiful, isn't it?" Jordan exclaimed. "I knew you'd love this place. What about you, Jenn? Do you love it or what?"

"Uhmmm, heck yeah I do," she cried out in exhilaration. "Our new make-out spot, hey Chase," she chided as she elbowed him gently in the ribs.

Chase, playfully pursued, cheeks blushing like a ripe tomato, emitted a slightly embarrassed, nervous laugh.

"Uh, yeah, I guess."

Jordan and Chase removed their backpacks and, like two knights in shining armour, they assembled a picnic, complete with sandwiches, cake and sparkling juice. Jordan flipped a blanket into the air and gently laid it out on the top of the clearing. It was the perfect spot to enjoy a romantic dinner and revel in the splendour surrounding us. I couldn't imagine anything more romantic.

"You guys have outdone yourselves," I said with an enamoured sigh. "This is honestly the most perfect distraction. Jenny and I must find a way to repay you two for such a perfect day."

"That isn't necessary, Kace," Jordan replied. "I love you and would do anything to make you happy. You should know by now that your presence in my life is enough. I don't need anything else."

My cheeks painted a subtle shade of rose; I nestled into the sturdy embrace of his broad shoulders, enveloped by the comforting warmth he exuded. In the lottery of love, I must have hit the jackpot to have won the heart of someone so flawlessly perfect. I snuck a peek at Jenny and Chase. They were equally enamoured with one another. I don't think things could have been any more perfect.

The day whispered its farewell, painting the sky with the gentle hues of a vanishing sunset, as the warm glow gracefully retreated beyond the western embrace of twilight. The stars made their evening debut one by one, twinkling with a soft shimmer. The full moon ascended majestically, casting its ethereal glow upon us, enchanting the waterfall with a magical luminescence that danced upon the cascading waters. I leaned in to kiss Jordan. His lips, soft as silk, met mine with a triumphant embrace, sealing a moment of victorious passion.

The moment was short-lived. Deep in the vast darkness of our forested retreat came a deep and threatening vocalization. Not the human kind, no. The kind you'd expect to hear in the haunted forest of OZ. The four of us froze, scared to move a muscle.

"What was that?" Chase whispered, his face frozen in pure terror.

Jordan rose, donning a facade of strength, determined not to cast shadows of apprehension upon me and Jenny.

"I'm not sure," Jordan replied with bravado.

I swept my gaze through the obsidian abyss, urgently tuning my sight to unveil the origin of that spine-chilling resonance. It wasn't long before I saw them, the menacing amber eyes staring out from the darkness. I screamed, then Jenny screamed. Jordan and Chase swiftly turned their heads toward our shared gaze, only now realizing the presence of those ominous amber eyes. They exchanged a nervous glance.

"What on earth is that?" Jordan attempted to call out, almost inaudibly. It was as though his voice had escaped him. Chase, equally as stunned, opened his mouth, but no noise escaped.

"Those are the amber eyes the townsfolk reported observing two years ago, you know the ones that appeared when Ellie vanished," I whispered. "Jenny and I saw them about a week ago."

"Wait, what?" Jordan asked with puzzlement and fear. You know what, we'll talk about this later. I think we'd better get out of here quickly."

Abandoning the blanket and picnic gear, Jordan

and Chase snatched their backpacks and our hands, enthusiastically bolting down the trail. It was pitch dark and we stumbled several times, tripping over rocks, shrubs and branches. I skidded down a slippery embankment in my clumsiness, halting just before teetering over the brink of a petite cliff. The ominous symphony of the creatures' growls echoed, orchestrating a crescendo of fear that surged through us from behind. We could hear the beast growling behind us, our fear escalating.

"Kacey, are you alright?" Jordan cried out in desperation. He reached for my hand, helping me to my feet.

"I'm good," I replied, somewhat shaken. "Let's keep going. I just want to get back to the car."

We pressed along the trail, moving swiftly as if chased by unseen wolves, our pace resembling the urgency of hunted rabbits. The ominous growls faded into silence, leaving only the distant hum of engines echoing from the far-off freeway. The sound was a welcome relief. As fast as our bodies would allow, we packed into the car like sardines and stormed off into the night. I reclined in my seat, gasping for breath, desperately trying to make sense of what had just happened. Jenny, usually calm and composed, looked frantic. Her breathing was fast-paced, so much so that I worried for her safety.

"Guys, I think Jenny needs help. Her breathing is too fast, and she's breaking into a cold sweat. Maybe we should take her to the hospital emergency."

"Already on it," Jordan replied in a heroic tone.

Jordan maneuvered with Nascar-like precision, protecting his lead as he raced, determined to get Jenny the help she needed. Jordan's stealthy maneuvering through the twisted streets of Fort Richfield caught me by surprise, showcasing a skillful navigation that left an impression. This guy not only had the looks but the skill too, I thought. How lucky am I? In that moment, I had to reprimand myself, reminding myself that daydreaming about Jordan's allure wasn't the priority; focus was needed.

Upon arriving at the emergency entrance, Jordan and Chase carefully carried Jenny out of the car. I promptly approached the front desk receptionist and completed Jenny's check-in process. The triage nurse inquired about Jenny's condition. I shared the complete story with her, omitting the part involving the amber eyes. She asked about Jenny's possession of an asthma inhaler. I don't ever recall Jenny having an asthmatic attack, so I replied with a confident "No." She requested that I take a seat and assured me that Jenny would be called to see a doctor once one became available.

I was both relieved and anxious that Jenny was now out of harm's way, nervous because the amber-eyes made a second appearance, and I was still no closer to knowing what monstrosity hid behind them. Jordan suddenly interrupted my thoughts with a slight tap on my shoulder.

"Hey, can we talk about what happened at the waterfall?" Jordan asked. His eyes gazed into mine with such intensity that I hesitated momentarily.

"Um, yeah sure."

"Let's go sit over there by the coffee shop," he said, gesturing with his hands. "It's closed, so talking will be more private."

We sauntered to the coffee shop and picked a few high barstools. I always preferred sitting in them when the option was available. They made me feel taller and gave me a sense of confidence. Jordan glanced over at me, as though he were expecting me to start talking. When I didn't, he drew in a deep breath and began his questioning investigation.

"So, what exactly was that?" Jordan asked with both curiosity and shock."

"You wouldn't believe me even if I tried to explain it," I replied hesitantly.

"Try me," Jordan said.

I looked him in the eye and started regaling the events surrounding my first sighting of the amber eyes. He looked at me so intently that I felt his eyes were X-rays penetrating my soul. It intimidated me to be honest. We were suddenly interrupted by a voice that seemingly came out of nowhere.

"Excuse me," a woman dressed in a white coat called out. "We're ready to see Jenny Forester now."

We got up from our seats and assisted Jenny into a wheelchair and watched with cautious optimism as the woman in white wheeled her away.

"Should we say a little prayer for Jenny?" I asked.

"Yes," Jordan replied coldly, "but first you owe me an explanation. I need to know why you chose not to tell me about your first sighting of the amber-eyes. Do you not trust me?"

I could feel a lump forming in my throat, and as I swallowed, I could feel Jordan's gaze intensify. What sort of girlfriend was I? I didn't feel as though I had earned his trust and love at this particular moment.

"Jordan, will you let me explain?" I begged.

"I'm all ears, Kace."

CHAPTER SIX

Friday, May 6th, 2022

The four of us made a stylish entrance to the dance. Jordan and Chase had collaborated to rent a limousine for the occasion. Made up in our finest clothing, make-up and hair done to the nines, Jenny and I each felt like Cinderella going to the grand ball. The only thing missing was the glass slippers, but I couldn't imagine how uncomfortable wearing them for hours would be. No thanks, I'd keep my stylish pink flats, thank you very much. I had never ridden in a limousine before. The sheer elegance surprised me - the dazzling lights, spacious interior, stereo, and the mini fridge. It was essentially a luxury hotel on wheels. I was awestruck, and by the expression on Jenny's face, I could tell she was feeling the same way. Wow, did these boys ever know how to win our hearts. As the limousine reached the school entrance, I was on the verge of opening the door for my grand exit when Jordan hurriedly approached, seizing the door handle.

"No, no my lady, let me."

He exited first, making a grand gesture as he extended his arm to gently lead me out of the limousine. Chase quickly followed, taking Jenny's arm and gracefully helping her out of the limousine. The school was lit with spotlights, and there was a red carpet awaiting the arrival of the elegantly dressed students. There were people with cameras ready to take photos as each person descended the red carpet and into the cleverly designed archway leading into the school. I felt like a celebrity. Richfield High went all out; there was no flaw in their budget, no expense spared. My heart palpitated in my chest, not because I was nervous, but because I was excited. My first dance ever, and this was the experience that greeted me. How exciting for a Sophomore such as myself. Equally as impressed, Jenny looked over at me with a wide grin and a sparkle in her eyes. We didn't have to exchange words; we knew this would be one exceptional evening.

Entering the school, we were embraced by the pulsating beat and dancing lights, a comforting welcome that felt like reconnecting with an old friend. Balloons and streamers adorned every corner, catching the vibrant reflections from the feverish disco ball, turning the room into a kaleidoscope of celebration. Our classmates' faded chatter and laughter echoed in harmony with the pulsating music, creating a lively symphony that enveloped the atmosphere. This was a spectacle unlike any I had ever experienced before. Jenny and I gazed in awe as Jordan and Chase escorted us, arm in arm, onto the dance floor, embodying the princesses we had always imagined ourselves to be. The slow, rhythmic beat of the music set the perfect tone for Jordan and my first-ever dance together. The disco ball, spinning overhead, created a magical scene forever etched in my mind. Shania Twain's "Still the One," playing in unison with the hypnotic sway of Jordan's hips, was pure perfection. It was one of those moments that I wished would last for eternity. I snuck a glance at Jenny and Chase. Jenny's head gently rested on his shoulder, and his arms wrapped tightly around her waist, as though he was holding on for dear life. They truly were the perfect couple. If fairy tales were real, the enchanting dance floor would be graced by the presence of a modern-day Cinderella and Prince Charming, epitomizing the magic of this grand ball.

When Shania Twain's "Still the One" transitioned into Lady Gaga's "Poker Face," Jenny and I seized the opportunity to grab a drink from the makeshift drink bar. This wasn't the type of bar that served alcoholic beverages, of course, but it crafted sophisticated mocktails like Shirley Temples, Virgin Strawberry Daiquiris, and Virgin Mai Tai's. During the serene pause for our libations, curiosity nudged me to gracefully weave into the conversation, inquiring about Jenny's evening adventures.

"So, how are things going with Chase?"

"It's like a dream," she swooned. "His arms are so strong, and when he held me there on the dance floor, I felt like I had been swept away into a magical time-warp. It was literally as though time stood still. Kace, I think I'm in love."

I smiled with jubilation. I was ecstatic for Jenny.

"I know what you're thinking, Kace," Jenny said in haste, "but I mean it this time. He's the one. I have no doubt that he's the man for me."

"I never doubted it for a minute," I replied. "I can tell

just by looking at you both that you are really in love with one another."

Jenny smiled, almost with relief. This was new. Jenny usually danced to her own rhythm, a melody composed of her confidence and straightforward nature, indifferent to the opinion of others. This moment of vulnerability took me by surprise. With its enchanting touch, love has a knack for transforming even the most assertive and most confident women into delightful balls of mush.

"What about you and Jordan?" Jenny asked coyly. "What's the story there?"

"Jordan," I replied almost questioningly, "Uhm… he's great."

"Just great?"

"Well, I uhmm…" I hesitated. I wasn't one to share my deepest feelings with anyone. My constant self-doubt always got in the way of that, even if I were with those I trusted most. Damn, I hated how my mind played these nonsensical games with me. "I mean, he's amazing," I continued. "What's not to love?"

"Kacey, you're too funny. I don't even have to look you in the eyes to see how crazy you are about Jordan. Your body language says it all."

"My body language?" I asked quizzically. "What do you mean?"

"Oh, come on, Kace. Every time he walks into the room, your eyes light up like stars in the night sky. Your body tenses up, but in a good way, like you're anticipating his tender kiss or gentle touch. It doesn't take a rocket scientist to know that you're head over heels in love with the guy."

I stared at Jenny in awe. Did my body language truly

reveal that much about my feelings for Jordan? I rarely considered my body language, to be honest. While I observed others' body language, I never fully grasped how much my nonverbal cues revealed about my feelings.

"I guess there's no hiding anything from you," I replied, winking at Jenny as we headed back to the boys, drinks in hand.

Jenny and I dashed with enthusiasm back to the boys, who, with anxious eyes, watched our two-step shuffle with amusement.

"What's the hold-up?" Chase asked, somewhat amused. "Did you fall into a bottomless pit, or what?"

"Come on now, Chase," Jenny replied coyly, "do you really think if I had actually gotten trapped in a dark and dingy pit, I would have called out to you for rescue? I'm a strong and independent woman, after all."

"Touche," Chase replied.

"How about you, Kace?" Jordan asked with a faint grin. "Did you need any rescuing? I mean, I thought you had drowned in a pool of punch."

I laughed, trying my best to maintain an air of confidence. I didn't want Jordan to feel trapped by my persistent need for self-assurance.

"I'm all good, Jordan. No need for rescuing here."

"Well, good then. What do you think? Should we go to the photo booth and take a group photo? You know, to preserve memories and all that jazz."

"Absolutely," Jenny replied, speaking in turn for me.

I suspect she used her body language reading superpower again, sensing my self-doubt creeping back in.

I turned to Jenny, and without saying a word, she nodded, acknowledging my gratitude.

Navigating toward the photo booth, I kept inadvertently tripping on my gown, while Jenny struggled to maintain balance in her towering 4-inch heels, adding a touch of chaos to our journey. I suspect Jenny regretted wearing those heels. She should have stuck to flats, like me. The lineup was longer than the line for a Disneyland attraction, or so it felt. Jenny kept shifting her weight from one foot to the other. It was obvious those heels were not performing the job she had intended.

"I don't know, guys," I started hesitantly, "Is it worth it to wait in this gargantuan line? We'll miss the entire dance if we wait here all night."

Jenny nodded in agreement.

"Yeah, boys. I think maybe we should abandon ship. I'd rather spend my time cuddling up to this stud muffin anyhow." She looked over at Chase playfully.

Jordan and Chase reluctantly concurred with our evaluation, acknowledging the circumstances. Leaving the photo booth line, regret lingered as we wished we had opted to capture moments earlier in the evening. We meandered our way back to the dance floor. I couldn't wait to be back in Jordan's arms, swaying to the rhythm of the music. From the look in his eyes, I'm certain Jordan felt the same way. Our rendezvous with the dance floor, however, was cut short by the abrupt appearance of, you guessed it, Ellie Mason. Shocker!!! Ellie and her abysmal band of misfits, bathed in the spotlight as if starring in a solo act, obstructed our way, creating a theatrical barrier between us and the boys. Ellie's blonde hair glistened under the kaleidoscope of the disco ball, curls rolling effortlessly over her shoulders. Her stunning white gown cascaded like a silk scarf, dancing in the breeze, reminiscent of Marilyn Monroe's iconic moment with her billowing white dress. Her band of misfits were equally dressed to impress. Loa Abrahams, second in command after Ellie, wore a scarlet coloured gown with a jewelled tiara atop her head. She and Ellie exchanged sly grins, enjoying the rift they were causing between Jenny, me and the boys. The whole group laughed, pointing at us as if we were sad clowns at a circus.

"Lookie what we got here," Ellie spat out with disgust. "Silly girls. You actually think those boys want to be here with you at the dance? Not likely. They want girls like us, girls with gorgeous hair, gorgeous faces and most of all sparkling personalities. Girls like you two, well, they'd have to be desperate to tango with the likes of you."

Loa and the other girls in the misfit squad giggled in pure delight. They basked in the glory that came along with being friends with Ellie.

I loathed Ellie. This was mine and Jenny's night. How dare she ruin it for us! Months of anticipation, countless nights planning, and envisioning the magic of this experience, all shattered instantly as she swiftly dismantled our dreams. It took every fibre of my being to hold my tongue. Despite my usual lack of self-confidence, Ellie had a remarkable ability to dissolve all the lingering doubts I harboured about myself. In its place, my anger surged forth with an unmistakable force. My hands clenched, fists so tight my knuckles were white. I could feel my jaw tense and my teeth clench in fury. This seemed to amuse Jenny. She looked my way, almost as if to say this is your rodeo, have at it. My gaze remained fixed on Ellie, seething with unbridled animosity as an eternal fire raged within me.

I know it's cliche, but if looks could kill, Ellie would be D.E.A.D.

"What the hell is your problem, you narcissistic bitch?" My words shot out like a poisonous arrow ready to strike Ellie dead. "Do you enjoy destroying lives? What is your deal? Why don't you just die already?"

Ellie and her misfit crew were in hysterics. This is precisely what they wanted. This was the Ellie show; the world was her stage and her misfit friends, her puppets. She held the strings and crafted the script.

"You hear that, everybody?" she yelled to anyone within earshot. "Kacey wants me dead. If I suddenly disappear one day, you'll know who to question first."

Jenny began to lose her temper. She initially handed me the reins to handle the situation, but at this point, she couldn't stand idly by and do nothing. She walked straight up to Ellie and pulled her body so close that they stood nose to nose. With their eyes affixed on one another, I could hear the rapid pace of their breathing. The moment's intensity felt like we were watching a UFC fight.

"Look bitch," Jenny snarled, "that's my friend you're talking smack about. You'll have more than her to worry about if you're not careful. As a matter of fact, I'm pretty sure more than half of the people in this room wish you'd just vanish forever. I suggest you back off, or you won't like what will happen next."

Ellie stared in disbelief. It appeared that Jenny had caught her off guard. I had to admit, it gave me such satisfaction to know that Ellie had finally been dealt a blow, and she had no clue how to handle it. However, the moment was fleeting; before long, Ellie had regained her composure.

"Did you hear that everyone?" Ellie cried out. "Another one wishing me harm. Hmmm, the suspect list is growing. If something happens to me, you all know who the top suspects are. Oh, and don't forget about their sappy little boy toys over there. I wouldn't count them out of the suspect list either."

By now, the music had stopped, and the entire dance floor was still and in shock at the events that had just transpired. Teachers and students alike were quiet as mice. The silence was deafening, so quiet you could hear a pin drop. After a few moments of awkward silence, Mrs Laughlin stepped up on stage and grabbed a microphone.

"Ladies and gentlemen," she started in a flustered voice, "let's return to enjoying the evening. DJ, start up that music."

Looking straight at us with eyes of daggers, Mrs Laughlin sternly requested that Ellie, Jenny and I follow her immediately.

Jenny and I walked away in defeat, staring forlornly at Jordan and Chase, who looked stunned by what had just occurred. With a quick and fleeting glance, I saw Jordan mouth the words, "It's okay, I still love you." Despite the circumstances, I felt a warmth bubbling up in my chest. Jordan just told me that he loved me. This was the first time those words had ever been uttered to me. I smiled at Jenny; she knew exactly what I felt, just like always. She clutched my hand tightly as we walked down the dark and silent hall, preparing ourselves for the aftermath of our impromptu outburst.

CHAPTER SEVEN

Friday, May 3rd, 2024

Jordan fixed a penetrating stare on me, sharply, awaiting my explanation. Why hadn't I told him about the amber eyes in the first place? It was evident that I experienced a profound escalation of anxiety and struggled with self-reassurance. After all these years, Jordan likely recognized my reluctance to open up and share feelings, fearing judgment. He should go easy on me, I thought. He knows that I love and trust him. He won't hold my minor transgression against me, will he? I consistently tried to reassure myself that everything would be okay, believing that Jordan and I would emerge from this situation stronger than before. We had been through so much together over the past few years, especially with the mystery surrounding Ellie's disappearance. I could not imagine that this would be the nail in our coffin. I gathered my composure, took a deep breath, and articulated my perspective.

"Jordan," I began, "I'm so sorry. I should have informed

you earlier about my encounter with the amber-eyes. Honestly, I was hesitant to say anything to Jenny, too. I know I can trust you, that's not the issue. The issue is me and my lack of self-confidence. I know I need to work on that, and I promise I will get some counselling or something. Right now, though, I just want to focus on Jenny. Can we please just do that?" I begged.

"Kacey, look. Am I a bit upset? Absolutely. I was already aware that you had certain confidence-related concerns. And that's ok. I'm not judging you for that. But I want you to know that you never have to hide anything from me. You should never doubt yourself. You're smart, beautiful and kind. I will always be in your corner, no matter what. People do that when they love somebody, and I love you more than you realize. You and I, we are a team."

I gazed up at Jordan lovingly as he reached over, pulling me closer, his strong arms embracing me. The scent of his cologne sent ripples of sensations through my entire body. He emanated warmth, his soft hair complemented by eyes that seemed to pierce through me, as if gazing into my soul. His embrace was just what I needed at that moment.

Time crawled at a snail's pace, turning minutes into seemingly endless hours. What was taking so long? Why hadn't anyone given us an update on Jenny? I was beginning to feel my anxiety creep back in. Jordan could sense it. He approached me, enveloping me with his strong arms, embracing me reassuringly as if to convey that everything would be alright.

"I wonder if there are any updates on Jenny," I asked. "She's been with the doctor for a while now. Maybe I should go ask the lady at reception."

"Good idea," Jordan responded. "Maybe Chase should

go with you. I know he's been quiet all night, but he needs to know how Jenny's doing. I can't imagine how anxious he must be right now."

I approached Chase, gently resting my hand on his shoulder. He had his head down, his hands gently cupping the sides of his face. His body language revealed signs of anxiety and fatigue, evident before he even spoke. I suppose Jenny's expertise in body language rubbed off on me. It's funny, but I had forgotten all about Jenny's superpower. It had been two years since the Spring Fling Dance, and only now did that specific memory resurface in my mind. Funny how that works. Chase looked up at me with tired red eyes. He looked rough, as though he hadn't slept in days.

"Chase," I whispered, "did you want to come with me and check to see how Jenny is doing?"

"Yeah," he said, yawning. "How long has it been? Two hours?"

"Something like that," I replied.

He mustered the will to stand, and together we trudged at the pace of a sloth to the reception desk. The lady on the other end of the desk was engrossed in reading some sort of chart or letter on the screen before her. She motioned to us to wait a few moments as she finished her task. After what seemed like an unusually long time, she finally greeted us.

"How can I help you?"

"Uhm, yes, hi," I replied. "We want to check in on our friend Jenny Forester. She was admitted to see a doctor a few hours ago."

"Give me a few minutes to pull up her file," the receptionist said in a monotone voice.

Chase and I waited patiently, exchanging worried glances. It was absolute torture not knowing if Jenny was alright.

"Yes, I have the file right here. It looks as though there were some complications, and she's been taken in for surgery."

"Wait, what?" Chase and I cried out in unison.

"Why didn't anybody come and tell us?" I asked with exasperation. "We were the ones who brought her here in the first place. Shouldn't somebody have come out and given us an update or something? Why is she in surgery? What happened? What's going on? Is she going to be okay?"

"Unfortunately," the receptionist started, "we only contact immediate family in these circumstances. If you ask, I can only tell you her status, but I can't give you more information about her condition. Patient confidentiality and all that. You understand, right?"

"Yeah, I get it, but I don't think it's fair that we have to sit here in a panic," I replied huffily.

"I'm sorry I can't give you more information," the receptionist said. "I believe the doctor has contacted her parents. Maybe you can give them a call for an update."

"I think I'll do just that. Thanks for the help," I replied somewhat sarcastically.

"You're welcome," the receptionist replied, not even noticing the sarcasm dripping from my voice.

Chase and I turned to walk away; it wasn't long before he lost control. I don't believe he was angry, not at me or anyone else; instead, he seemed overwhelmed with all that was happening. I truly felt sorry for him.

"What the hell, Kacey?" Chase blurted out. "What on earth is going on? Jenny seemed perfectly fine earlier. Why on earth is she in surgery?"

"Chase, if I had all the answers, I wouldn't have been bickering back and forth with the receptionist. Let's find a quiet spot, and I'll call Mr. and Mrs. Forester. They must be on their way here to see Jenny."

He reluctantly agreed. We returned to Jordan, and I informed him about Jenny's condition. While shocked, he understood why the receptionist couldn't give us more detailed information. He opted to join us as we searched for a tranquil place to reach out to Jenny's parents. We made our way down the long, narrow hallway, sterile and white, searching for the perfect spot to make our call. As we rounded the corner, I spotted Mr. and Mrs. Forester frantically going to the reception desk. I attempted to wave them down, but in their panic and haste, they overlooked my long, spindly hand flapping awkwardly in the air.

"Hey guys, I just saw the Foresters. They were heading to reception. I'm just going to go over there and talk to them. I should probably fill them in on what happened."

"Did you want any company?" Jordan asked, "You know, for support."

I smiled at Jordan with sincerity. Gosh, I loved this man. Always thinking about me and my ever-so-wild emotions.

"Thanks," I replied lovingly, "but I think I've got this. You know Jordan, I've been thinking about what you said, about not being afraid to speak out and to have faith in myself. I think I'm going to try that, starting today."

Jordan leaned in and gave me a gentle peck on the cheek. "You've got this, babe. Never doubt yourself."

I flashed Jordan a confident grin and approached the front desk reception. The Foresters had every right to know what happened and how Jenny ended up in the hospital. I wasn't going to let fear control me anymore. I was determined to bury all of my self-doubt six feet under where it belonged. I would conquer this internal struggle once and for all. As I approached the reception desk, I could see Mr. Forester's arms around Mrs. Forester, comforting her with his embrace. I hesitated for a moment, unsure if I should interrupt. Nope, that was my fear talking again. I need to tell them, I chided myself. They deserve to know why Jenny ended up here at the hospital.

"Mr. and Mrs. Forester," I called out hesitantly, "I have some information about Jenny. We should find a quiet place to sit so I can fill you in."

Mr. Forester stared at me, almost as if he didn't recognize me at first. Mrs. Forester couldn't find the strength to lift her head from Mr. Forester's shoulder. Neither of them tried to move, so I took a deep breath, bracing myself for whatever outcome was to follow the news I was about to share.

"I was with Jenny, sir. We were having a picnic with Jordan and Chase out in the forest just outside town. It was quite a long and steep hike. I don't think either of us was prepared for it. We had been there for quite some time, and shortly after dark, we heard a bizarre and unusual noise coming from the bush. None of us could see anything at first, but that changed abruptly. Jenny and I spotted amber eyes staring back at us from the forested brush. All four of us panicked, and before we knew it, we were running down the steep path from an unknown assailant. By the time we got to the car, Jenny was breathing heavily, and she looked as though she was about to pass out. That's when we decided to bring her here to the hospital."

It seemed the words came tumbling out of my mouth with ease, but it didn't feel that way. I hesitated to look Mr. Forester in the eyes, terrified that his gaze might stun me like a loaded weapon. To my surprise, his eyes were kind and sympathetic.

"Kacey," he said softly, "I'm so glad you were there with Jenny. How terrifying that ordeal must have been for you all. I just spoke to the nice receptionist here, and she told me what is happening with Jenny."

I listened intently as Mr. Forester continued.

"Jenny had a severe anxiety attack that resulted in heart palpitations and dysregulated breathing. Jenny has an existing heart condition, and the doctors were worried about any long-term effects and stress this could place on her heart. They opted to perform a minor surgery and place a loop recorder in her chest to monitor her heartbeat. She's okay though. She just got out of surgery, and she's resting. I bet she'd love to see you and the boys."

I stared at Mr. Forester, puzzled by his words. From the body language I had witnessed earlier with Mrs. Forester, I was under the impression that they had just received some awful news. Maybe I hadn't inherited Jenny's superpower after all.

"Kacey, before you go, though," he hesitated momentarily. "I'd like to ask you for more information about the amber eyes you observed in the forest. Are these the same eyes that people reported observing a few years back on the night that girl disappeared?"

"Uhm, yes, they are," I replied nervously. "They're back.

I don't know why, but they're back. Jenny and I saw them in the brush out back of my house last week, too."

"Hey, Kacey. I think it's best to keep this between us right now," Mr. Forester replied. "I want to do a bit of research on these amber eyes before we jump to any conclusions. I don't want to cause unnecessary panic around town. I can count on you to keep this hushed, right? Just between us, Jenny and the boys."

I thought it was a strange request. Why was Mr. Forester so invested in hiding the triumphant return of the amber eyes from people? I didn't have time to ponder that now; I had to prioritize time with Jenny.

"Of course, Mr. Forester. I won't say a word."

"Great," he replied. "Now, why don't you and Jenny go have a visit? Let her know I'll be there in a short while."

Mr. Forester and I parted ways. Heading to Jenny's room, my mind raced with wild scenarios involving Mr. Forester. Great, I thought, my anxiety-fueled drivel is on overdrive. Maybe I should ask Jenny about her father's interest in the amber eyes, or perhaps I should just let it go for now. I sighed. Just when I thought my internal struggles had been resolved, here they were, making a grand reappearance.

CHAPTER EIGHT

Friday, May 6th, 2022

Ellie, Jenny and I remained silent, nervously twirling our thumbs, our gaze fixed on the ceiling. We had no inkling about the punishment Mrs. Laughlin would dole out. Describing my anxiety as merely "anxious" would be an understatement; my stomach heaved, my head pounded like I had been hit with a hammer. This was not an experience I wanted to repeat, yet here I was once again with Ellie. The only source of comfort was having Jenny by my side. Mrs. Laughlin sat in her reclining leather chair, her steel-cold eyes staring us down from across the desk. I dreaded what would come next. Mrs. Laughlin cleared her throat.

"So, who wants to explain to me what ensued between the three of you? Jenny, Kacey, Ellie?"

We all sat in silence. Not a single sound escaped our mouths; the mouths that had been recently filled with anger and hatred. I snuck a glance at Jenny, who met my eyes questioningly. I could sense her reluctance to stir up more drama, yet her frustration with Ellie's perpetual victim role was unmistakable. On the other hand, Ellie portrayed an air of smug confidence, as if she had no role in the events that had just transpired. How typical, I thought. Just like Ellie, to assume no responsibility. I had to admit I was slightly jealous of Ellie's confidence. It's not that I aimed to instill fear in others or perpetually play the victim, but bidding farewell to the fear and anxiety that had taken up near-permanent residence in my mind would be a relief. Jenny looked away and turned slowly toward Mrs. Laughlin.

"I'm going to tell you something about Ellie, Mrs. Laughlin," Jenny said with unbridled anger. "Everyone here at school, whether they want to admit it or not, is fed up with Ellie and her antics. Maybe they're too scared to say anything and don't want to stir the pot, but I assure you, the rumblings going around in the halls and on social media support my claim."

Ellie's eyes pierced through Jenny like the sharp blade of a knife. The intensity of her stare was intimidating. I wanted to come to Jenny's defence and give her the support to back up her claims, but my voice had mysteriously vanished.

"Like you're any better, Jenny," Ellie huffed. "For your information, Mrs. Laughlin, Jenny and Kacey threatened me. Everybody heard it. Just ask Loa, River, Autumn and Adrienne. Hell, even their boy toys, Chase and Jordan, heard it."

Jenny scoffed, a look of annoyance plastered across her face.

"You know, Ellie, it's just like you to use your crew of misfits as witnesses as if they are reliable sources. My goodness, what's next, princess? You gonna pull some random transcript of our conversations out of thin air? Nobody threatened you. All we did was speak the truth, and the truth hurts, doesn't it?"

"Jenny, Ellie," Mrs. Laughlin shouted, "enough. I didn't call the three of you here to spark a debate. No, I called you here to get to the bottom of this mess. This has been ongoing for quite some time, and I think we need to find a solution to resolve this. Kacey, I'd like to hear your take on this matter."

"Me?" I replied with hesitancy in my voice. "I think Jenny covered it all. I'm not sure if I would have anything worthwhile to add."

"Kacey," Mrs. Laughlin said scornfully, "You and Ellie were in my office earlier. Would you care to elaborate on why I am sitting here with the two of you once again? There must be something that you can add to Jenny's remarks because it certainly seems that there is some sort of animosity between the two of you."

"Honestly, Mrs. Laughlin," I began, "I don't know what sort of problem Ellie has with me or Jenny or anyone else, for that matter. But for some reason, she can't resist the urge to verbally attack us at every opportunity. Neither of us ever talks to Ellie. We only interact with her when she's verbally assaulting us, and I mean, should we not be defending ourselves?"

"Kacey, that's not what I am implying at all," Mrs. Laughlin said defensively. "Of course, you have every right to defend yourself, but I believe there is a better way to do that than to cause an unnecessary scene in front of your peers. Perhaps you and Jenny could ask Ellie to leave you alone. Maybe you could say I don't feel like talking to you, and walk away. Even coming to me or another teacher would have been better than the public spectacle the three of you engaged in. Not to mention uttering words such as why don't you just die already or half of the people in this room wish you'd just vanish forever, could legally be considered threats. I don't think anybody wants to be charged with uttering threats, and I certainly don't believe that you wish harm to one another. That said, the three of you are forbidden to return to the dance, so go home and consider how you will resolve this matter and make better choices in the future."

Jenny and I didn't bother to argue with Mrs. Laughlin. We felt defeated enough and truthfully didn't want any more drama to ensue. Were we upset about leaving the boys hanging? Absolutely, but we knew they would understand, and we both knew that they would likely call us later to catch up on the gossip of our meeting with Mrs. Laughlin. On the other hand, Ellie cried out in typical princess fashion, protesting every single point made by Mrs. Laughlin and finding every reason to make herself the only victim in this scenario.

"Mrs. Laughlin, this isn't fair. I did absolutely nothing. Why am I being expelled from the dance? They are the ones who threatened me," she snarled, pointing her finger precisely at Jenny and me.

"Well, Ellie, you see," Mrs. Laughlin began, "all three of you were involved in this dispute, and it's only fair that all three of you are expelled from the dance. I can't be picking sides here. That wouldn't be very professional of me, now would it?"

Ellie sighed in exasperation, not bothering to hide her displeasure. I couldn't help but grin. Nothing gave me more satisfaction than when Princess Ellie was put in her place. Jenny, equally as amused, winked at me as we left Mrs. Laughlin's office and made our way home on foot.

"Gonna be a long walk home," Jenny sighed. "I feel bad that the boys spent all that money on a limousine, and we can't even enjoy it. Ouch. My feet are going to pay the price for this little misdemeanour. There's no way I'm walking all the way home in these ridiculous heels."

Jenny gracefully removed her heels, delicately retrieving them from the sidewalk, her stockinged feet meeting the pavement with unapologetic confidence. This was one of those moments where I was thankful for my pretty pink flats. I'm unsure how, but I had forgotten all about the limousine. I suppose the enchantment of the evening, before the incident with Ellie, had encompassed me, sweeping me away into a seemingly dreamlike realm of serene bliss. All my mind could conjure was an image of Jordan and me swaying in perfect harmony on the dance floor. I could feel the gentle twinge of a smile forming in the corners of my mouth.

"You know, Jenn," I mocked playfully, "I did tell you not to wear those insanely tall heels."

"Yeah, I know, I know…" Jenn replied hastily, attempting to change the subject. "I wonder if the princess will have to walk home, too? I think her parents are at some fancy business dinner, and I certainly don't think she'll call Jason to come pick her up. She's way too stubborn for that."

Jason was Ellie's older brother. He had graduated from Richfield High a few years back and undoubtedly caught the attention of many girls, including me and Jenny. We often contemplated where we would get married, how many children we'd have, what kind of house we'd live in and how amazing his body was under those tight t-shirts he always teased us with. He was a gym brat, and the rippled, toned muscles protruding from his too-tight shirts were a sure sign of his athletic prowess. His hair was a messy nest of dark, wavy chestnut hair, his eyes piercing blue sapphires. When his gaze locked onto you, it felt like being ensnared in the captivating spell of a hypnotist, drawn irresistibly into his realm of allure and enigma. There was no way of resisting his charm. But now that Jenny and I had Chase and Jordan in our lives, his charm had gradually withered into obscurity. Our fantasies now revolved around our current relationships with the boys, and nothing could distract us from our growing feelings towards them.

"You're probably right, Jenn. I don't think Jason would even be an option for her. She'd never swallow her pride and admit that she needs help. She'd rather walk the whole way home in the dark, carrying the train of her gown in her hand. She'd never let someone come to her rescue. That's not the Ellie way. And you know what? I don't even feel a bit sorry for her. She brought this on herself. We would still be at the dance if she minded her own business. This is all on her. I really do hope she disappears and never comes back."

"Whoah, Kacey," Jenny replied abruptly, "sounds like you're on the brink of losing it. I don't blame you, really. This was supposed to be our night. We had planned out every last detail for weeks, only to have it all come crashing down on us. I know how you feel, I really do, but I think Mrs. Laughlin does have a point. We may have taken it too far when we told Ellie we wanted her to vanish without a trace. I'm not coming to her defence or anything, I'd never be on the Ellie bandwagon, but I don't think wishing harm to someone is the right way to handle things. We're better than that."

I would be lying if I didn't admit that Jenny's moment of clarity surprised me. Typically, I was the shyer and more reserved one, hesitant to get involved in public charades. Jenny was usually the firecracker with confidence oozing like lava from a newly erupted volcano. She never backed down from a fight. It was as though a light bulb erupted inside her brain tonight, highlighting a new and improved Jenny. I had to admit, I was impressed by her calm and composed demeanour.

"I know you're right, Jenny," I said, somewhat embarrassed by my previous comment. "It's just while in the heat of the moment, sometimes your emotions take over and you just can't resist the urge to get things off your chest."

"Sounds like I'm starting to rub off on you a bit, huh?" Jenny smirked. "This newfound confidence, it's kinda nice to see. Now, if only you could let self-doubt disappear permanently, that would be something."

Jenny had a point. It felt nice to have the ability to stand up for myself, to have the desire to put myself first and not let people walk all over me. I wanted to make a promise to myself to let my fears go and be more confident. Still, every time I felt that I was making significant strides in building my self-confidence, there was that nagging feeling just waiting around the corner, ready to drag me back under the waves of doubt. It was odd, but my confidence only came out to play when Ellie pushed me. Strange, I thought. What was it about Ellie that pushed my buttons?

"It would be nice, but I'm not sure I have it in me to be confident all of the time," I replied. It's almost as if I need Ellie to give me that push. I don't know why, but she always brings out my hidden rage."

"Well, you're not the only one, Kacey. Ellie brings out the rage in me, too. She just has that magical way of pushing one's buttons. I wish I knew her secret. I'd love to know how to push her buttons. She only ever gets defensive when she gets caught by Mrs. Laughlin. Otherwise, she just laughs smugly with her little minion followers. I'm honestly tired of it."

The entire student population was tired of Ellie and her antics. The problem was that most people were too scared to say anything. They wanted to do all they could to avoid ending up on Ellie's hitlist, and who could blame them? Being on the receiving end of one of her targeted outbursts didn't feel nice.

As Jenny and I continued Westbound on Main St. toward our homes, we heard the distant wail of sirens approaching. I didn't think much of it at first. It wasn't unusual for the occasional siren to make its presence known throughout our small town. There were occasional medical emergencies or rare neighbourhood disturbances, like anywhere else. It wasn't until we saw a barrage of police vehicles racing down Main St. with blue and red lights strobing like disco balls that we began to suspect there was something more sinister taking place. Jenny and I exchanged a worried glance. Should we be out here alone in the darkness, with no other people around? Was there some sort of danger lurking within our town, waiting to stalk its next prey?

"Jenny, we'd better stick to the well-lit areas and do everything possible to get home as quickly as possible."

"Absolutely, Kacey. Let's walk a little faster."

I considered myself fortunate that Jenny resided just one block away from me. Neither of us would have to walk alone for long. The sirens gave us a sense of fear; fear that something was afoot in our small town. Whatever was going on, it could not have been anything good. Neither Jenny nor I had seen so many police vehicles in one place. It was both unusual and alarming.

Describing the relief of returning home, being enveloped by the comforting embrace of its familiar walls felt like finding sanctuary, a genuine reassurance rather than an overstatement. I'm sure Jenny felt a similar sense of relief. I was too engulfed by emotions to relax and settle in for the night. The excitement of the evening was still fresh in my mind: the limousine ride, the romance-fueled slow dance with Jordan, the drama with Ellie, the barrage of police vehicles. It was a lot to take in. No matter how diligently I attempted to coax my mind into dwelling on the positive aspects of the evening, it stubbornly gravitated back to the latter moments. Something about the sirens and flashing red and blue lights alarmed me, I couldn't put my finger on it. My thoughts were abruptly shaken back to reality when the phone rang. I picked up the phone, almost hesitantly.

"Hello."

"Kacey, it's Jordan. I just wanted to check to make sure you got home alright. The police shut the dance down. There was some sort of police incident, and the school was asked to close up and send everyone home. They just sent out an email to all parents notifying them of the early closure. Chase just called Jenny, and she's safe at home."

"Yeah, I know. We walked home together," I replied.

"Did you two notice anything unusual?" Jordan asked with concern in his voice.

"We did see all of those police vehicles go racing by," I replied. "Did the police mention anything about what was going on or why they shut the dance down?"

"Nothing definitive," Jordan replied. "But I did overhear some of the officers mentioning that some townsfolk reported hearing the shrill scream of a young woman. I thought I overheard something about someone seeing some strange coloured eyes lurking in the bush just on the outskirts of town, too. Seems a little far-fetched to me."

"So strange. I wonder what's going on?" I asked with concerned curiosity.

"No idea, Kace. All I know is I'm glad both you and Jenny are safe. Not that I want to bring up Ellie or anything, but she was walking alone too, right?"

"Oh shit Jordan, you're right. I don't like the girl, but I don't want anything bad to happen to her. I think Jenny might have Loa's number. Maybe I should phone her and see if she's heard from Ellie."

I gave Jenny a call and retrieved Loa's number. It would seem strange to some that Jenny would have Loa's number, considering she was Ellie's second in command. However, there was a time when the three of us were close before Ellie came to our middle school. Our relationship with Loa rapidly changed when Ellie made her middle school debut. Loa always sought approval and wanted nothing more than to fit in and be part of the "it" crowd. A friendship with Ellie provided her with that path to popularity. We soon became nothing more than a distant memory. Jenny, being the amazing friend she was, asked if she should call Loa. I suspect she was trying to spare me the anxiety of it all, especially after the events that had transpired that evening. I politely refused, knowing I had to commit to continually improving my self-esteem. I hung up with Jenny, drew deep breaths, and slowly dialled the numbers. The phone rang endlessly like a raging river making its way to the edge of a waterfall. After a few rings, I heard a deafening silence on the other end.

"Hello…" a voice said cautiously.

"Loa? It's Kacey."

"Kacey?" she replied questioningly. "Why are you calling me? What do you want?"

"Look, I know we're not exactly friends," I replied, "but I wanted to check in and see if you had heard from Ellie. With all the crazy shit going on tonight, I wanted to make sure she got home alright. I don't exactly want to call her, you know, in case things flare up again, but I thought maybe you might be a little more approachable. Have you heard anything from her?"

"Uh… no actually," Loa replied with fear in her voice. "I called her parents, but they said they hadn't heard from her. They even asked Jason, but he hasn't seen or heard from her either. They're getting worried, and honestly, so am I."

"Did you hear about what happened?" I asked. " About all of the police cars flying down the road, the woman's scream, and the strange colored eyes sighted in the bush?"

"Of course, it's all over the local news," Loa replied. "I sure hope Ellie shows up soon. I can't even imagine what I'd do without her."

"I do too, Loa. As strange as it sounds, I wouldn't wish harm on anyone, even Ellie. If you hear anything, could you give me a call?"

"Of course. Hey Kacey, just so you know, I don't have anything against you or Jenny. I just go along with Ellie, so that she knows I'm loyal and stuff. I just don't want to make her mad or anything."

"I already figured, Loa. Try to get some sleep. Good night."

"Good night, Kacey."

CHAPTER NINE

Friday, May 3rd, 2024

I reached Jenny's hospital room, still pondering my discussion with Mr. Forester. No matter how many scenarios I could muster, none seemed plausible, and of course, others were so far-fetched that I almost had to shake my head in disbelief. When anxiety takes control, your mind conjures countless outlandish notions, pulling you into the depths of conspiracy theories. I had to muster the strength to brush it aside, if not for my well-being, then for Jenny's sake.

Jenny was lying in bed, a white sheet pulled up to her chin, a pulse oximeter clipped to her fingertips, and a monitor beside her displaying her vital signs. I could hear the rhythmic thumping of her heartbeat synchronized with the monitor. Her eyes were closed, but I could tell she wasn't asleep. Her head swayed gently to an invisible melody streaming through her earbuds. Upon feeling my presence, she opened her eyes and greeted me with her trademark Jenny smile.

"Fancy meeting you here," she quipped. "Guess you thought I was done for, huh?"

"Well, you did give us quite the scare," I replied sincerely. "How are you feeling?"

"I'm okay, considering the circumstances. I didn't plan on landing in the hospital, though. I'm glad you, Jordan and Chase were there to help a sister out."

"How much do you remember, Jenny?" I asked with hesitation in my voice.

"I remember a steep hike and a waterfall. A picnic, cuddling with Chase in the moonlight." Suddenly, her pupils dilated as wide as saucers. She stared at me, fear emanating from her eyes.

"What is it, Jenn? What do you remember?"

"Amber eyes in the forest? Running away? Did that really happen, Kacey? Everything is so foggy."

"Uh, yeah, it did. That's why you ended up here in the hospital. We were running so fast to get away, and you were pretty much hyperventilating by the time we returned to the car. We rushed you here as quickly as we could."

Jenny paused, the moment stretching on endlessly. It felt akin to a cinematic scene, where time slowed as if the clock's hands were suspended mid-motion, each second stretching into eternity. My face remained fixated on hers, her pupils still dilated from the shock of remembering the events of the evening. "How? Why?" she muttered. "We really saw those glowing eyes again?"

"Yeah, only this time it was accompanied by the most ferocious and menacing growl, unlike any I've ever heard. There's no way it was a wolf or a bear. They don't have eyes like that or make that type of noise. I'm honestly stumped.

I have no idea what it was, and I don't want to find out either."

"Kacey, do you think this might be related to the night of the Spring Fling Dance? People did report seeing those same glowing eyes and hearing that woman's scream. I know it has been speculated before, but do you think it was Ellie? She did vanish that night. We could have been next. I'm so glad you and the boys were at the waterfall. Otherwise, I'm not sure what would have happened."

I had to admit, the thought had crossed my mind. Did that mysterious scream belong to Ellie? Did the source of the glowing amber eyes and the menacing growl ultimately play a role in her disappearance? These were all questions that the townsfolk had tirelessly mulled over, endlessly debating their answers. Although there had been a police investigation, no conclusive evidence had ever been recorded. It remained a mystery, but I suspected the case was about to be resurrected.

"I feel the same way, Jenn. I couldn't have survived that ordeal if it hadn't been for you and the boys. As for Ellie, I have my suspicions. We were all walking home alone from the dance. I'm sure she was all by herself. She would have been the perfect target for something sinister lurking in the shadows."

"I feel awful, Kace. We both told Ellie that we wished she would vanish forever. I can't help but feel guilty, almost as though we willed this to happen. Did we curse her?"

"I feel guilty, too, Jenn. But there is nothing that we could have done to prevent this from happening. We're not witches. It's not like we're experts at cursing people. It was going to happen regardless of what was said or done."

"I know Kace," Jenny sighed. "I honestly wish this whole thing would just go away."

"Me too, Jenn, me too."

I pondered approaching Jenny about her father and whether he had ever brought up anything regarding the amber eyes. I still could not fathom his involvement in this situation. Our conversation felt peculiar. Why did he not want me to disclose what had happened to anyone beyond our small circle? Keeping a secret from Jenny didn't feel right, I thought. I should ask Jenny about her father to find out what he knows about the situation. But what if she thinks I'm accusing him of something? What if she gets angry with me? Once more, I found myself in doubt. I compelled myself to dismiss my doubts and summon the courage to broach the topic. A recurring theme in my life, I mused. I must commit to work on my self-confidence.

"Hey, Jenny?" I asked with a hint of hesitation. "Has your father ever mentioned anything about the amber-coloured eyes, like now or even back when they were first spotted two years ago? I'm only asking because when I first saw him here at the hospital, I filled him in on what had happened to us at the waterfall. He seemed concerned about how the incident could have affected us both physically and emotionally. Still, he seemed more concerned with me not telling anyone outside of our group about what had happened tonight."

Jenny's gaze lingered on me momentarily, her eyes scanning me like a self-checkout machine at the grocery store. She bore an expression blending bewilderment and worry as if she were pondering how to formulate a response to my inquiry. My cheeks flushed, not from embarrassment but from deeply seeded anger that Jenny would hesitate to divulge crucial information about the recent events. Jenny and I didn't keep secrets from one another, or so I thought. However, her hesitation to my questions conveyed a conflicting narrative.

"I'm not really sure how to answer that, Kacey. In all transparency, I don't know much about the events from the night Ellie disappeared or if my father was involved. I can confirm that on the night Ellie vanished, my father engaged in a hushed conversation over the phone with someone. It was very clear that he didn't want anyone to hear. When he hung up, he saw me standing in the hallway, but he didn't seem flustered or the least bit bothered. I didn't think anything of it. I just assumed he was on a business call and was trying his best not to disturb the rest of us watching TV in the next room."

"I'm not sure why, Jenn, but it just really strikes me odd that he doesn't want others to know about what happened to us tonight. It just doesn't make sense. There's got to be more to it than either of us knows. I know this is asking too much, but could you talk to your dad? Maybe just find out why this needs to remain a secret."

"Of course, Kacey. I'm curious about it myself. It's not like the whole town doesn't know what happened to Ellie two years ago; everyone knows about the amber-eyed sighting. Would it shake the town up again to know that the mysterious glowing eyes have resurfaced? Probably. But isn't that information that everyone deserves to know? People might want to take precautions to protect themselves."

It was a relief to know that Jenny understood my stance on our experience and her father's reluctance to have anyone else become aware of the situation. I needed answers, especially after this shocking and scary conundrum we had found ourselves in. It would be hard to bite my tongue and keep things hushed, but I knew I had to give Jenny ample opportunity to have a discussion with her father. I had no choice but to patiently wait.

"I'll let you get some rest, Jenn," I said, satisfied that our conversation would lead to long-awaited answers. "The sooner you get out of here, the better."

I slowly walked with cautious optimism to the hospital room door, turning to flash Jenny a confident grin before exiting into the sterile white starkness of the hallway. I had to find Chase and Jordan and update them on Jenny's condition and the strange occurrence with her father. I could not wait to solve this mystery. It was time to finally get the answers the whole town had been contemplating over the past two years.

CHAPTER TEN

Saturday, May 7th, 2022

I woke up feeling like I had emerged from a tumultuous nightmare. My eyes were heavy, my head ached, and my heart palpitated like a rhythmic drum at a rock concert. I was surprised that I had slept at all. Last evening's events were akin to a horror movie, simultaneously mysterious, chilling, and unfathomable. I got up from the comfort of my warm bed, stretching my arms far above my head to wake up my tense muscles. I sauntered out of my bedroom and down the hall into the bathroom, the smell of bacon and toast greeting me like an old friend. I could hear the clanking of dishes from the kitchen below me; my parents were already in weekend hustle mode. I'm unsure why, but I half expected things to play out differently this Saturday morning. After all, it wasn't your usual start to the weekend. As I was about to close the bathroom door and hop into the shower, my mother's voice echoed up the stairs like a gentle summer breeze.

"Kacey! Breakfast is ready."

"I'm just about to hop in the shower. I'll be down in a few minutes," I called out.

"Kacey, your father and I want to talk to you. Could you hold off on your shower for the time being?"

With some hesitation, I descended the winding staircase, cautiously entering the kitchen. I knew my parents had likely seen the news and had already gotten wind of last night's unusual events. I have no idea why my heart rate spiked so sharply, nor why my stomach churned as though I had just been on a drunken bender. It's not like I had done anything wrong.

"So…" I hesitated, "what's going on?"

"We just wanted to talk to you about what happened last night," my father started. "We heard about last night's occurrences; the police cars, the woman's scream, and those… those…amber coloured eyes," he stuttered. "We heard you come in early last night, and we received an email from the school notifying us that the dance had been shut down. We would be lying if we told you we weren't concerned for your safety. We didn't say anything last night because we thought you had probably been through enough and thought it best to let you sleep. But I think we should talk about it now over breakfast."

I stared at my father, my eyes brimming with tears. He was right. We needed to talk about what had happened, and I needed to tell them about my conversation with Loa. If for no other reason, I just needed to talk to someone to relieve this heavy burden. Keeping it secret would do no good for anyone, especially for Ellie, who, as far as I knew, was missing.

"Dad," I choked out with angst, "I'm so scared. Jenny and I got sent home from the dance last night. We had a confrontation with Ellie, and Mrs. Laughlin thought it would be best if the three of us left. I didn't want to bother you and Mom, so Jenny and I decided to walk home. We felt safe. It wasn't too late, and we walked home together. You know, safety in numbers, right?"

"Safety in numbers, absolutely," my dad responded sympathetically. "So… did the two of you see anything on your way home?"

"No, nothing… except for the police vehicles racing down Main St. We thought it was unusual, but we didn't think anything more of it until I spoke to Jordan."

"What did Jordan say about it?" my father quipped.

"He told me that the police asked the school to end the dance early and send all students home immediately. He thought he had overheard a few officers mention a woman screaming and that there had been a sighting of some strange-coloured glowing eyes in the bush on the outskirts of town. Jenny and I didn't see anything or hear any screaming." I hesitated briefly, fear welling up deep within me. "Dad," I called out, somewhat frightened. "Ellie was walking alone. I phoned Loa after talking to Jordan. She said Ellie never made it home."

"What?" my dad called out with shock and concern. "The news didn't mention that last night. Why wouldn't the police make a statement?"

"I have no idea, Dad. Maybe Ellie's parents wanted to contact all their friends and family first to see if they had seen her."

"Well, if it were me and you had gone missing," he

retorted, "I'd sure be contacting more than friends and family, that's for sure."

He wasn't wrong. If I were the parent of a missing child, I'd certainly be contacting the authorities immediately. But I had to have faith that the Mason family had their reasons for not reporting their daughter missing last night. Whatever the reason, I wouldn't hold it against them; they were already going through something unimaginable.

My father fixed himself a plate of bacon, eggs, and toast, poured himself a cup of coffee, and perched comfortably in his easy chair. He casually reached over to the end table, gripping the TV remote precisely, and turned on the morning news. Mitchell Murphy, Fort Richfield's top reporter, echoed from the television speakers. I had difficulty hearing what he was saying, so I meandered my way into the living room, arms in a balancing act, holding a plate of scrumptious eggs, bacon and toast in one hand and a cup of hot coffee in the other. As I began to place my enticing meal down and plunk myself comfortably onto the couch, Mitchell Murphy's voice captured my attention.

"Ellie Mason, a student at Richfield High, has been reported as missing early this morning. She was last seen leaving Richfield High at approximately 9:00 pm, departing the Spring Fling Dance. Sources tell us that she and two other students, Jenny Forester and Kacey Lundgren, had some sort of a confrontation and were asked to leave the dance by the school principal, Mrs. Rachael Laughlin. At around 9:15 pm, some of the town residents reported hearing a woman's scream coming from the east side of town, and others have reported witnessing what can only be described as glowing amber-coloured eyes peering out from the dense underbrush of the forest on the edge of town. We currently have Mr. and Mrs. Mason here to give a statement."

I glanced over at my father, whose eyes remained fixated with what could only be described as a mix of fear and fascination as the familiar faces of the Masons flashed across the screen.

"We are making a public plea to anyone in town who may have any information about the disappearance of our daughter, Ellie," Mr. Mason pleaded. "She did not make it home last night after leaving the Spring Fling Dance. There have been reports of a woman's scream, but we have no evidence to prove that it was Ellie. Please contact the authorities if you have any information that may lead us to Ellie. We are offering a cash reward of $10,000 for any information that leads to the safe return of our daughter."

"If anyone has any information about the disappearance of Ellie Mason or her whereabouts, please call our toll-free hotline at 1-888-254-8957. This is Mitchell Murphy with Fort Richfield News."

Just as my father clicked off the TV and set the remote on the side table, my mother poked her head in from the kitchen. She stared at my father, almost as though she were waiting for him to give her permission to speak. Her eyes caught mine in a fleeting glance, and she quickly scurried back into the kitchen, fumbling with oven mitts and attempting to look busy. My father wasn't the domineering type, and their relationship had always seemed solid, so this behaviour struck me as unusual. My father had not noticed my mother's strange behaviour, but I certainly had. I meandered to the kitchen, trying not to rouse suspicion with my father. I wanted to talk to my mother privately without any interruption.

"Hey, Mom," I whispered. "Is everything alright? You looked like you wanted to say something to Dad, but then you took off in such a hurry."

"I'm fine, Sweetie. I wanted to talk to your father about something I had overheard the neighbours discussing last night. I didn't think much of it then, but I'm unsure after hearing the news report. I didn't want to interrupt your father during his breakfast, and I didn't want to alarm you."

"What is it, Mom? You don't have to worry about me. I would appreciate knowing what the neighbours were discussing. It might jog my memory. Maybe I'll have something to add to it. After all, Jenny and I may have been two of the last people to see Ellie."

"I never thought of that, Kacey." You're right; you two may have been the last people to see Ellie before she disappeared. Ok, I'll fill you in on what I overheard. Mr. and Mrs. Grays mentioned that they had been walking their dog on the east side of town between 9 and 9:30 pm. They had seen a young girl with blonde hair matching Ellie's description walking alone along the side of the road. She was heading toward a forested area on the eastern edge of town."

"What?" I gasped. "That doesn't make any sense. Ellie lives nowhere near the forested area. First, why were Mr. and Mrs. Grays walking their dog way over there, and second, why would Ellie go into the forest?"

"All great questions," my mother replied, "and ones I don't have the answers to. Mr and Mrs. Grays aren't aware that I had overheard their conversation. There was no mention of Ellie by name, but as of last night, nobody knew that Ellie had gone missing. For all we know, it could have been someone else that they witnessed heading into the forested area, but after hearing Mitchell Murphy on the news this morning, I began to cautiously connect the dots."

"Should we call the hotline that they posted on the news?" I inquired. "Anything could be considered relevant at this point, right?"

"Yes," my mother replied. "Anything we can do to help is a good thing. Even if the Grays have already reported their sighting, giving our statement is still a good idea. I hope that the town folk would give us the same respect if you had gone missing."

"Do you want me to call Mom?"

"How about we call together," she suggested.

I smiled warmly at my mother, praying that this information would lead to something, anything. I wasn't Ellie's greatest fan, but I certainly couldn't fathom what her parents were going through or her for that matter. My mind wandered to thoughts of fear and anxiety. "Was she cold? Was she hungry? Was she hurt? Was she safe? Was she scared? Stop it," I chided myself. "Don't think those types of thoughts. She's okay; she's got to be."

CHAPTER ELEVEN

Monday, May 6th, 2024

The weekend came and went like a thunderstorm on a hot summer day. I spent my time reading books and writing in my journal. It was a relief to have something to distract me from the ever-present drama that seemingly followed me like a dark cloud hovering overhead. Unfortunately, the reprieve was all too swift, and the grip of reality again swooped upon me like a raptor catching its prey.

How could it possibly be Monday already? I wasn't ready to return to school yet after the traumatizing events that had occurred last Friday. Jenny spent Friday night in the hospital and then the weekend at home resting. As for Jordan and Chase, the amazing boyfriends that they were, arranged to have flowers delivered to us over the weekend. Jenny and I spent an hour or two texting over the weekend and swooning over how in love we were. Some might argue that we were too young to know real love, but I didn't pay much attention to that banter. I knew how I felt; Jenny knew how she felt, and that was all that mattered. As I lay in bed contemplating the decision to get up and start my day, my thoughts were swiftly interrupted by the loud thump thump thump of someone banging on my bedroom door.

"Yeah, what is it?" I called out, somewhat annoyed that my moment of tranquillity had been yanked away so abruptly.

"You better get up, Kacey. You're going to be late for school," a familiar voice chanted from the other side of the door.

"Jenny," I exclaimed, both surprised and delighted.

"The one and only," she exclaimed.

I hopped out of bed, quick as a flash of lightning, nearly barreling down the door. I had not expected Jenny to return to school for at least a couple more days. What a pleasant surprise.

"Jenn, what the hell are you doing here?" I squealed in pure delight.

"Wild horses couldn't keep me from hanging with my best friend and boyfriend. Besides, I'm feeling alright, and I need the distraction."

"Well, I'm glad I can be one of your distractions," I laughed. "What do you say? Should we get to school early and surprise the boys? I don't believe they expected you to be back so soon."

"I've got a better idea. Let's grab some breakfast and bring something for the boys. I was thinking of something hot, like breakfast sandwiches or something. Nothing like showing the boys how much we love them than presenting them with a hot and fresh breakfast."

"Sounds like a plan," I exclaimed. "Let me get myself dressed and ready. I'll be ready to go in like ten minutes."

Jenny made her way down the stairs as I barricaded myself in the washroom, frantically brushing my hair and teeth and grabbing whatever was immediately accessible in my closet. No time to waste; we had to make it to school before the boys.

We arrived at school twenty minutes before the warning bell. The boys typically arrived ten minutes before the start of the first period, so we knew that we would be delivering them a surprise in the form of breakfast and Jenny's return. It wasn't long before we saw the familiar gleam of Jordan's car glinting in the morning sunlight. They casually pulled into the parking lot and stealthily backed into their assigned parking spot. Upon seeing Jenny and me, Chase and Jordan immediately grabbed their backpacks and ran at a marathon pace, greeting the two of us with wide-open arms and a warm embrace.

"Hey, Jenn," Jordan greeted, sounding somewhat surprised. "Didn't expect to see you here today. How are ya feeling?"

"Oh, you know, battered, bruised and beaten. The usual stuff that comes with a hospital visit," Jenny replied sarcastically.

Chase smiled at Jenny, relishing every moment of sarcastic drama. "I'm so glad you're back, Jenn. School isn't the same without your lovely smiling face to greet me."

"Right back at ya, kid," Jenny replied with a wink.

The back-and-forth banter between Jenny and Chase was a mixture of sweetness with a hint of sarcasm. It was their special way of communicating, and it worked for them.

I loved listening to it. Jordan and I, however, were more straightforward in our communication style. We said what we meant, and we meant what we said, and I was okay with that. I wasn't one to read between the lines anyway.

"So, boys…" I chimed in. "Jenny and I have a surprise for you."

"You mean the surprise wasn't Jenny's return?" Chase exclaimed with amusement.

"As amazing as Jenny's impromptu return is, no, Chase, that isn't the surprise."

Both Jordan and Chase exchanged nervous glances. I'm unsure what they were expecting, but I highly doubt it warranted a case of the jitters. I smiled, half amused, half concerned that they'd think I'd spring something unsettling on them, especially after what we had all experienced. I reached into my backpack, slowly pulling the breakfast bag out to create a sense of mystery and suspense. Jordan and Chase, like dogs awaiting a scrap of food, gazed intently at my hand, almost as if trying to summon the power of X-ray vision. I looked over at Jenny, who seemed amused by the drama. Finally, I ended the suspense and revealed the paper bag with the contents of a hot and delicious breakfast hiding inside. The boys glanced at one another, bewildered by what I was presenting.

"Breakfast?" Jordan asked quizzically.

"Yeah, breakfast. What were you expecting, contraband or something?"

"Of course not," Jordan scoffed, sounding somewhat annoyed that I would suggest such a thing. "I'm just confused, is all. Why the big production over breakfast?"

"Why not?" I replied. "After all the shit the four of us

went through, we deserve a treat."

The boys didn't argue with that logic and quickly scarfed down their breakfast like they hadn't eaten in weeks, yet still appreciative of our thoughtfulness.

"I needed this today, Jenn," Chase said, his voice full of gratitude. Thanks so much for this amazing surprise. You too, Kace. I haven't been able to eat much over the last several days, and I honestly didn't even realize how hungry I was."

"Me too," Jordan chimed in. "I've been so stressed out lately. That whole incident on Friday has been all I've thought about. I just haven't been able to eat, sleep, or even think straight. It's a miracle that Chase and I even managed to send you ladies flowers."

"I think we've all been stressed, to be honest," Jenny replied. "Not that I want to rehash the events of Friday night, but I think we need to sit down together and go over all of the details; see what we remember."

"I agree, Jenn," I replied, anxious to piece everything together. "Have you talked to your father yet? You know about why he wants us all to stay quiet?"

"What?" Jordan and Chase exclaim in unison. "What does Mr. Forester have to do with this?"

Jenny looked at Jordan and Chase and then shifted her gaze to me. She looked worried as if something had been weighing on her. She opened her mouth to say something, but no noise escaped. I stared at her, concern in my eyes.

"Jenn? Are you ok? What's the matter?" I asked.

"I…I…I just didn't know what to say to him," she stammered. "I intended to say something but didn't know how he'd react."

"I know it must be hard, Jenn," I replied emphatically, "but I think your dad might know more than he's letting on. Would you feel better if I came with you to talk to him? I mean, I was there too, so I think he owes all of us an explanation."

"No," Jenny replied with authority, "I need to do this alone. I will summon up the courage to go and talk to him tonight. He is my father, after all. Who can I talk to if I can't talk to him?"

"Is that a rhetorical question?" I asked slyly with a wink.

Jenny smiled. "I can always count on you to make me laugh, Kace."

The warning bell for the first period rang out with authority, and the four of us exchanged glances, knowing that this conversation would have to continue later.

"I'll see you all later," I called out as I swiftly walked away to English class. Jenny and the boys gave an enthusiastic wave as they made their way to their classes. Despite knowing that our conversation would pick up later, I couldn't help but wonder what juicy details Jenny might uncover. Her father acted suspiciously at the hospital; there was no question about that. What I couldn't wrap my mind around was what connection he could have to our sighting, or the one from two years ago, for that matter. Did he know something that the police didn't already know? Was he involved in some way? So many questions, yet I had to force myself to put them to the back of my mind. School was the priority now, and everything else would have to wait.

The day dragged on endlessly. Have you ever been so anxious about something that you could only focus on getting answers? Yeah, it was that kind of day. Despite making every attempt to shut off my brain, the endless loop of questions concerning Jenny's father's involvement played on repeat. When the dismissal bell finally announced the end of the school day, I triumphantly picked up my backpack and raced out the door eagerly. I wanted to make sure that I caught Jenny before she headed home. I knew how nervous she was feeling when it came to talking to her father.

I made my way to Jenny's locker with lightning speed, dodging my way in and out of student obstacles. It wasn't long before I saw Jenny's familiar smile turn the corner and head in my direction. I smiled back, unsure if Jenny's smile was sincere or a facade.

"Hey, Jenn," I said with a hint of hesitation. "How are you feeling?"

"Well, if I said I was perfectly fine, that would be a blatant lie," Jenny replied. "I love my father, and I know that he would never be upset with me for asking a sincere and honest question, but I can't help but feel this dreadful feeling in the pit of my stomach. I don't even know why I feel that way. It's not like he had anything to do with what happened, right?" Jenny's voice wavered as though she wasn't entirely convinced that what she was saying was valid.

"Right," I replied, not confident that my voice reflected the credence I was attempting to portray. "Jen, you've got this. You don't think you do, but you've got this. I'm just a phone call away if you need any support."

"Thanks, Kace. You are an amazing friend."

With that last pep talk, Jenny and I hugged and parted

ways. I couldn't help but feel anxious for Jenny. Even the idea that her father could have some involvement in this scenario was mind-blowing, if not ludicrous. But was it, though? There was just something off about how he persisted that we not share what happened to us with anyone outside our circle. I had to put it out of my mind for now and find some other distraction until Jenny had found the opportune time to have that conversation with her father. So, I did what any anxious teenager would do; I went home, grabbed some snacks, plopped down on the sofa, grabbed the TV remote and attempted to engross myself in other people's drama. Reality TV was just what the doctor ordered, except my hand kept a tight grip on my phone, constantly sneaking worried glances at my text messages to see if Jenny had any news to share. This was going to be a long evening.

CHAPTER TWELVE

Saturday, May 7th, 2022

My mother dialled the hotline number with tensed fingers. Although she was doing the right thing, I believe she was worried about what revelations might come to light with this newfound information. Perhaps this information had already been reported by Mr. and Mrs. Grays, and nothing new would have come to light. We just didn't know. She put the speaker on so we could hear and contribute to the conversation. She inhaled deeply as the ringing on the other end of the phone echoed loudly throughout our kitchen. When the woman on the other end of the phone finally picked up and greeted us, my mother let out an anguished sigh. I could see the tension building in her neck and shoulders, her bright blue eyes wide with worry and anticipation.

"Yes, hello," my mother greeted the woman on the other end of the phone. "Is this the right number to report any information about Ellie Mason?"

"It sure is, ma'am," the woman responded. "Did you have something you'd like to report?"

"Well, I'm not entirely sure," she said uncertainly. "I overheard my neighbours talking this morning, and they mentioned that they had seen a young lady fitting Ellie's description last night down near the woods at the east end of town. I didn't think much of it until I saw the news report on TV."

"Okay, ma'am, and do you know if your neighbours have formally reported their sighting?" the woman asked.

"I'm not sure, to be honest. I overheard the neighbours talking maybe an hour ago, and I never thought to ask because I wasn't aware at the time that Ellie was missing."

"Okay, ma'am. Is there anything else you'd like to add to your report?"

"I don't think so," my mom responded. She looked up at me suddenly and gestured toward the phone. "My daughter is here with me. She and Ellie went to the same high school. She and her friend Jenny had some sort of an altercation with Eliie last night, and the three of them were ejected from the dance. They may have been the last two people to see Ellie before she disappeared. Would you like to speak to her?"

"That would be wonderful, ma'am," the woman responded. "Any information is crucial at this point in the investigation."

My mother held the phone out toward me, the bright white screen blinding me like the sun reflecting off a mound of freshly fallen snow. My hand moved as if in a slow-motion action scene, gripping the phone tightly before touching my ear. "Hello," I said, somewhat hesitantly.

"Good morning," the hotline woman greeted me cheerfully. "Your mother tells me that you and your friend had an altercation last night with the missing subject, Ellie. Is that correct?"

"Uhmm… Ye…yes," I stammered.

"Firstly, what's your name, sweetie?" she asked, her voice dripping with sweetness like honey.

"Kacey, Kacey Lundgren."

"Ah, so you're the Kacey Lundgren they mentioned on the news this morning. And your friend Jenny Forester? She was involved in the altercation, too?"

"Yes, ma'am. All three of us were involved."

"I see," she replied calmly. "Could you give me some details on what happened that resulted in the three of you being asked to leave the dance?"

"Uhmm… yeah, sure," I responded, fearful and worried. "Jenny and I arrived at the dance with Jordan and Chase around 6:50 pm. We walked the red carpet, had our photos taken, you know, the usual stuff."

"Who are Jordan and Chase?" the hotline woman asked quizzically.

"They're mine and Jenny's boyfriends," I responded hastily, "but they had nothing to do with our altercation with Ellie."

"I see," she responded. "Okay then, continue."

"Jenny and I had gone to get some drinks, and on our way back to the dance floor, Ellie and her clique decided it was the opportune time to obstruct us from getting back to the boys. She told us that no boys would ever want us and that she and her clique were the only ones worthy of a boy's attention."

"I see. How did that make you feel?" the hotline woman asked, prying for more details.

"I just lost it. I'm not normally the type to get confrontational, but Ellie had been picking away at Jenny and me for so long that I just snapped."

"And how did Jenny get involved?"

"Jenny jumped in to defend me. She and Ellie were nose to nose. I thought they might throw some punches, but Mrs. Laughlin stepped in and broke it up."

"I see," the hotline woman said in a skeptical tone. "And I understand that there were witnesses who overheard the two of you wishing Ellie would die or go missing?"

"WAIT, what now?" I yelled out in shock.

"We have statements from several witnesses who overheard the two of you wish harm on Ms. Mason."

Still in shock, I had to force myself to revisit that awful night and tap my brain for the details I had so conveniently forgotten. I replayed the scene in my head. The epiphany came on suddenly. Shit, I did, in fact, wish Ellie dead. And Jenny? She did indeed threaten Ellie and say that most people hoped she would vanish forever. This did not look good for Jenny and me. "Ye...ye...yeah, you're right," the words tumbled out of my mouth like falling rocks in a landslide. "I didn't remember that until you just mentioned it. We didn't mean it, though. You know what it's like when you're heated and in the moment, right? You just spout off stuff. We would never wish harm to anyone."

"Yes, I get it," the hotline woman responded. "I've been in a verbal confrontation a time or two, but you must understand how this looks, right?"

"I know exactly how it looks, but I assure you that Jenny and I are not involved with Ellie's disappearance in any way, shape or form."

"That's good to hear, but deciding whether you're involved is not up to me. That's up to the authorities. I'm only responsible for asking you questions and recording the information."

"Yes, I understand," I replied, feeling somewhat defeated. "So what happens next?"

"Well, I do have a few more questions for you. Then I will send this report to the local authorities, and they may contact you and Jenny for more information."

"Okay, so what else would you like to know?"

"After the three of you left the dance, were there any more words exchanged between the three of you?"

"No," I replied. "Jenny and I live a few blocks from one another, so the two of us walked home together, heading west on Main St. Ellie lives on the east end of town, so she was walking home in the opposite direction."

"Do you know if Ellie was walking home alone?" the hotline woman asked.

"Yes, as far as I know. She left the dance alone, and later, after getting home, I spoke to my boyfriend, Jordan. He suggested I call Ellie's friend Loa to see if Ellie had made it home safely. He had overheard the police talking about some sort of weird amber-coloured eyes spotted on the eastern end of town and reports of a woman screaming."

"Did you end up speaking with Loa?"

"I did," I responded defensively. "She informed me that she had checked in with Ellie's parents that night, and nobody had heard from her."

"I see. Did Loa mention anything else?"

"No… well, just that she had nothing against Jenny or me. She claims she only joins the tirade to avoid betraying Ellie's trust. So, technically, even Loa knows that Ellie is a bully."

"I don't see the relevance in that last comment," the hotline woman replied sternly.

"I don't know," I replied sarcastically, "perhaps it means that others out there hold ill will toward Ellie, but they're too scared to do anything about it. Maybe the authorities should consider questioning everyone at the school who has ever interacted with Ellie. I have to be honest; this conversation has made me feel that Jenny and I are the prime targets of suspicion, and I don't exactly appreciate the implication."

My mother sat idly by on the kitchen barstool next to me. I hadn't noticed her gaze shifting from concerned to annoyed and angered. She motioned at me to hand over the phone, her eyes blazing with fire and brimstone.

"Hi, this is Mrs. Lundgren again," my mother said abruptly. "I'm not exactly thrilled to hear where this conversation is leading and the implications you are placing upon my daughter and her friend."

"Ma'am, I'm not making any implications toward your daughter and her friend," the hotline woman replied defensively. "I'm simply doing my due diligence and asking logical questions about the disappearance of Ms. Mason. That is my job, after all."

"No, your job is to take statements from eyewitness accounts. What you're doing is interrogating my daughter, which I assure you is not your job. What's your name, ma'am? I'd like to formally complain to your supervisor about your method of taking public statements."

"Ma'am," the hotline woman cried in exasperation, "there's no need to get a supervisor involved. I'm sure we can resolve this issue here and now."

"No," my mother belted out, angry and frustrated. "Please connect me with a supervisor now. This conversation we're having is over."

"Very well, ma'am. It'll be just a moment."

My mother exchanged a nervous glance in my direction and smiled. I could see that she was heated but was trying to keep her composure in check, not to alarm me. It was too late for that. I was already on edge and nervously anticipating what would happen next. Even with Ellie not present, she had a hold on me. Fuck, I thought. Will this girl ever set me free?"

It wasn't long before my mother focused her attention back on the conversation on the other end of the phone. A supervisor must have finally heeded her wishes to discuss the antics of the woman who took it upon herself to interrogate me. "Yes, hello," my mother greeted the person on the other end of the phone. "I'd like to file a complaint against one of your hotline employees."

"May I ask why, ma'am?" the supervisor inquired.

"She was leading my daughter to reveal information about last night and her relationship with Ellie."

"I see. Could you tell me a little bit more about what happened?"

"I'm fairly certain your conversations are recorded, are they not? Could you not go back and review the file? I don't particularly want to waste any more of my time rehashing the entire conversation."

"I understand, ma'am. Let me formally apologize for our employee's misstep in her communication. You're correct. She had no right to interrogate your daughter. That is the job of the authorities. However, if your daughter willingly answered the questions, we have the right to forward that information to the authorities. I hope you can understand that."

"No, actually. I don't understand. My daughter is a minor and should be informed of her rights before she is led to reveal certain details of her relationship with Ellie. You know what? Since neither you nor your employee can help, I will go to the authorities with my daughter and our lawyer. I will be sure to file a formal complaint about the incident with your employee, too. It's quite obvious you are not taking the correct steps to train your employees and inform them of callers' rights, particularly when they are minors."

"I'm sorry you feel that way, ma'am. I sincerely hope that you have a wonderful day."

Without saying goodbye, my mother slammed the phone with such gusto that the table shook. I had never seen her so infuriated. "Go get dressed, Kacey. We're going to the police station."

I stared at my mother, shocked but equally impressed. This was a new side to her that I had never witnessed before. It's true what they say; when it comes to her children, a woman transforms into a fierce mama bear. I could only hope that her raw and fierce side would be inherited by me when I had my own children.

CHAPTER THIRTEEN

Monday, May 6th, 2024

The phone rang, loud like an alarm clock, jolting me from my temporary distraction of reality TV drama. I knew it had to be Jenny, or rather, I hoped it was Jenny. I wasn't in the mood for idle chit-chat. There was too much on my mind, and I wouldn't have the drive or the energy to feign interest. I raced to my phone, sitting on the table on the opposite side of the room, grasping it as though my life depended on it. "Jenny?" I asked.

"Yeah, Kace. It's me."

"Thank goodness. I was beginning to think you'd fallen into the abyss or something. So… what happened? What did your father say?" She hesitated briefly before pulling in a deep breath as though she were attempting to calm her fluttering nerves.

"Where do I start?" Jenny replied in exasperation. "There's so much to tell, and I honestly think I have yet to comprehend any of it."

"It's alright, Jenny. Just take a moment to gather yourself and start whenever you're ready." Truthfully, I wanted Jenny to spill everything instantly, but I knew I wouldn't be an ideal friend if I pressured her before she was ready to share.

Jenny drew another deep breath and began delineating the details of her conversation with her father. "So, you obviously know that my father works for Encore Enterprises," Jenny began.

Encore Enterprises was a reasonably new, highly accredited scientific research center that opened only three years ago. Their main area of research focused on extracting DNA from fossilized remains of long-extinct creatures. Typically, extracting DNA from fossilized remains is not the easiest of tasks. For one thing, DNA diminishes after approximately 1 to 1.5 million years under the best preservation conditions, and more often than not, the DNA fragments are too short to assemble into a correct genetic sequence. However, the research center was testing a new method for DNA extraction, so there was quite a buzz about how much success would be achieved. The goal, they claimed, was to learn more about these creatures, their diet, habitat, mating habits, and so on. Many rumours were circulating that something more sinister was at play at Encore Enterprises. The talk of the town was that the extracted DNA was being used to resurrect some of the creatures. However, other rumours claim that the DNA of multiple creatures was being combined to create some sort of genetically engineered hybrid super creature. Jenny had never spoken much about her father's work at the research center, and I never bothered to ask. Like several other people in town, I chalked the rumours up to paranoid conspiracies.

Jenny continued, "Well, he was tasked with testing some fancy new equipment. He says there was some sort of malfunction, and the DNA sample was contaminated. He thought he had heard the faint sound of growling inside the chamber where the DNA was extracted. But, as he made his way to investigate, the power mysteriously went out, leaving him in complete darkness."

"Jenn, are you serious? Something isn't right about that. How could it be possible that a power outage occurs right at that moment?"

"I don't know, Kace," Jenny replied, a perplexed look on her face. "But that's not even the strangest part... when the lights powered back on, he opened the door to the chamber only to find the DNA sample missing and..."

Jenny hesitated.

"And what, Jenn?" I asked, my voice dripping with urgency.

"And there were claw marks on the thick steel walls of the chamber."

"What!" I cried out, equally shocked and concerned. "When did this happen? I don't recall any recent power outages."

"Well, that's the thing," Jenny began. "It happened on the night of the Spring Fling Dance two years ago."

My jaw dropped. My eyes fixated intensely on Jenny's. Why hadn't this information been reported to the authorities? Was this incident related to what the townsfolk reported seeing that night, the glowing amber eyes? Did this have any link to what happened to Ellie? Did this have anything to do with what happened to us a few nights back? My mind was racing; there were so many questions and no definitive answers.

"Jenny," I exclaimed, "Your father has been keeping this secret all this time? Why wouldn't he say something sooner?"

"I asked him that very question, Kace. He danced around the subject a bit. All he would say was that he worried the authorities wouldn't take him seriously. He was scared that they would accuse him of covering something up and arrest him for tampering with biological substances."

"I do understand that. It does sound far-fetched, and to be honest, hearing it now seems surreal. But did your father even consider that what he witnessed could be connected with Ellie's disappearance? I mean, the townsfolk reported those strangely coloured eyes appearing that night. Then, factor in Ellie's disappearance? Doesn't it seem strange that those things occurred in conjunction?"

"Absolutely," Jenny replied. "It's all strange, and like I said, I'm still having difficulty comprehending it all. But, Kace, I believe my father. I don't think he was covering up anything. I do think he's just as confused as you and I. As for the connection to Ellie's disappearance and our scare last week, all he would say was that he never really considered that the events at the research center were related to Ellie until we reported our experience at the waterfall. According to him, the similarities between that night two years ago and our incident were too convenient to be coincidental."

"Right?" I agreed. "There is no way that the sighting of the amber-coloured eyes on the night of Ellie's disappearance and our experience last week aren't related. Even stranger are the claw marks on the walls of the chamber. Does your father have any idea what could have made them?"

"He didn't say, but I'm sure he would have told me if he had any inclination. Anyway, the reason he wanted us to keep quiet about what happened to us was that he thought the authorities would connect Ellie's disappearance to our incident. He then worried that what happened at the research center could potentially come to light, and he would be accused of knowingly withholding information that could have been pertinent to Ellie's missing persons case."

"But your father said that he didn't make the connection to Ellie's case until he heard about what happened to us. Why not tell the police exactly that?"

"Like I said, Kace... he's worried that the authorities will think he's intentionally covering something up. The story is so far-fetched that he fears they will automatically implicate him in Ellie's disappearance, regardless of what claims he makes. Truthfully, I don't think we should say anything. I know my father; he isn't the type to make up some wild story like that, and he certainly doesn't have it in him to hurt anyone, even Ellie."

"I don't doubt that for a minute, Jenn. And you're right. We'll keep things quiet. Let's fill Jordan and Chase in on the new revelations. Even if we plan to keep things hushed about our experience at the waterfall, the boys deserve to know what's going on. They are victims, too, and I'm pretty sure they were just as alarmed by everything that went down as we were."

"Definitely," Jenny replied. "But could we wait until tomorrow morning before school? After all of these shocking revelations tonight, I need a brain break. I just need to veg out on the couch and watch some nonsensical scripted TV drama."

"Of course, Jenn," I answered emphatically. "To be truthful, I could use some quiet time, too. I need to process a lot of information, and I don't think rehashing our conversation for a second time tonight will help me do that."

"Thanks, Kace," Jenny sighed, relieved by my understanding. "I'll see you tomorrow. Try to rest."

"You too, Jenn. Good night."

I hung up and immediately grabbed a notepad from my father's office. I wanted to create a list of all the events from the night of the Spring Fling Dance and those from the past several days. Although I knew I couldn't tell anyone about what had happened to us at the waterfall, I felt I owed it to myself to investigate further, connect the dots, and fill in the blanks, so to speak. I owed it to myself, Jenny, the boys, and hell, even Ellie. It would seem that Jenny's father was also an unintentional victim in this drama. If I could do anything to help keep his name free and clear and solve the mystery of Ellie's disappearance, I would consider it a massive achievement. After all these years, our town deserved some answers, and I was determined to bring those answers to them. Detective Kacey Lundgren, at your service.

CHAPTER FOURTEEN

Saturday, May 7th, 2022

I glided up the stairs as fast as I could to my bedroom, wasting no time rifling through my closet for the perfect outfit. My mother was enraged; this was no time to test her patience. As soon as I was dressed, I returned to the kitchen, racing like an out-of-control tornado. My mother grabbed her purse and keys, storming out to the car. I followed in close pursuit. I did not want to do anything to aggravate her further. She opened the car door aggressively, and I feared she might damage the springs. I climbed into the passenger seat post-haste, buckling my belt and sitting in complete silence, anxiously awaiting the gentle hum of the engine. She sat in silence for several minutes as though contemplating her next move. It wasn't long before she turned toward me, staring at me with stone-cold eyes.

"Kacey," she started in an eerily calm voice, "When we get to the police station, I don't want you to say a single word until Mr. Grieves arrives, do you understand?"

Mr. Grieves was our long-time lawyer and a close personal friend of the family. My parents first met him years ago when I was in grade school. He helped my parents out of a jam when their SUV lost control and collided with another vehicle, resulting in a debilitating injury to one of the passengers.

"Yes, Mom. I understand."

No sooner had I acknowledged my mother's request, Mr. Grieves made his grand arrival: gray suit and black tie, polished shoes and a folder with a stack of paper hanging out the side. He and my mother exchanged glances and a subtle nod.

"Good morning, Kacey," Mr. Grieves greeted me. "Your mother filled me in on all the details of your conversation with the woman at the missing persons hotline. She also filled me in on the events from the night of the Spring Fling Dance. Firstly, let me apologize on behalf of those involved for putting you through that gruelling type of questioning. You are a minor and have the right to have a lawyer present during intensive questioning. The woman working at the hotline was not following proper protocol and should never have subjected you to that. Secondly, I would appreciate it if you let me direct the flow of conversation with the authorities and only speak when I have given you a nod of approval. Is that okay with you, Kacey?"

I nodded my head in agreement.

"Great. Then why don't we head in and see what we can accomplish? I assure you, Kacey, you've done nothing wrong. You have nothing to worry about."

"But what about that comment I made at the Spring Fling Dance? You know, the one about wanting something to happen to Ellie?"

"You were understandably upset, and in the moment, you said something you didn't mean. It happens to the best of us. I wouldn't focus too much on that, Kacey. I've got your back."

I nodded my head once again, hesitantly, but also heeding his words. I would try my best to relax and let Mr. Grieves take the reins.

"So what do you say? Should we head in now?"

"Sure, I guess," I replied apprehensively.

The three of us made our way up the stairs of the police precinct. Each step felt like weights were wrapped around my ankles, undercutting me and forcing me to exude more energy. I let out an exasperated sigh. I was not looking forward to this, despite the reassurance by Mr Grieves. We finally made our way to the top of the stairs, and Mr. Grieves, the gentleman he was, held the door open for my mother and me.

"After you, ladies."

"Thank you," my mother replied with a gracious smile.

A woman at the front desk greeted us with a smile and a voice that could only be described as chipper.

"Well, good morning. How can I help you all today?"

"Good morning," Mr. Grieves replied. "We are here to file a complaint against a woman from the missing persons hotline."

"I see. May I ask why you are filing a complaint?" the woman asked.

"My client here, Ms. Lundgren, was wrongfully interrogated. The line of questioning led her to reveal certain details irrelevant to the situation. Additionally, she is a minor. She should have had an adult or a lawyer present if an interrogation was to occur."

"Thank you for bringing this to our attention, Mr...." the woman hesitated.

"Mr. Grieves."

"Thank you, Mr. Grieves. You are correct. The hotline's purpose is not to interrogate but to take note of potential tips that may lead us to the missing person's location. Any other questions unrelated to the information willingly offered by the caller are off-limits. You are also correct that a minor should always have an adult or lawyer present during these types of scenarios. Please provide me with the phone call's time and date so we may check our call logs to determine which hotline operator you spoke to.

"Absolutely," Mr. Grieves replied. "The call occurred this morning at approximately 9:30 am. The hotline operator was a woman, but we unfortunately did not get her name."

"That's okay, Mr. Grieves. We will check our logs to see which calls occurred during that time frame and which were answered by a woman."

Mr. Grieves glanced over at my mother and me with a thin smile of victory. "Thank you, ma'am. We very much appreciate your efforts."

"You're welcome, sir. Let me check our call logs. While I'm gone, please feel free to help yourself to some coffee or hot chocolate. I'll be back as soon as possible."

Mr. Grieves motioned for my mother and me to follow him to a small table and chairs tucked away in the corner of the police precinct waiting room. As we took our seats, he rifled through the stack of papers in the folder he had clutched tightly against his chest. Within moments, he had a sealed manila envelope that he eloquently placed on the table before us.

"So," he began. "I've been keeping tabs on all the happenings around Fort Richfield that may be connected to Ellie's disappearance. I know she was only reported missing late last night. Still, from the moment I got word of the mysterious sightings of the amber-coloured eyes and then Ellie's disappearance, I thought it might be useful to do my homework, just in case someone might need my help. And it's a good thing I did because when your mother called me this morning and filled me in on some of your interactions with Ellie last night at the dance, I knew I may have my work cut out for me. She told me that multiple witnesses overheard your words to Ellie. Could you tell me a little bit more about what occurred last night, Kacey? What prompted you and Jenny to confront Ellie?"

"Of course, Mr. Grieves," I replied. "Ellie approached the two of us and, in front of the entire school, told us that we were unworthy of our boyfriend's attention. Things with Ellie have been escalating for quite some time, and Jenny and I had both lost patience with it all, you know. We both said things in the heat of the moment that we didn't mean. But Ellie, being Ellie, took full advantage of that and used it against us by outing us to the entire school. She accused the two of us of wanting to hurt her."

"Did you want to hurt Ellie?" Mr. Grieves asked questioningly.

"No, of course not," I replied. "Like I said earlier, we said things we didn't mean. It was one of those situations where you're pushed to the edge and can no longer idly sit by and take it."

"I believe you, and like I mentioned earlier, I understand how things can become heated," Mr. Grieves explained. "Words are exchanged in the moment but aren't necessarily meant to be taken seriously. But the fact is that these words were uttered on the same night that Ellie disappeared, and we cannot ignore that it makes you and Jenny appear suspicious, especially in the eyes of the law. I don't want you to volunteer any information if we are summoned to speak to an officer. Let the officer ask you the questions and, as mentioned earlier, wait for me to give you a nod before you give a reply. You got it?"

"Yes, Mr. Grieves."

A few moments later, the woman who greeted us at the front desk returned and motioned for us to follow her down a long corridor. As I trudged down the corridor, my eyes observed all the fine details that the average person would likely not pay any attention to. The wall was adorned with employee of the month photos, advertisements for local community outreach centers, and old, outdated artwork. The carpet was ripped and torn in places and desperately needed updating. I wondered how people could come to work here day in and day out and maintain a positive attitude with such a dreary backdrop. I had to give myself a headshake because the decor is the last thing most people in these circumstances would notice. I suppose when I'm feeling anxious, my mind looks for ways to distract me from my stressors.

"You can take a seat in here," the woman said as she closed the door behind her. She hesitated briefly and turned around. "Officer Tarik will be right with you."

"Thank you, ma'am," Mr. Grieves replied.

I sat nervously at the table, my left leg shaking and my

fingers tapping in a rhythmic motion on the table. Mr. Grieves looked up at me, and he could instantly tell I was a mess. His eyes were soft and kind, yet that did nothing to quell my fears.

"Everything is going to be alright, Kacey. Follow my lead, just like I told you. Alright?"

I nodded in acknowledgement. If only I truly believed that.

CHAPTER FIFTEEN

Saturday, May 11th, 2024

The school week moved by at a snail's pace. I had difficulty comprehending how time could pass so slowly. You know the saying time flies when you're having fun? Well, in the case of Jordan, Chase, Jenny, and me, when you're nervous as hell, time seems to freeze.

Jenny and I had filled Jordan and Chase in on the details of Jenny's discussion with her father on Tuesday morning. They were equal parts confused, shocked, and curious. No surprise there; so were we. Upon waking up on Saturday morning, I decided to take another gander at the notes I had compiled about the whole amber eyes, research center and Ellie's disappearance scenario. Jenny, the boys, and I added to the notes all week, creating a timeline of events. It was as though we were actual detectives. We had made significant headway into our mock investigation, yet some things still left me to ponder. My thoughts were interrupted by an obnoxiously loud pounding at the front door. Who on earth was knocking at 8 am on a Saturday? I half grumbled and half yawned as I wiped the sleep from my eyes and forced myself to meander to the front door. I slowly turned the knob and opened the door unenthusiastically, hoping that whoever was on the other side of the door was worthy of my efforts.

"Hey, sleepyhead! What's happening? Anything new to share?"

"Jenny," I exclaimed, somewhat annoyed by the early arrival. "What on earth are you doing here, and why so early?"

"Good detectives never rest when there's a case to solve," Jenny replied triumphantly.

"I can't argue with that logic," I laughed. "I have nothing new to report; however, I just woke up and was about to examine the evidence we managed to compile, so to speak. Care to join me?"

"Would I?" Jenny grinned slyly. "Absofreakinlutely."

"Well," I giggled, "somebody's overly enthusiastic."

"You gotta be if you want to be a good detective," Jenny replied with a wink.

Jenny and I made our way to the kitchen table, pulling out our chairs with a loud screeching sound, which I must admit closely resembled the sound of nails on a chalkboard. I winced. That sound drove me up the wall. I quickly bypassed the moment, grabbing the stack of papers in a mangled heap on the table's left corner. Some of the documents clumsily floated to the floor in an effortless whoosh. I must make a note to be more organized, I thought to myself. I spent a good few minutes rifling through the stack until I found the timeline that the two of us and the boys had created. I slapped it down dramatically, face up on the table so that Jenny could see its detailed intricacies.

"Somebody's been busy," Jenny retorted playfully. "Look at all of those colours and highlights?"

"If you're going to make a timeline, you may as well do it right," I replied. "It's easier to follow and keep track of events when things are colour-coded, don't you think?"

"Umm… yeah. I'm just teasing you, Kace. You know, I think it's fabulous. Besides, what kind of detectives would we be if we didn't have some level of organization?"

I smiled, happy to know that I had the best and most supportive friend I could ever have hoped for. I began scanning the timeline, refreshing my memory of all the dates and events we had noted. The first entry occurred on the night of the Spring Fling Dance and Ellie's disappearance.

"So," I began reluctantly, "we know that when we left the dance, it was shortly before 9 pm. We also know that my neighbours, Mr. and Mrs. Grays, reported seeing a young woman fitting Ellie's description walking toward the forested area on the east side of town between 9 pm and 9:30 pm."

"We also know that on that same night, my father was working at the scientific research center, and the power mysteriously shut off, leaving them in complete and utter darkness," Jenny replied. "And, let's not forget that my father reported the DNA sample he was examining went missing and that in its place were strange claw marks left behind in the extraction chamber."

"That must somehow connect to the amber eyes reported that night and the ones we encountered at the waterfall," I said inquisitively. "Didn't your father mention hearing a growling noise from the extraction chamber, too, right before the power went out?"

"He did, and I must admit that got me thinking about the growls we heard at the waterfall," Jenny replied shakily. "I don't know, Kace. This is all so bizarre, like something out of a supernatural thriller."

"Tell me about it," I replied in agreement. "Another thing that has been eating away at me these past two years is why Ellie's parents didn't report her missing that night. Why did they wait until morning? Something was going down that night. We heard the sirens and saw the police cars racing down Main St. When she didn't arrive home, especially after receiving notification from the school that the dance was shut down early, you'd think they'd have been in a panic."

"Yeah, that part is certainly strange, and truthfully, I don't understand it any more than you, Kace. Mr. Mason works at the research center with my father. Maybe he could arrange a meeting between Mr. Mason and us, you know, to try to get some answers? It might seem strange that we're bringing this up two years later, especially since my father doesn't want anyone to know about what we experienced at the waterfall. Still, we could tell him we are working on an investigative report for the school. We could say we want to speak to people with firsthand experience in cases of missing persons. I just hope that it doesn't come across as insensitive."

"Wait," I exclaimed, shocked by Jenny's revelation. "Did you just say Mr. Mason works at the research center?"

"Yeah… why?"

"How long has he worked there?" I asked.

"Since it first opened, just like my father."

"So, he probably knows all about the power outage, the missing DNA sample, and the claw marks inside the extraction chamber?" I questioned.

"I imagine he would," Jenny replied. "How exactly is that relevant?"

"Think, Jenn," I cried out sternly. "If he knew what occurred that night, why wasn't he more concerned about Ellie's whereabouts? Why wait until morning to report her missing? I know this isn't the first time we've brought this up; hell, it isn't even the first time this morning. But seriously, why wait? Didn't you say that the Mason's were at some sort of business dinner Jenn?"

"I did mention that they were out for dinner, but maybe that information wasn't entirely accurate, who knows? If he had known about the power outage that evening, why would he have waited until morning to report Ellie missing? I know I'm not a parent, but I could not imagine knowing about the events at the research center and not being the slightest bit concerned about the whereabouts of my child."

"There's something off about the whole thing, that's for sure. I guess we've got more investigation work to do than, Jenn?"

"I'd say. You think we should call Jordan and Chase?"

"Yeah, I do," I replied matter-of-factly. "The more heads we put together, the better. I hate to do this to you, Jenn, but could you confirm whether Mr. Mason worked the night Ellie disappeared? I know it was difficult to engage in a discussion with your father in the first place, but I think this information could be relevant in cracking the case."

"No worries, Kace. The initial conversation was difficult, but shouldn't be as awkward or stressful this time. I've got this."

"Thanks, Jenn. Now, what do you say, call the boys?" Jenny nodded in agreement.

I picked up the phone and called Jordan while Jenny dialled Chase's number. I was anxious to start compiling the collected evidence and discussing this newly revealed information about Mr. Mason. How could this have slipped past me all of these years? How did I not know that Mr. Mason worked for Encore Enterprises? How could Jenny not have realized the relevance of Mr. Mason working there? What information did Mr. Mason know? Was he there the night of the blackout? Did he know about the claw marks on the inside walls of the chambers? Did Mr. Forester know what animal the DNA sample belonged to, for that matter? So many questions and possibilities. Where would our investigation lead us? I had no clue, but I was anxious to find out.

CHAPTER
SIXTEEN

Saturday, May 7th, 2022

The three of us sat waiting for Officer Tarik: my mother, Mr. Grieves, and I. We had been waiting for what felt like an eternity; however, a glance at the old analog clock above the door revealed that it had only been about five minutes. I was becoming increasingly anxious and beginning to lose patience. Mr. Grieves and my mother could sense this as they glanced at me with thin-lipped smiles. This was their attempt to reassure me that everything would be fine, but their efforts fell short of the intended goal. It wasn't too long after that, a tall man with dark hair, dark skin and dark brown eyes entered the room. His hair was combed back neatly with a wisp that fell slightly over his left eye. He wore a gray suit and a colourful tie with various anime cartoons plastered across it. His shoes were dressy and shiny black, making a scuffing noise as he walked across the carpeted floor. His eyes met mine, and despite the playful tie, I could instantly tell that he wasn't the type to beat around the bush. This man was all business.

"Good morning, everyone," he greeted us in a monotone voice. "The file I was perusing a few moments ago informs me that you are here to discuss an incident that occurred earlier this morning with one of our missing persons hotline operators. Is that correct?"

"Good morning, Officer Tarik," Mr. Grieves greeted nonchalantly. "Yes, that is correct."

"Please provide me with the nature of your complaint. I read that you are concerned with the questioning that Ms. Lundgren was subjected to."

"Yes, sir, that is correct," Mr. Grieves responded, sounding slightly sharp. "Ms. Lundgren was attempting to be a model citizen by phoning in and sharing information about her last sighting of Ms. Mason. She was unjustifiably subjected to personal questions that led her to reveal some information that should have only been discussed in the presence of a lawyer or trusted adult. Additionally, she is a minor, and in the eyes of the law, she is not required to answer any questions without an adult present."

"I see," OfficerTarik answered. "So, are you looking to press charges against our telephone operator?"

"No, sir, I wouldn't take it that far, but I request that you review proper protocol with your staff at the hotline and perhaps scratch any information that Ms. Lundgren was unjustifiably subjected to disclose from the record."

"Here's the problem with that, Mr. Grieves," Officer Tarik began. "While our hotline operator wrongfully asked questions that were not in line with her job description, she wouldn't have had that information, to start with, if other callers had not reported it to the hotline, too.

Several witnesses overheard some banter between Ms. Lundgren, Ms. Forester, and Ms. Mason on the night of the Spring Fling Dance. These witnesses willingly disclosed this information to our hotline operators. So, while our operator should not have used Ms. Lundgren to verify the validity of these statements, the information was already out there before Ms. Lundgren spoke a word. You must understand that because the source of the information did not originate with Ms. Lundgren herself, there is nothing that we can do to strike it from the record."

"I understand that just fine, Officer Tarik. However, any use of my client's statement to verify these reports must be stricken from the record. If you want to question my client again to validate the claims made against her, now is the opportune time since both I and her mother are present."

"Well, then," Officer Tarik replied, amused, "let's get started if it's convenient for you, of course, Ms. Lundgren."

I glanced at Mr. Grieves just like he directed me, and he nodded. "Yeah, sure. I guess," I replied hesitantly. Admittedly, I was none too thrilled about regaling the details all over again for what felt like the billionth time, but Ellie was missing, and it was my duty to do my part and help her find her way back home."

An hour and a half later, we emerged from the police precinct, all exhausted and ready to call it a day. Looking more exhausted and dishevelled than I, my mother gave me a weak smile. I knew she was proud of how I had handled myself. She knew all too well how anxiety and self-doubt had a habit of creeping up on me. Hell, I was proud of myself. If something like this had happened a year ago, I would have had a meltdown. Mr. Grieves once again fumbled with his papers as he attempted to maintain a look of professionalism. Once he gathered himself and his belongings, he glanced at my mother and me, giving us a triumphant wink.

"Well, ladies, we came out on top today. It's good that we had the opportunity to discuss your case properly, with me and your mother present, Kacey. All of the allegations against both you and Jenny are circumstantial at best. Words are just that, words. There's no solid evidence to prove that either of you had any affiliation with Ellie's disappearance. As a matter of fact, the two of you and Ellie live on opposite sides of town. There are no witnesses to confirm or deny that the three of you were together once you left the school dance. Your neighbours reported a sighting of a young woman fitting Ellie's description on the opposite end of town, with no sight of anyone else around. Unless there's some mystery person out there with solid evidence proving the three of you were together, there's nothing more the authorities can do. I reckon it's safe to say you are free and clear, Kacey."

"Thanks, Mr. Grieves," I replied, thankful to have such an intelligent and diligent person on my side. "Hopefully, this will be the last time I have to deal with all this."

"You're welcome, Kacey. I do believe you will have no further issues. And with that, ladies, I bid you adieu. If you need anything else, do not hesitate to contact me."

Mr. Grieves waved goodbye, smiling at us as he climbed into his shiny sports car and drove away.

Still looking tired and dishevelled, my mother turned to me and smiled. "Do you want to go get some lunch? After this ridiculously long morning, I'm famished. Maybe we could talk a bit about all the shenanigans that have been happening lately. By the way, why didn't you say anything sooner about how Ellie treated you?"

"Yes, to lunch, but can we talk about anything other than Ellie? If that's okay with you, I want to put this all behind me."

"Sure, honey. I completely understand. If you ever want to talk, just know that your father and I are here for you, okay?"

"Thanks, Mom. I appreciate everything you and Dad do for me."

My mother, looking a little embarrassed by all the mushy stuff but also thankful for the kind words, smiled. "Where should we go for lunch? You choose. After the day you had, you deserve to eat wherever you want."

"How about McGonigal's?" I asked.

"Absolutely," my mother replied enthusiastically. "They do have the best burgers in town."

"And the best milkshakes, too," I said excitedly.

My mother and I made our way to the car. After glancing at the side mirrors to check for vehicles, we pulled into traffic and headed off for our lunch date.

CHAPTER SEVENTEEN

Friday, May 17th, and Saturday, May 18th, 2024

Another week passed by in the blink of an eye. Things had been hectic at school, so much so that Jenny, Chase, Jordan and I barely had time to get together to discuss the notes on our investigation. Jenny made several attempts to further interrogate her father on the events that unfolded at the research center on the night of Ellie's disappearance, but he was swamped with work. The warmer spring temperatures created a backlog of work at Encore Enterprises. It wasn't unusual for business to pick up at this time of year; after all, digging for fossils was far more efficient after the ground frost melted. Fort Richfield High students were also prepping for the last weeks of the semester and final exams. It was a constant buzz of activity. Admittedly, I was disappointed in our lack of constructive gains in our efforts to seek out the truth surrounding that night's events, but I had no choice but to accept it. I possessed zero magical powers and could not erase the numerous tasks continuously heaped onto our laps. I could sense Jenny's frustration, too, as she constantly complained about being overwhelmed and overworked.

"I'm going to attempt to talk to my father tonight about Mr. Mason," Jenny informed me. "It's Friday, and he should be home early tonight to kick off the weekend. I don't have any homework or exams to study for next week either, so I have all the free time in the world. I hope he'll find the time to hear me out and answer all my questions."

"Keep me posted, alright, Jenn? I will be on edge all evening waiting for your call."

"Don't worry," Jenny laughed. "I wouldn't dare leave you hanging."

"You better not," I scoffed. Jenny winked and hurried along to her after-school job at Shelby's Diner.

I arrived home, exhausted yet anxious to continue piecing together this intricate puzzle. My detective's brain was on overdrive, and although I was fully aware that I needed a brain break, I had difficulty pulling myself away from the string of messy papers strewn across the top of my bedroom desk. I grabbed my journal and decided to document my experiences with the investigation. Writing was an outlet I frequently visited to allow me to decompress and compile all my thoughts in one place. It was beneficial to write everything down so I could revisit those thoughts later if the need arose. I was desperate to find a distraction so my brain could settle down from the constant replay of Jenny's conversation earlier in the afternoon. Journal writing was the perfect reprieve. It was going to be a long, drawn-out evening of waiting, that's for sure.

I opened my eyes and blinked rapidly, confusion plastered

all over my face. Had I fallen asleep? It was now dark, and only the light from the streetlamp across the street peeked through the blinds. Shit. Had I missed Jenny's call? I scrambled in the dark, desperately reaching around for my phone. What time was it anyway? 10 pm? Whoa, I must have been exhausted. I swiftly checked my recent calls only to find that Jenny had not called as expected. Perhaps she hadn't spoken to her father yet about Mr. Mason. I struggled internally back and forth with myself, trying to debate whether I should call Jenny myself. On the one hand, I desperately wanted to know if she had any news to share, but on the other hand, I remembered she had promised me that she wouldn't leave me hanging. I ultimately decided to give her the benefit of the doubt. Perhaps she had worked late and hadn't arrived home yet. Or perhaps her father was working the late shift and wasn't available to have a discussion with her. Either way, I knew Jenny would fill me in when she had news to share. I sighed, disappointed but aware that this was how life sometimes worked. Now, I had to decide if I should get up for a while and have something to eat or just go back to sleep. Sleep beckoned to me, and it was good as my mind could rest in slumber. I curled back under my thick, velvety blanket, my legs hunched up in the fetal position, and I gently fell asleep.

I suddenly felt a familiar warmth brushing my cheek as a glint of sunlight peeked through the blinds, enveloping me in a golden halo. It was Saturday morning, and a glorious one at that. I squinted my eyes, trying to focus them on the big white numbers on my phone screen—9 am. I quickly checked my call log. No call or text from Jenny. Damn, what on earth was happening? I thought for sure she'd at least call or text me. I felt the sudden urge to call her, but quickly remembered that I had vowed to give her the benefit of the doubt. But it did seem odd that she wouldn't have at least texted me, even if there was no news to share. I went to the washroom, swiftly prepping my shower and toiletries. Maybe by the time I finished my morning ritual, Jenny would have called. Wishful thinking. Still not a peep out of her. The clock now read 9:32 am. I was beginning to grow anxious. Where on earth was Jenny? Why hadn't she called or texted yet? Just then, as though I had planned it, the phone rang. I jumped up from my comfy chair as quickly as a startled cat and anxiously grasped my phone. The name on the screen read Jordan. No, not Jordan, I thought, feeling completely and utterly disappointed. I knew we were all working on this investigation together, but his name was not the one I was eagerly anticipating. Of course, I loved it when Jordan called. He was my boyfriend, after all. However, right now, at this moment, Jenny was the only person I wanted to hear from. I begrudgingly picked up the phone, and with obvious disappointment emanating from my voice, I said, "Hello."

"Well, aren't you a ray of sunshine today?" Jordan teased.

"Not right now, Jordan. I'm not in the mood for fun and games."

"Well, Kacey, you'd be surprised to know I'm not in the mood either."

"What do you mean by that, Jordan?" I asked, more curious than all heck.

"Haven't you heard, Kacey?"

"Heard what?" I asked.

"Chase called me late last night," he began hesitantly. "He told me that Jenny's parents called to let him know that Jenny was back in the hospital."

"What?" I screamed in pure shock. "Why? What happened?"

"I have no idea," Jordan replied. "Chase didn't say. He was far too upset when I spoke to him, and it was difficult to understand what he said. All I learned from that conversation was that Jenny was back in the hospital."

"Should we go to the hospital to check on Jenny?" I asked.

"Absolutely. Give me about 20 minutes. I'll come pick you up."

"Thanks, Jordan. I'll get myself ready. Thank you for calling me and letting me know. I just had this awful feeling that something wasn't right when Jenny didn't call or text me last night." I hung up the phone and raced up the stairs to my bedroom. Rounding the corner of the stairs, I nearly barreled into my mother, who was performing a balancing act with a basket of laundry and a bucket full of cleaning supplies.

"Whoa there, Kacey. You almost knocked me over. Where are you off to in such a hurry?"

"Jordan's on his way to pick me up. We're going to the hospital to see Jenny. Something happened last night, and we have no idea how she's doing or what's wrong with her."

"Oh my, not again," my mother replied in shock. "Please let me know how Jenny's doing once you get there, okay, Kacey?"

"Don't worry, I will, Mom." I continued to my room, flinging the door open with such force that I thought the hinges might break. I raced straight to my closet, tearing out whatever my hands grasped first. This wasn't a fashion show, and I had no care about how dishevelled or organized my clothes looked. The only concern I had was finding out what had happened to Jenny. Once dressed, I attacked the stairs like a ninja warrior ready for battle and bee-lined to the front door. Jordan was approaching my house, and as he pulled into my driveway, he waved at me frantically.

"Hurry, get in," he demanded. "Chase is going to meet us at the hospital and fill us in on the events from last night."

I hopped into the vehicle at record speed, and Jordan sped off, tires squealing on the pavement. I barely had time to put on my seat belt, but I was okay with that. Getting to Jenny was the top priority.

In under 15 minutes, we arrived at the hospital. Jordan pulled into the underground parking lot. He would attempt to park wherever he could fit his vehicle, regardless of whether it was a legal parking spot. Although I was rushing to talk to Chase and visit with Jenny, I reminded Jordan that it was best that he take the time to park in a legal spot to avoid more parking tickets. He already had several that were unpaid.

Once parked, Jordan and I made our way to the elevator lobby. I pressed the button with heavy fingers, and the number pad began to glow with each stop that the elevator made. I was getting anxious. Each time the glow of the numbers paused during the elevator's descent, I held my breath. It was taking a painstakingly long time. When the familiar ding of the elevator bell chimed, I grabbed Jordan's hand and pulled him forcefully onto the elevator. He looked at me, caught off guard by my assertiveness.

"I'm sorry," I apologized. "I'm just really anxious to talk to Chase and, of course, to see Jenny."

"No need to apologize," Jordan replied sympathetically.

"I get it. I'm anxious, too. I did not expect Jenny to be back in the hospital. My mind is cooking up all sorts of crazy scenarios. I can only imagine the elaborate ideas your brain is manifesting."

Jordan was right. My mind swirled like an out-of-control tornado, thoughts like debris violently tossed about aimlessly. With each floor the elevator climbed, I would take a deep breath, trying to silence the dark thoughts invading my personal space. After what felt like an infinite cycle of torture, the number 1 finally lit up on the number pad. We had finally made our way to the patient's reception area. I rushed to the reception desk at record speed, only to find Chase waiting there for us. His face was filled with anguish, tears streaming down his face. A horrifying thought popped into my head. Was Jenny hurt? Was she unconscious? Was she in a coma? Was she waiting for surgery? Or worse, was she, was she, dead?

CHAPTER EIGHTEEN

Friday, May 20th, 2022

More than a week had passed since my interview with the authorities. Nothing new had surfaced, and things had calmed down in and around the town. People at school had reverted to a relatively everyday existence, sharing Instagram posts and regaling themselves with their upcoming plans for the weekend. It was almost as if Ellie had never existed. Usually, this would have been the ideal scenario for Jenny and me. Still, because of the history between us and our involvement in the police investigation, it wasn't as easy for us to carry on as though nothing had ever happened. Although Mr. Grieves reassured me that this was likely the last time I would be subjected to any police questioning, I couldn't shake the feeling that things were only just beginning. My intuition was correct. When school let out at the end of the day, Jenny and I made our way home, excited that our last few weeks of school were on the horizon and that we would soon be enjoying our free time in the sun. Pool lounging and picnics couldn't come soon enough, especially after the last few months we had endured. When Jenny arrived at the edge of her street, we warmly embraced each other and waved goodbye. I went to the end of my block, meandering without a care. It was a welcome feeling I had not experienced in weeks, perhaps even months. Upon arriving home, I noticed that my mother and father had arrived early. Their vehicles were parked in the driveway, and I wondered what had prompted this unexpected surprise. My mother was in the kitchen rummaging around in the junk drawer, you know, the one where you keep all of the knick-knacks and other random stuff.

"Hey, Mom," I greeted. "What are you and Dad doing home so early?

"Oh, hey, honey. How was your day at school?"

"It was okay. Nothing out of the ordinary. So, will you tell me why you guys are home so early?"

"About that, honey. Mr. Grieves called me today."

"Really? About what?" I asked in bewilderment.

"Well, here's the thing," my mother started. "Ellie's clutch purse from the night of the dance was found deep in the forested area, close to where Mr. and Mrs. Grays reported seeing the woman fitting Ellie's description."

"Whoa… really?" I asked, shocked by the revelation.

"Yes, but that's not all," my mother stuttered.

"Well, what else was there?" I asked, starting to feel concerned.

"Inside the clutch, they found your and Jenny's matching friendship necklaces engraved with your names."

"But… but…" I stuttered. "That's impossible. Jenny and I lost those months ago, long before the Spring Fling Dance. We had to take them off to participate in women's wrestling during P.E. When we went to the locker room to get changed, they were missing. We assumed someone accidentally picked them up with their belongings, and they got lost somewhere along the way."

"Unfortunately, they somehow ended up in Ellie's clutch," my mom replied with genuine concern. "I believe you, but it doesn't look good for you or Jenny. Can you imagine how they could have ended up in Ellie's clutch?"

"No," I replied in complete bewilderment. "Unless Ellie or someone else intentionally stole them during gym class. She was in the same class as us, as were all her groupies. But Jenny and I never wore them outside of our clothes. We always kept them tucked into our shirts. How could anyone have even known about them?"

"I can't answer that question, honey. But you and Jenny should put your heads together; consider whether there were any opportunities for the necklaces to go missing."

"So, what did Mr. Grieves say?" I asked. "Does he think the authorities will want to question Jenny and me?"

"He isn't sure, but he did say to be prepared," my mother replied. "I'm going to be honest with you, Kacey. The authorities aren't going to brush this aside, especially knowing the relationship between the two of you and Ellie."

"Yeah, I figured. This sucks so much. I just want all of this to go away already. Jenny and I had nothing to do with Ellie's disappearance. Just because we had a conflict with her doesn't mean anything. As for the missing necklaces, is it all that unusual for things to go missing? Things are always going missing at our school."

"I completely understand, and I'm so sorry you are going through this, honey."

"Thanks, Mom. I'm going to go to my room and give Jenny a call. I'll take your suggestion and see if the two of us can figure out the mystery of how our missing necklaces ended up in Ellie's clutch."

"Great idea, honey. I'll see you later. Your father and I will go and talk to Mr. Grieves and see what the next steps are if the authorities decide to investigate this further."

"Thanks, Mom, for being so supportive." My mother smiled and strolled into the living room, leaning over my father's shoulder and whispering into his ear. He carefully placed down his glass of water, grabbed his wallet and keys off the side table, and slipped on his shoes. He gave me a fleeting glance as he exited the front door. I smiled bravely and grabbed my phone, quickly dialling Jenny's number.

"Hey, Kace. What's up?" Jenny greeted me, surprised to hear from me.

"My parents were home when I got here, which was unusual. My mom immediately approached me and told me that Mr. Grieves had called."

"Why was he calling? I thought all of this interrogation stuff was over," Jenny replied.

"So did I, but unfortunately, the authorities found something."

"What!" Jenny exclaimed, shocked. "What did they find?"

"Well, that's the strange part. Remember those friendship necklaces we bought?"

"Yeah, but we lost those months ago. What would the necklaces have to do with anything?"

"A lot apparently," I replied.

"What do you mean by a lot?" Jenny asked, puzzled.

"Well, they found Ellie's clutch in the wooded area. You know, the one she carried around at the Spring Fling Dance."

"Okay, so that proves she was there and that it was likely her that your neighbours witnessed while they were walking their dog," Jenny replied, confused. "But I still don't know what that has to do with our missing necklaces."

"That's the strange part. Apparently, our necklaces were found inside the clutch."

"Are you fucking kidding me," Jenny screamed in shock. "That's impossible. Firstly, nobody but us and our parents knew about them, not even Jordan and Chase. We always kept them tucked under our shirts. Secondly, those went missing months before the Spring Fling Dance. How would Ellie have even gotten hold of them?"

"That's exactly what I told my mom. I haven't got a clue how any of this is possible."

"Do you think the authorities will want to talk to us?" Jenny asked.

"I asked my mom that question, and she wasn't sure. All she said was that we should be prepared. Honestly, Jenn, I'm sick of this. We didn't do anything. I just want to go back to our normal lives."

"I hear you," Jenny replied. Frankly, I never expected Ellie to haunt us still, even after she vanished."

"Neither did I," I sighed. "So, I suppose we just sit and

wait. No point in stressing until there's a reason to stress."

"Pretty much. I still don't understand how those necklaces suddenly reappeared and in Ellie's clutch, no less," Jenny pondered. "Do you think somebody is setting us up to take the fall for Ellie's disappearance?"

"I don't know, Jenn," I replied. "I know I'm famous for manifesting some wild scenarios, but even this one is a little over the top."

"Maybe we should interrogate Ellie's henchmen," Jenny suggested. "You know, to see if they know something. Maybe one of them will slip up if they do."

"Do you think Loa, River, Autumn and the others would rat her out?" I asked. "Even if they know something, I think that might be a secret they take to the grave."

A secret they take to the grave. What an ironic yet bleak thought. I had to shake my head in disbelief. Since when did our lives become akin to a true crime documentary?

Jenny and I pondered our circumstances for several more minutes and then took a siesta. We weren't accomplishing anything, and the stress of the entire ordeal was only taking a toll on our mental health. We agreed to pick this up on Monday at school and bring Chase and Jordan in on the drama that was now our lives. I bid Jenny goodbye and went up to my room. I changed into comfy pyjamas, played lively music and aimlessly scrolled through my phone. What a screwed-up start to the weekend, I thought.

CHAPTER NINETEEN

Saturday, May 18th, 2024

Chase greeted Jordan and me with red, puffy eyes. He looked awful, as if he hadn't slept in days. His rough exterior only served to heighten my anxiety. I had to admit, though, that the experience with Ellie's disappearance and, most recently, our encounter with the mysterious amber eyes had worked wonders on teaching me techniques to keep my anxiety in check. I felt accomplished.

"Hey, guys. Sorry that I look like shit." Chase rubbed his eyes, attempting to make himself look more alert. "I haven't slept a wink all night."

"Chase, what happened?" I asked, my voice wavering. "Is Jenny okay?"

"She's in stable condition, just resting right now. She was cut up pretty badly and lost quite a bit of blood. She needed to be stitched up."

"What the hell, Chase? What on earth happened?" I

yelled. I wasn't angry with Chase; I was just confused and worried about Jenny.

"I went to pick her up after work at about 9 pm. When I arrived, I called her to tell her I was waiting outside. When she didn't pick up, I knew something was wrong. I left my car and started across the parking lot to the diner's front door. I gave her another call and heard her phone ringing. That's when I knew something was not right."

"So, where was she?" I inquired.

"I didn't know at first," Chase replied. "I followed the sound of her ringtone. When I got close to the garbage bins, it was then that I noticed Jenny on the ground, bleeding profusely. I panicked and started screaming for help. As I dialled 911, I scanned the area and saw those amber eyes again, peering out from the trees across the street."

"Whoa... what?" I replied, perplexed. "The same eyes we saw up at the waterfall?"

"Exactly the same ones," Chase replied. "I think whatever it was, it attacked Jenny."

"Holy shit," Jordan exclaimed. "That's new. All previous sightings were just that, sightings. There's been no report of attacks in conjunction with the amber-eyes appearance."

"True," I replied. "But don't forget that we heard threatening growls up at the waterfall, and I'm fairly certain that thing was pursuing us."

"You're absolutely right, Kacey," Jordan agreed. "I know none of us actually saw anything, but whatever it was, it was growling, and it didn't seem to get any quieter the further we fled."

"For now, I think we'll put this discussion on the back

burner," I replied. "I want to investigate it further, but I want to see Jenny now. Chase, can you take me to Jenny's room?" Chase nodded his head and turned the corner past the nurses' station.

I don't know what it was about hospitals that gave me the chills, but I shivered every time I strolled through the sterile white halls. Maybe it was the smell of antiseptic, the random beeps from various machines, or worse yet, the occasional groans and cries from patients within their rooms. Either way, I just wanted to get to Jenny's room to distract myself from all the commotion inside my brain. We rounded the corner, and Chase slowly pushed open the door to Jenny's room. I was not prepared for what I saw. Jenny was bandaged up all over the right side of her arm. She was hooked up to machines, an IV dripping some sort of fluid into her body. Her eyes were closed, and she appeared relatively peaceful despite her injuries. She must have heard the door creaking because she looked up from her restful slumber after a moment or two to see who was entering her private oasis.

"Hey, sleepyhead," I greeted. "How are you feeling?"

"I've been better," Jenny attempted to joke with a half grin.

"You've definitely looked better, too," I laughed, attempting to lighten the mood.

"Gee, thanks," Jenny scoffed jokingly. "Some best friend you are."

"So, what happened, Jenn?" I asked.

"I was taking out the garbage at the end of the night like I always do, when I heard something rustling in the trees across the street. Then I heard the most surreal sound I've ever heard. It was like something out of a horror movie.

You never expect something like that to happen in real life."

"Jeeze, Jenny. That sounds terrifying. I'm not sure if I would have survived such an ordeal. My anxiety would have been in overdrive. I'd probably have had a heart attack."

"Well, I pretty much did. That heart-monitoring device of mine proved it. My heart rate was through the roof."

"Did you see it?" I asked with insatiable curiosity.

"Not entirely, just a glimpse. It was dark out. I saw a dark, hulking mass with black or brown fur, long razor-like claws, sharp needle-point teeth, and glowing amber eyes."

"Holy shit Jenn. That's quite the description. Any ideas on what it may have been?"

"No. I couldn't distinguish any shape, just certain features. It was massive, though, like a person, but more muscular, more threatening."

"Woah, Jenn. Once you're feeling better, we'd better update our investigation notes. And not that I want to push or anything, but you still need to ask your dad about Mr. Mason."

"Yeah, I know. I'll get to it as soon as the doctors spring me out of here. But right now, I'm just too tired and sore."

"Get some rest, Jenn. Hopefully, they'll let you out of here tomorrow."

"That's what I'm aiming for, Kace. I'll call you when I get released from this makeshift prison."

I had to laugh. Jenny was always so dramatic and witty. "Gotcha, superstar," I replied with a wink. "Hey Jenny," I called out as I made my not-so-hasty exit. "Try not to leave me hanging this time."

"I'll try my best not to get attacked again, you know, so

144

as not to inconvenience you," Jenny replied sarcastically.

"Haha, you're so funny, Jenn," I retorted as I waved goodbye and walked through the hospital room door. As Jordan, Chase and I made our way back to the nurses' station, I couldn't help but notice Chase still looking as though his entire world had ended.

"You okay?" I asked. "You look as though you'd lost your Grandma."

"I'm good, I promise," Chase replied. "Just tired, overwhelmed, and I suppose upset. The last thing I ever wanted was for Jenny to get hurt."

"I can't even imagine what went through your mind when you found Jenny like that," I sympathized. "No wonder you're an emotional wreck. I asked Jenny if she could identify what attacked her, but all she could make out was dark fur, sharp claws and teeth, amber-coloured eyes, and a vast, hulking body. Did you happen to see anything that could help identify what the creature is?"

"Not definitively, no. But I did capture a glimpse of something watching Jenny and me from the grove of trees across the street while waiting for the ambulance.

"What did it look like, Chase?" I prodded.

"I know it sounds crazy, Kacey, but it looked like a wolf. Only it was standing upright on two legs and far taller than any wolf I've ever seen. I thought my mind was playing tricks on me, so I didn't say anything earlier. I thought the stress of everything that's gone down the last little while had finally taken its toll on me."

I gasped as a sudden realization hit me. Maybe those rumours about the Scientific Research Center weren't so far-fetched. Maybe, just maybe, they were performing experimental genetic modification procedures. It's nothing new for scientists to create genetically modified organisms. This could be the key to explaining how those claw marks ended up in the DNA extraction chamber. Perhaps when the power went out, something went awry. Jenny needed to talk to her father about Mr. Mason. He may be harbouring some crucial information we need to crack the case. He probably isn't even aware of it. At this juncture, I had no choice but to wait for Jenny to be released from the hospital. The waiting was going to eat me alive.

CHAPTER TWENTY

Monday, May 23rd, 2022

The weekend came and went without a hitch. Things were quiet, much quieter than expected. Jenny and I resolved to take the weekend off from the excess drama and only engage if the drama sought us out first. Lucky for us, it didn't. Come Monday morning, the two of us were committed to updating the boys on our current hardship and how that discovery would impact the authority's investigation.

"Hey ladies," Jordan called out as Jenny and I trudged across the concrete jungle of the parking lot. "What's new?"

"What isn't new is more like it," I replied with an eye roll.

"What's that supposed to mean?" Jordan countered back in sheer curiosity.

"Well…" Jenny began sarcastically, "Kacey and I have been implicated again in Ellie's disappearance."

"No, you're joking, right?" Jordan exclaimed.

"I wish she were," I replied. "Unfortunately, they found something that belonged to us in the clutch purse that Ellie was carrying. Apparently, they found it lying in the woods close to where a young woman fitting her description was spotted."

"What on earth could Ellie have had in her possession that belonged to you?" Jordan inquired. "It's not like you guys were close or anything. How would she have gotten her hands on anything?"

"We have racked our brains trying to come up with a logical explanation to that question, Jordan," I replied. "We just don't know."

"So what was it that they found in the clutch? How can they link it back to you and Jenny?" Jordan asked.

"It was a set of friendship necklaces with our names on them. We had gotten them together a long time ago," I replied. We never really wore them in plain sight. They were constantly under our shirts. Logically speaking, there should be no reason that anyone knew of their existence unless we told them, of course."

"Neither Chase nor I knew about their existence, so I highly doubt anyone else could have known about them," Jordan quipped. "Did you ever take them off and leave them lying around where someone could have snatched them up?"

"That's the thing. We rarely took them off, except for one time in P.E., I replied. We had to take them off to participate in women's wrestling. When we came back to our lockers, they were gone."

"And let me guess," Jordan exclaimed, "Ellie and her clique were in that class, too."

"You would be correct," I replied.

"So, do you think you were set up or something?" Jordan asked. "It's obvious that neither you nor Jenny was involved in Ellie's disappearance, so there has to be another explanation for how those necklaces got inside her clutch."

"Jenny already brought that up, but I don't know. It sounds sort of crazy. No offence or anything, Jenn. Ellie wasn't our biggest fan; her clique would do anything she asked of them, but this seems a little over the top. What purpose would it serve anyone to frame us for Ellie's disappearance?"

"Well," Jenny replied, "that's what we have to figure out. There's someone out there who knows how our necklaces got into Ellie's clutch, unless it was Ellie herself, in which case we have to figure out if she's still alive or not."

"I suppose then," I started, "we better put on our thinking caps and kick this investigation into overdrive."

The four of us trudged off to our morning classes; however, school would be the last thing on our minds. I knew, without any doubt, that our minds would be preoccupied with the incessant questions surrounding the appearance of the clutch and its contents.

I sat patiently in my English class, every word seemingly stretched to ridiculous lengths. My mind danced back and forth with thoughts of Shakespearean lore and mysterious reappearing personal artifacts. My eyes constantly shifted from the clock on the wall to my desk and back. I must have looked like one of those old clocks from the '50s and '60s where the cat's eyes moved back and forth; a ridiculous sight, I'm sure.

When the dismissal bell rang triumphantly, I tried to

intercept Jenny at her locker. The hallway was a sea of straggling bodies carrying books, backpacks, papers and other artifacts. It felt like navigating through a maze, trying to zigzag back and forth between the mindless, wandering souls. Miraculously, I made it to Jenny's locker and we exchanged anxious glances.

"Did you manage to learn anything today?" I asked in the most sarcastic tone I could muster.

"Yeah, no," Jenny replied, returning my sarcasm. "My mind was a wandering leaf dancing briskly in the morning breeze. I learnt fuck all."

"Same," I replied. "I'm honestly not sure how we'll get through the rest of the day. My mind is on overdrive, and I'm focused on only one thing: proving that we had nothing to do with Ellie's disappearance."

"Do you think the authorities have contacted our parents yet?" Jenny asked. "Have you or your parents heard anything more from Mr. Grieves?"

"Nothing yet that I'm aware of. I'm sure my mom would call the school if there were any critical updates on the situation."

"You're right," Jenny agreed. "She definitely wouldn't leave you hanging."

The second bell rang for the start of our second-period class. We both hugged each other and scurried off to our classes. Another class of struggling to tame the anxiety brewing within myself. This day would drag on endlessly; I could already feel it. I sighed.

The end of the school day finally arrived. I felt like a young child again, awaiting Santa Claus's arrival. The anxiety was overwhelming, yet a sense of relief washed over me the minute the final dismissal bell sang, signalling the end of the day. Floating like a surfer riding an ocean wave, my legs carried me to Jenny's locker. Jenny, Jordan, and Chase were already waiting for me when I arrived.

"Jeeze, Kacey," Jordan mused. "Slow much?"

"While I appreciate the sarcastic humour, Jordan," I quipped, "I need us to maintain a sense of urgency here. I'd prefer to figure out how our necklaces ended up in Ellie's clutch before the authorities question us."

"Yeah, I know," Jordan replied in a serious tone. "I was just trying to find a way to lighten the mood. You know me, I'm the guy who's always trying to keep things light."

"I get it. And you're right; we do need that. So thank you," I replied, giving Jordan a hurried peck on the cheek.

"So, what do you guys want to do?" Jenny asked. "Where do we start? Do we talk to Loa, Autumn and River? Ask them if they know anything about our missing necklaces?"

"That's as good a start as any," I replied, somewhat unsure and hesitant.

It's not that I was scared to approach them; it was more that I was worried they would try to cover up the truth or, worse yet, that one of them was trying to frame us. How awkward would that be, talking to the person attempting to sabotage you? I forced myself to shake off the nerves. This was what good investigative work consisted of.

"Who wants to do the questioning?" Jenny asked. "Should I start with Autumn? Should you start with Loa, Kace?"

"I've got a decent relationship with Loa, at least I think I do," I recalled. "I called her on the night of the dance to check in on Ellie. You know, to make sure she got home okay. After all the sirens and the sightings of the amber eyes, I figured I should at least practice being a decent human being and do a check-in."

"I love that you're concerned about Ellie," Jenn said. "It's one of the things I love most about you. It's not as though Ellie would return the favour, though."

"I know, but still… I'd feel bad if something happened to anyone and I didn't do my due diligence and check in on them."

Jenny smiled warmly at me. "Well, I guess we'd better get our dialling fingers ready," she said. "I suspect this won't go over as smoothly as we hoped."

Jordan and Chase said their goodbyes and took off for home. Jenny and I steadied ourselves on a bench, took a deep breath, and started the arduous task of reaching out to Jenny's squad. This was not going to be fun, I thought to myself. It was not fun at all.

CHAPTER TWENTY-ONE

Sunday, May 26th, 2024

After a week's stay, Jenny was finally released from the hospital. I was thrilled that she was on the mend, but I was also anxious about any revelations that Jenny might uncover when she finally sat down with her father. Despite the circumstances of Jenny's hospital visit, I still hungered for information that would lead us one step closer to solving the mystery of Ellie's disappearance and the reappearance of the amber eyes. I decided the best course of action was to wait until late afternoon or early evening. Jenny should return home by then and settle in from her hospital stay. I felt tremendous guilt for putting so much pressure on Jenny, but this was important for our investigation. We needed to put this chapter of our lives to bed once and for all.

I decided the best way to pass the time was to sit and read my newest addition to my mini personal library. Becoming engrossed in a good read was always a favourite pastime.

I settled on my bed, curled up warm and cozy under the covers, and began to immerse myself in the fictional world of Freyville. This would keep my mind from wandering back to my current dilemma.

Hours passed swiftly, and I was shocked to see the hands of the clock read 4:06 pm. Whoa, I thought to myself, I really did immerse myself in the fantastical world of Freyville. What a relief to have had my book to preoccupy my mind. My thoughts were interrupted by the obnoxious sound of my ringtone, blaring at a deafening volume. I nearly jumped out of my skin.

"Please be Jenny, please be Jenny," I whispered out loud. I quickly picked up the phone.

"Hey, it's me," the familiar voice on the other end of the phone greeted me.

"Jenny?" I replied, almost questioningly.

"Yeah, it's me."

"How are you feeling? Are you still sore and tired?"

"I'm okay. Feeling much better after a week's worth of pampering at the hospital. They really took care of me. I almost didn't want to go home."

"I bet," I replied. "So, not that I'm trying to be pushy or anything, but did you have a chance to talk to your father about Mr. Mason?"

"Actually, I did," Jenny replied. "Some pretty interesting information came about due to that conversation."

"Really," I exclaimed. "Like what?"

"Well, firstly, he confirmed that Mr. Mason was working that night. So it would be impossible for him not to have known about the power outage."

"Interesting. So, did Mr. Mason know what happened in the DNA extraction chamber?" I asked.

"Well, that's the exciting part," Jenny exclaimed. "According to my father, Mr. Mason was tasked with the project manager position for this research experiment. Apparently, he had discovered the fossilized remains of an extinct Dire Wolf on an expedition in the glaciers of the Alaskan wilderness several years back. After months of excavation, the remains were sent to the scientific research center. My father was recruited to join the team working with Mr. Mason and his DNA research on the fossilized remains."

"That is interesting. I wonder if this might be part of why your father wanted things to remain hushed about our sighting of the amber eyes at the waterfall. He didn't want to be implicated in any nefarious activity by the authorities, but maybe he was also trying to protect the research center's reputation and Mr. Mason's."

"Exactly," Jenny nodded in agreement. "There were already so many rumours swirling about the place when they first opened, too, so bringing this up would add fuel to the fire."

"Did your father say anything else, Jenny?" I asked. "Like what they were planning on doing with the Dire Wolf DNA? In Social Studies, I remember learning that the last Dire Wolf went extinct about 10,000 years ago. Can they even get a DNA sample from a fossil that old?"

"I remember my father mentioning in our previous conversation that he was asked to test this new fancy piece of equipment. I'm assuming this new equipment has capabilities we're unaware of yet. Last year in Social Studies, Mrs. Leighton mentioned that DNA could be extracted from older fossilized specimens if well preserved in permafrost. This specimen may have been discovered well-preserved with some assistance from climate change and the subsequent melting of glacial ice in Alaska. As for the plan for the DNA, if they did extract anything viable, who knows? I'm sure the intent is for it to be used for educational and research purposes, not for anything nefarious, as some of the rumours around town claim."

"I'm sure you're right, Jenn. But I can't be the only one connecting the dots here regarding the growling and the claw marks inside the DNA extraction chamber. Isn't it odd that the DNA being tested belonged to a species of extinct wolf? I mean, they growl, and they certainly have sharp claws. And what about the glowing amber eyes and the fact that you were attacked by something that Chase described as wolf-like?"

"WHAT NOW!" Jenny bellowed out in surprise. "Chase, saw what attacked me? Why didn't he say anything to me?"

"You mean you didn't know, Jenn?" I exclaimed in sheer surprise.

"No. He didn't say anything to me. Not one single word."

"I'm not going to get involved in that drama; that's between you and Chase. But the fact that he saw a wolf-like creature and the DNA sample went missing after the power outage seems far too convenient to be a coincidence. There must be some connection between all of these events. We just need to piece everything together and figure out what that connection is."

"So, Detective Lundgren, where do we start?" Jenny inquired.

"Well, Detective Forester, we meet with Detectives Bally

and Drieger to review our notes. Look for connections, fill in the missing pieces of the puzzle."

Jenny and I said our goodbyes as she anxiously texted Chase. My fingers simultaneously tapped the bright glass screen, texting Jordan. We arranged to meet at Gunderson Park, just down the road from my place, at 6:30 pm. Gunderson Park wasn't typically busy on Sunday evenings, and it would be the perfect spot to lay out all of our notes and have serious discussions without fear of being scrutinized.

By this time, the clock read 5:30 pm. One more hour to entertain myself, I thought. What on earth will I do to keep my thoughts at bay? As usual, my mind began to manifest wild scenarios of conspiracy, deceit, and lies, all dusted with a touch of mystery and intrigue. If Jenny could have read my thoughts at that moment, she would have scolded me for being utterly and completely paranoid and ridiculous. I loathed her ability to remain calm, even when she was the one who had every reason to fall down the rabbit hole. I contemplated for several minutes before deciding that the best way to keep my mind from wandering down a dark path of destruction was to bake, a favourite pastime. Besides, what better way to prepare for an intense discussion session and compare notes than indulging in the gooey deliciousness of golden brown sugar and chocolate chips? Cookies were just what the doctor ordered, I mused. I gathered all the ingredients from the pantry and went to town, creating the best chocolate chip cookies ever. Perhaps I was being a little bit cocky, believing that my cookies were the best in the infinite expanse of the Universe, but after all of the craziness that had made its home in the depths of my brain, I deserved this one victory. I wasn't about to let anyone or anything take that away.

It wasn't long before the sweet and fragrant aroma of cookies swirled in the air, enticing my nostrils. I removed the cookies from the oven and transferred them to a cooling rack before packing them for our investigative update. I glanced at the clock and noticed it was now 6:25 pm. I decided to gather my notes and prepare for our meeting of the minds. I ran upstairs, gathered everything I needed and hastily stuffed the entire pile into my backpack. Just as I was about to head out the door, I craned my head back toward the kitchen. "The cookies! Mustn't forget the cookies." I found a plastic container and placed the cookies gently into it, taking care not to break any. I stuffed one into my mouth, exited the front door, and headed to Gunderson Park. This was sure to be an eventful evening, that much I was sure about.

CHAPTER TWENTY-TWO

Monday, May 23rd, 2022

I held my breath as the phone's ringing echoed in my ear. The last time Loa and I spoke, we both admitted that neither of us had anything personal against one another. Ellie's influence was the determining factor in our non-existent relationship. I heard a faint crackle on the other end of the phone, followed by a barely audible "Hello."

"Loa? It's me, Kacey."

"Kacey? What do you want? Why are you calling me?"

"Well, I was hoping you could help me solve this little problem," I replied.

"Huh! What problem? Why would you ask me to help?"

"Well, that's because it has something to do with Ellie, and considering how close the two of you were, I thought you might be the best person to ask."

"Ummm… okay, so what can I help you with?"

"Do you remember last semester when we participated in women's wrestling in P.E.?"

"Yeah, what about it?

"So Jenny and I had these matching friendship necklaces, you know, the ones that have two halves? So, we had to take them off for wrestling and put them in a locker, but when we returned to the locker room to get changed, the necklaces were missing."

"What does that have to do with Ellie?" Loa asked, puzzled.

"Well, I'm not sure if you've heard yet, but they found something of Ellie's in the forested area on the east side of town." Awkward silence greeted me for several seconds. Then Loa finally replied, shocked by my revelation.

"They did?" she exclaimed. "What did they find?"

"Well, that's the part I need your help with, Loa. Those necklaces I just told you about; well, they found Ellie's clutch from the dance in the forested area with both of them inside."

"What?" Loa cried in a burst of confusion. "But how, why? That makes no sense. I don't think Ellie even knew you had those necklaces. She never mentioned them, and I'm certain she would have made a spectacle out of the two of you had she known about them."

"That's what I'm trying to figure out. And by your reaction, you have absolutely no knowledge of how the necklaces went missing in the first place or how they ended up in Ellie's clutch."

"No, no clue at all. I didn't even know that the necklaces existed," Loa replied.

"We hid them well. We always wore them under our shirts. Jordan and Chase didn't even know about them. You don't think somebody from your group knew about them, do you? Perhaps Autumn or River?"

"If they did know about them, they sure kept it tight-lipped," Loa said confidently. "We shared virtually everything. We were a very tight group. The three of us still are, even without Ellie."

"What about Ellie? I know you said you were certain she didn't know about the necklaces, but how do you know?" I inquired. "Isn't it possible that she kept things from you all? You did, after all, keep things from her. I remember you saying you only joined in on the verbal attacks against Jenny and me to appease her, correct?"

"I mean, yes. You've got a point. Despite being close with Ellie, I always suspected that she had secrets that she didn't share with the rest of us. This one time, I asked her if she wanted to go to the mall after school, and she blew it off. She gave me some excuse, saying she had to help her parents with some stuff at home. If you knew Ellie like I did, you'd find it suspicious that she would pass up a trip to the mall to help her parents with something. She wasn't exactly the helping type, and passing up a trip to the mall was not likely."

"So, did you confront her about it?" I questioned.

"Sort of. I didn't want to push too hard for information. I knew my place with Ellie and didn't want to risk putting myself in a precarious position. It's not like I was popular before we started hanging out together. I couldn't risk losing my credibility as a friend."

"I get that," I replied empathetically. "I know firsthand

what it's like to be on Ellie's hit list. I don't blame you for wanting to stay in Ellie's good graces. Secretly, I was a bit envious of you, Autumn, and River. I always wondered what life could have been like had I been one of the popular girls."

"Wanna know a secret ?" Loa asked.

"Uhmm… yeah, sure," I replied curiously.

"I was always jealous of your and Jenny's friendship."

My eyebrows shot up in surprise. "Really?" I replied, somewhat confused. "Why on earth would you be jealous of our friendship? You were friends with the queen herself. How could you possibly wish for something different?"

"It wasn't exactly all sunshine and rainbows. Trying to meet Ellie's expectations for our group was a challenge. All I ever wanted was to have the quintessential teenage experience, but I never expected there to be so much pressure to be perfect all the time. It honestly was exhausting. Don't get me wrong, I wouldn't trade my high school years for anything, but sometimes I wish things were just easier, you know. Just natural and easygoing like yours and Jenny's friendship was."

Admittedly, I was taken aback by Loa's confession. Never in my wildest dreams would I have suspected I was the subject of someone's jealousy. I never really thought about the perspective of the other players in Ellie's group. I never once considered how much pressure there would be to appease Ellie and maintain friendship status. There was a lot of expectation to be perfect, and I pitied Loa, Autumn, and River for the first time.

"So what happens next?" Loa asked. "Have the authorities questioned you and Jenny yet about the necklaces?"

"Not yet, but my lawyer told my mother they will likely reach out this week. Hence, I'm being proactive and trying to do my due diligence and figure out how our necklaces ended up in Ellie's clutch."

"Well, let me know if there's anything I can do to help. I'll do whatever I can."

"Thanks, Loa, and thank you for confiding in me. It's nice to know you trust me in what I can only imagine is a really tough time for you."

"Anytime, Kacey. Have a great evening. Goodnight."

"Goodnight," I replied.

I had a brief feeling of peace wash over me despite the precarious situation that Jenny and I currently found ourselves in. It was a nice feeling to know that even our distant enemies were actually allies in what could only be described as a shared struggle for the truth. I placed my phone into the pocket of my jeans and glanced over at Jenny, who was still conversing with Autumn. Our eyes briefly met, and Jenny gave me a wink, hinting she may have some relevant information to share. I waited patiently, but began to get fidgety after about ten minutes. I quickly walked to the park down the street to calm my mind. I gestured to Jenny, who, as usual, could read my thoughts. She gave me a thumbs up as I turned my back to her and headed down the winding path leading me to the park. I couldn't wait to see what information Jenny had compiled from her discussion with Autumn.

I strolled toward the park, enticing my senses with the crisp air and the beautiful scent of flowers. As I closed in on the forested area, I hesitated briefly. Did I really want to go in there, especially after all the sightings of the amber eyes around town? Did I want to become another missing teenage statistic? I chastised myself for thinking such foolish things. I continued on the path. I told myself just one loop, and then I'd head back to Jenny for an update. As I rounded a bend in the path, I heard a rustling sound to my left. I spun myself around so violently that I nearly lost my footing. A squirrel was digging aimlessly amongst the fallen leaves, perhaps searching for a long-lost treasure. I had to laugh at myself for being so jittery. How ridiculous, I thought to myself. Scared of a little squirrel. I watched as the squirrel rejoiced in his triumphant success, happily chattering away with his prize stuffed into his cheeks. I continued down the path, anxious to finish the loop to rejoin Jenny and regale the details of our conversations, but life had another plan for me. I once again heard the familiar rustling leaves. Expecting to find the little squirrel hunting for hidden treasures again, I heard a strange yet threatening growl. It was enough to send me hightailing it back to Jenny as fast as my legs would carry me. I wasn't about to stick around to find out what the source of the growling was. When I returned to Jenny, she finished her call with Autumn. I huffed loudly, desperately trying to catch my breath.

"What's the matter with you?" Jenny asked, concern plastered across her face.

"You wouldn't believe me even if you wanted to," I replied.

"Try me," Jenny prodded.

I sat beside Jenny and began recounting the details of my experience as they were still fresh in my mind.

CHAPTER TWENTY-THREE

Sunday, May 26th, 2024

I arrived at Gunderson Park with cookies and notes in hand. Jenny and the boys were already awaiting my arrival, sitting cross-legged on a large blanket with stacks of papers in front of them.

"What's all this?" I asked.

"You didn't think you were the only one taking notes, did you?" Jenny asked sarcastically.

"No, but I wasn't expecting this large a pile," I replied.

"Well, Ms. Detective, we figured that the best way to tackle this investigation was for us to take notes and compare and contrast our findings, you know, to get the most thorough information."

"Jenny, super detective," I giggled. "So, anything new and interesting?"

"So Chase has suggested that we visit Mr. Mason in

person. He thinks going straight to the source and asking about the research project and what he hopes to accomplish could fill in some of the blanks for us. My father already informed me that they were working with a Dire Wolf's fossilized remains, but we don't know if they successfully extracted the DNA."

"It would certainly be interesting to get his perspective on this," I agreed. "I'm sure he could answer all of our unanswered questions. I'm just hesitant to bring this up two years later. I'm fully aware that he has likely made peace with what happened to Ellie, but I can't help but wonder if our prodding could set off some long-buried trauma."

"I think that's a risk we're going to have to take," Jenny replied sharply. "We deserve answers, too. I've landed in the hospital twice due to these mysterious amber eyes. If there's a connection between these incidents and what happened at the research center, I deserve an answer."

"You're right, you're absolutely right," I agreed. "I don't think we can continue on this path, not knowing what the hell is happening in our little town. I think we should do it. We should make plans to go see Mr. Mason."

Jenny smiled, almost with relief. Jordan and Chase's eyes met mine, and they nodded in agreement. The only remaining question was who would bite the bullet and contact Mr. Mason? Jenny had been through enough trauma already; two hospital visits and two difficult conversations with her father were enough for her to handle on her own. This time, either Chase, Jordan, or I would have to make the sacrifice. I swallowed hard and took a deep breath to calm my nerves. I would bite the bullet for Jenny, Jordan, Chase, me, and the whole town. It was time to get some answers and put this two-year saga to rest once and for all. My eyes shifted from one side to the other, silently observing the stillness between us. I finally broke the silence and announced my intentions to approach Mr. Mason with our questions.

"I'll do it," I blurted out. "I'll go talk to Mr. Mason."

"Kacey, are you sure you want to do this?" Jenny asked with concern in her voice.

"I'll be fine, Jenny, I promise. You've been through enough already, and honestly, this is just something I need to do. I've been anxious for many years and must learn not to let it control me. This will be good for me, for us, for everyone in the town. We need to put an end to this dark cloud hovering over us. We must return Fort Richfield to its former glory, where residents can raise a family without fear and trepidation."

"I'll go with you, Kace," Jordan announced, placing his arm around my shoulder in a warm embrace. "I applaud your bravery in tackling this alone and sparing Jenny from more trauma. But what kind of boyfriend would I be if I didn't do my darndest to support you?"

"Jordan, you never cease to amaze me. I'd love it if you'd accompany me. Thank you for always being so kind and supportive. I often ask myself how I landed such an amazing guy like you."

"It isn't really much of a mystery, Kace. You're smart, kind, thoughtful and most of all…" he hesitated, "hot."

I burst out laughing. "Hot, huh. Really, Jordan. So that's why you love me so much?"

"Well, having eye candy hanging off your arm certainly doesn't hurt," Jordan replied with a sly smile and a wink.

I blushed twenty shades of red and proceeded to press

my lips against his in a passionate kiss, his strong arms wrapping around me ever so tightly. It was one of those moments that you only see in the movies. The world seemed to spin, and time moved slowly, enveloping us in a magical time warp.

"Geeze, guys, get a room," Jenny chided.

Jordan and I glanced up from our magical romantic moment, meeting Jenny's eyes and feeling the heat of embarrassment creep across our cheeks.

"Sorry, Jenn," we both replied in unison.

"Don't be sorry," Jenny laughed. "I just thought you might be trying to upstage me and Chase." She grabbed Chase by the collar of his hoodie, pulled him closer and planted a sloppy, wet kiss on his lips. "Can't be the only ones putting on a show now, hey Chase?" Chase blushed all sorts of shades of red. Suddenly, to everyone's surprise, Chase grabbed Jenny by the waist, dipping her as though she were the belle of the ball and returned her kiss passionately. Jordan and I exchanged a shocked look, quickly changing to congratulatory applause.

"Congratulations, Chase," Jordan cheered. "You've finally learned to not give a crap about what others think. Feels liberating, doesn't it?"

"Yeah, it does. Honestly, I don't know why public displays of affection always make me feel awkward and as though I were on display."

"Trust me, dude," Jordan assured him. "Nobody even cares, except Jenny, of course." Jordan gave Jenny a sly wink, and she reciprocated with a mischievous smirk.

"Well, anyway," I interrupted, "perhaps we should compare our notes. I'd like to be armed with as much information as possible before attempting to speak with Mr. Mason."

"Yeah, probably a good idea," Jordan agreed.

"So, I'll start first," I volunteered. "We know that on the night of the Spring Fling Dance, Jenny and I witnessed multiple emergency vehicles heading to the east side of town while walking home from the dance. We also know that my neighbours, The Grays, were out walking their dog and reported seeing a young lady fitting Ellie's description near a forested area on the same side of town at about the same time we would have been walking home from the dance."

"And," Jenny interjected, "Jordan confirmed that everyone was sent home from the dance early due to some sort of police incident."

"Yes, that's right," Jordan agreed. "I also remember calling Kacey to ensure she and Jenny had made it home safely and then discussing that it might be a good idea to see if Ellie had made it home."

"Yes, that's correct," I agreed. "After hanging up with Jordan, I called Loa. I didn't have Ellie's number, but I also didn't want to rehash the events from the dance over the phone. She confirmed that Ellie had not contacted her since leaving the dance. There were also all of the reports from the townsfolk about the amber eyes sightings on that very same night," I recalled. "And then there was our incident earlier at the beginning of this month at the waterfall and the one I had a week earlier in the brush behind my house."

"Let's not forget, too, that Jenny was attacked by something resembling a wolf standing upright on two legs this past Friday night," Chase recollected.

"Yes, and my father confirmed that both he and Mr. Mason had been working at the research center on the night of the dance when the power mysteriously went out," Jenny replied. "Then he recalled that the DNA sample they had been researching had vanished, and claw marks were left in its place when the power came back on. Ironically, the DNA sample was that of an extinct Dire Wolf."

"Whoa, I never knew that," Jordan exclaimed. "They were extracting DNA from an extinct wolf?"

"Yeah," Jenny confirmed. "Even stranger yet is that Mr. Mason was head of the research project and was the one who had excavated the remains of the wolf a few months earlier in the Alaskan permafrost."

"That's a pretty big revelation, considering that you were attacked by something resembling a wolf," Chase replied.

"Tell me about it," Jenny replied. "And this is exactly why we need to talk to Mr. Mason."

"So what's the plan then?" Jordan asked, glancing curiously in my direction.

"I suppose we should make a plan then," I replied. We should decide when we will talk to Mr. Mason."

"Tonight's as good a night as any," Jordan suggested. "I have no plans tonight, and it's only 7 pm. I'm sure Mr. Mason will be home."

"Okay then," I replied, my stomach twisting in knots. "I guess we'd better pack up and head on out." Jenny and Chase stared intensely at Jordan and me. You could see the empathy dripping from their eyes.

"Good luck, guys," Jenny called out as we approached Jordan's car. I turned back to look at Jenny and managed a nervous smile. She waved slowly, almost as though she was afraid to convey too much enthusiasm in her movements.

"So," I began as I turned to face Jordan. "I guess it's time to solve this mystery, huh?"

"I guess," he replied. "Hopefully, we'll get some of the answers we seek."

We walked hand in hand, reaching his car faster than I anticipated. He held open the passenger door for me, and I stepped in gracefully. I sighed in anticipation. I certainly wasn't looking forward to this.

CHAPTER TWENTY-FOUR

Monday, May 23rd, 2022

Jenny's eyes fixated on mine, concentration at its fullest capacity. I hesitated to tell her at first what I had just experienced. My anxiety came creeping back in like a burglar in the night. Only a month ago, when I saw the amber eyes for the first time, I recalled my hesitation in calling Jenny, which was silly because Jenny was my best friend and support system. I always presumed that if people didn't see my point of view or understand my thoughts, they were against me somehow. I now know that this isn't true at all, which has immensely helped me control my anxious thoughts.

"While you were speaking with Autumn, I went for a walk along the trail just over there," I said, pointing with authority to the twisted path in the distance. "About halfway down the path, a forested area cropped up. Initially, I hesitated to enter it, but I convinced myself it was safe because it was daylight. That was my first mistake. I heard the sound of rustling leaves, so I glanced over, only to see a little squirrel digging for his buried treasure. I had to laugh at myself because my mind had me convinced that the little squirrel was something far more threatening. I continued my walk and heard the same sound of rustling leaves. I fully expected to see the same little squirrel stocking up on his buried treasure, but that did not happen. I looked around, but I didn't see anything. Then, a terrifying sound came booming out of the forest. It sort of sounded like a lion. That was when I came running back here to you."

"So you didn't see what made the noise?" Jenny asked, attempting to confirm my detailed report.

"No, nothing; there was only growling."

"So weird, especially right in the middle of the afternoon," Jenny pondered.

"Anyways, did you have any news to share after speaking with Autumn?" I questioned.

"Boy, do I ever," Jenny replied excitedly.

"Well, don't leave me hanging," I shouted.

"So it turns out that during gym that day, Autumn recalls Ellie running back to the locker room. She claims to have forgotten her mouthguard. Autumn claims she didn't question it because we were participating in wrestling, which seemed a valid reason."

"Hmmm… interesting. I wonder if Ellie was the only one who visited the locker room during P.E. that day?"

"I honestly don't recall," Jenny replied. "It was months ago, and if I didn't have a specific reason to be on alert, I would not remember something like that."

"Absolutely," I agreed. "I'm curious if the security cameras caught anything?"

"Maybe," Jenny replied.

"I'm not sure that the school would give us access to the security footage or if they would even have the recordings from months ago," I pondered. "Do you know who we could ask?"

"I have no idea, but I certainly know who we shouldn't ask," Jenny retorted.

"Who?" I asked quizzically.

"Mrs. Laughlin, that's who," Jenny scoffed. "She's got it out for us. It wouldn't surprise me if she were the one who planted the necklaces inside Ellie's clutch."

"Ok, I think that's maybe a bit of a stretch," I chided. "I'm fully aware that Mrs. Laughlin isn't our biggest fan, but she isn't a fan of Ellie's either. What purpose would it serve her to try to sabotage us? It's not like she has anything to gain."

"Gee, I don't know, Kace, maybe having us expelled from school. Then all three of us are out of her hair."

"Yeah, I'm not convinced, Jenn. I'm sure she wouldn't risk her reputation or career to set us up. Wouldn't the authorities ask for security footage or something like we are? If we tell them our side of the story, they'll surely want to see who was in and out of the locker room. If it were her, the security footage would incriminate her."

"I suppose," Jenny agreed somewhat hesitantly. "But I just can't shake this nagging feeling that something is awry."

"I get that," I replied empathetically. "There's nothing orthodox about this situation."

"So, what should we do then?" Jenny asked.

"Just go to the school office and be blunt about wanting to check out the security footage," I replied. "The worst they can do is say no."

"And what do we say if they question why we want to see the security footage?"

"The truth, I suppose.

"Tomorrow morning, then?" Jenny asked

"Tomorrow morning, it's a date."

CHAPTER TWENTY-FIVE

Sunday, May 26th, 2024

Jordan pulled up to the Mason's driveway, and the street lights illuminated the dewdrops that nestled onto the tall bushes surrounding the property like diamonds. The Mason's home loomed over us like a dark shadow in the night; it was so large and exuded an almost threatening tone. I felt my heart palpitate inside my chest as anxiety began to creep over me. I sighed, knowing that there was nothing I could do to quell this fear. Jordan clasped my hand, his fingers intertwined with mine. I was beginning to suspect that he may have inherited some of Jenny's superpowers. It was as though he knew just what I needed at that moment.

"You ready to do this?" Jordan questioned as he gazed at me with eyes of steel.

I knew Jordan was attempting to maintain an air of strength and courage for my benefit, but I could tell by the twinge of his upper lip that he was just as nervous as I was for our rendezvous with Mr. Mason.

"You bet," I replied with the best nonchalant attitude I could muster. "Wild horses couldn't keep me away." I cracked a forced smile at Jordan.

"You do know that you don't have to pretend that everything is just fine and dandy for my sake, don't you?" Jordan asked me.

"I know," I replied. "It's just that I've been working so hard on my internal struggle with anxiety that every time I feel it creep back in, I feel as though I'm relapsing to the old Kacey. Admitting it out loud just solidifies those feelings."

"I know you've worked hard to overcome your anxiety, Kace. I'm proud of how far you've come and how much you've accomplished. But there's no shame in admitting that you still feel some fear and anxiety every now and then. It's a normal part of life; sometimes, we all feel that way. Right now, my stomach is in knots. It's churning like the ocean's waves during a violent storm. You've got this. I've got this. We've got this."

I leaned over and kissed Jordan tenderly on the cheek. "Thank you for always being my superhero, Jordan."

Jordan smiled as we exited the car together. We strolled hand in hand, encompassing the long-winded driveway like snails on a mission. The dark mahogany front door loomed over us, casting an ominous shadow. I don't know if the threat was a product of our overactive imaginations or if there was some shred of reality. I tensed, but then reminded myself that I had to be brave. Jordan must have felt my grip tighten because he leaned in close and whispered.

"You are the bravest person I know, Kace. You've got

this."

He was right. I did have this. Jenny held her own and proved time and time again how brave she could be. Between confronting her dad for some truth and clarity and multiple hospital visits, she had proven to be the most courageous of us all. The least I could do was suck it up and talk to Mr. Mason. I breathed deeply, filling my lungs with the mid-evening air. I steadied myself and grabbed Jordan's hand with renewed strength and unwavering confidence. "Let's go," I blurted out.

"Yes, ma'am," he replied with a grin and a wink.

We made our way up the front stairs, the mahogany door no longer the threat we had initially perceived. I raised my hand, forming my fingers into a curled fist, and gave three swift knocks. The sound reverberated from the opposite side of the door. I could only imagine how vast the front foyer was. The Masons had money, and the house, large and elegant with a perfectly manicured lawn and a colourful, bountiful garden, did not hide that fact. I could hear the faint echo of footsteps approaching closer until the mahogany door slowly creaked open.

"May I help you?" a feminine, meek voice whispered.

A pair of small light blue eyes peered at Jordan and me from the darkness of the foyer, the mahogany door only slightly ajar. Their penetrating stare seemed to bore right through us; however, I could sense a calm and kind demeanour emanating from them.

"Hi. My name is Kacey Lundgren, and this is my boyfriend, Jordan," I whispered back. "We were hoping to talk to Mr. Mason."

"May I ask what business you have with Mr. Mason?" the

mystery woman asked.

"Uhm," I hesitated briefly before regaining my composure, "Sure. We were hoping to talk to him about the night that Ellie disappeared. I know it may be a sensitive topic, but we're trying to create a timeline of events to solve the mystery behind her disappearance and perhaps get some real closure for everyone involved."

"I see," the woman replied. "Isn't that a job for the authorities?"

"Yes, ma'am, you're correct. It's just that we think that whatever went on that night, whatever it was that people reported witnessing, it's beginning to resurface."

"Interesting," the woman pondered thoughtfully. "And what might that have to do with Mr. Mason?"

"I'd much rather just talk to Mr. Mason, ma'am, if you don't mind," I replied haughtily. I felt horrible for talking to the woman with such a tone, but I was getting impatient, and I just wanted to finish this conversation.

"Very well then," she replied as she stepped back to open the mahogany door even wider. She motioned for us to follow her. The entryway was even larger than I had envisioned it to be. Dim lights illuminated the hallway path, flickering ever so slightly like a flame from their perch on the dark walnut walls. It reminded me of one of those fancy mansions you see on TV, with the old family portraits proudly displayed.

"Mr. Mason is right through here," the woman whispered as she gestured toward the second door on the right. Jordan took charge and stepped through the door, holding my hand tightly. From behind a screen perched on a large wooden desk, cold, dark blue eyes peered curiously in our direction.

"Clara?" a voice emanated from behind the computer screen. "Who might these two fresh-faced young adults be?"

"This is Ms. Lundgren and ...," the woman paused. "I didn't get your last name, young man," she replied, looking at Jordan anxiously.

"Jordan is fine," he replied confidently.

"Thank you, Clara. You may go now. Could you please close the door behind you?" Mr. Mason asked.

Clara nodded at Mr. Mason in acknowledgement and then made her way out of the room, closing it with such care and precision that neither a squeak nor a creak emitted from the presumably old and tired hinges. Mr. Mason looked up from the screen of his computer at Jordan and me, motioning for us to take a seat. We exchanged nervous glances and hastily took our seats, taking care not to knock any of the neatly stacked piles of paper to the floor.

"So, Ms. Lundgren," Mr. Mason began. "I know who you are all too well. You were involved in an altercation with my daughter two years ago, the very same night that she disappeared."

"Yes, that's right. But I want you to know that neither Jenny nor I had anything to do with her going missing."

"I'm very much aware, and I'm sorry that you and your friend have had this guilt hanging over your head for so long," Mr. Mason declared.

"Guilt!" I exclaimed. "I have zero guilt hanging over me, and while I can't speak for Jenny, I'm pretty sure she harbours no guilt either. Why would we? We know we didn't do anything wrong. I only mentioned that we had nothing to do with Ellie's disappearance because you haven't said two words to either of us over the past two years. I wasn't sure if it was because you harboured some kind of resentment towards us or if you genuinely were aloof to how this whole scenario affected the two of us."

"I'm so sorry, Ms. Lundgren. I had no idea how much this whole conundrum affected the two of you. I should have spoken to the two of you earlier to let you know that I harboured no resentment or ill will toward you."

"Well, that's done and gone, and I'm not worried about it anymore. Truthfully, the two of us are here to ask you about your experience at the Scientific Research Center on the night Ellie disappeared."

"Oh, ummm… why would you want to know about that?" Mr. Mason asked, flustered.

"Well, as you are probably already aware," I continued, "Jenny Forester's dad works for the research center, too. He informed us about the power outage and the DNA extraction work performed that night. He also informed us that you were the project manager for that research project and had found the remains of a well-preserved Dire Wolf in Alaska months earlier."

"Yes, that's all true. But why do you want to speak to me? Sounds like you got all of the information you're looking for from Mr. Forester."

"Apparently, upon inspection of the DNA extraction chamber," I replied, "immediately following the power outage, Mr. Forester reported seeing claw marks inside and found the DNA sample missing. He informed us that you were also working that night. We thought you might have more information about the power outage and the whereabouts of the DNA sample. Or maybe even know what could have left the claw marks inside the extraction chamber. It seems awfully coincidental that work was being performed on extracting Dire Wolf DNA, and then suddenly, claw marks mysteriously appeared, and the sample went missing."

"I'm not sure what you're trying to imply, Ms. Lundgren," Mr. Mason replied in an annoyed and panicked tone, "but if you think that I had anything to do with that power outage, then you're sorely mistaken. If you don't mind, I'd appreciate it if you and your boyfriend would leave. Now!"

"But, but… Mr. Mason," I pleaded, "my friends and I are working hard to try and put all the puzzle pieces together, trying to solve the mystery of what went down that night. Don't you want to get some closure? Maybe find out what happened to Ellie once and for all?"

"I've made my peace with that. It's been two years. Now get out," Mr. Mason roared.

Jordan and I did not hesitate and heeded Mr. Mason's command. We bolted out of the room and into the hallway, where a concerned Clara sat, waiting at a small table and chairs. As we scurried by her, she rose from her seat, seemingly ready to show us out. However, we hurriedly passed her into the main foyer and straight to the large mahogany door. Clara grabbed my shoulder just as Jordan grabbed the handle to let us out.

"I couldn't help but overhear your conversation with Mr. Mason," she whispered. "I know some things that could maybe help your investigation."

Jordan and I spun around instantly, our heels squeaking

on the shiny tiled floor.

"What?" I exclaimed, both shocked and surprised.

"Can you come back tomorrow evening, around 9 pm? Don't come to the front door, though. Go around the side of the house and to the back shed. I can meet you there. I'll tell you everything I know."

Jordan and I looked at each other questioningly. He nodded in approval. "Yes, I can come back tomorrow night," I replied.

"Good," Clara responded, sounding almost relieved. "I can no longer keep this to myself. I will see you then."

Jordan held the car door open for me like the gentleman he was and held my hand as I slid into the front passenger seat. As he entered the vehicle and buckled his seatbelt, he turned to me, a smile plastered across his handsome face.

"I'm really proud of you, Kacey, for how you handled yourself there. You took the lead and didn't let me get a word in. This is the most confident I have seen you in a long time."

I smiled back at Jordan, beaming like I had just won the golden lottery. "Thanks, babe," I replied. "Now tell me, what on earth was going on with Mr. Mason? He was acting rather strange, wasn't he? It's like I struck a nerve or something."

"I don't even know how to interpret that conversation," Jordan replied. "It's almost as though he were trying to hide something."

"Tell me about it. Something certainly doesn't add up. I hope Clara can shed some light on the matter."

"Time will tell, I guess," Jordan replied. "Guess we'd better get home. It's getting late, and I imagine you will want to fill Jenny in on our meeting with Mr. Mason."

"Absolutely. Thanks, Jordan, for coming with me tonight. Just having you near is a real comfort."

"Anytime, Kace. You're my person. I'll always be there to support you."

I smiled warmly as Jordan started the engine and drove off into the dark of the night.

CHAPTER TWENTY-SIX

Tuesday, May 24th, 2022

Jenny and I arrived at school at 8:15 am sharp. We didn't wait for the boys like we usually did, no. This time we had important business to attend to. I know the boys would have joined us on our trip to the office and offered their full support, but this felt like something that Jenny and I needed to handle on our own. Jenny wasted no time prepping for our conversation and began to march with authority to the school office. She turned to me, eyes dead serious and said, "You coming or what? We've got no time to waste."

I laughed, then graced her with a military salute. "Yes, Lieutenant Forester."

The two of us marched so fast and with such authority across the school's front lawn that we must have appeared as though we were auditioning for a role in the school play as a Grand Marshall or some other important historical figure. I could feel other students' eyes penetrating us with blatant stares of disbelief, perhaps contemplating what mess we had gotten ourselves into this time. Determined and fierce, Jenny braced her foot upon the bottom of the entryway door and pushed herself into the handle with such force that the impact left a small red mark on her forearm. We continued down the hall, our feet marching together in perfect synchronization. It sounded like a marching band should have accompanied us to announce our imminent arrival at the office. We rounded a corner and then marched our way into the office, approaching the front desk, our facial expressions portraying innocent bystanders being accused of a crime they didn't commit.

"Can I help you, Ms. Forester and Ms. Lundgren?" Ms. Lythe, the secretary, asked.

"You absolutely can," Jenny announced abruptly. "We demand to see Mrs. Laughlin right now if you don't mind."

"Well, first of all, ladies," Ms. Lythe replied, "please don't take that tone of voice with me. It's not very becoming. Secondly, Mrs. Laughlin is scheduled for a meeting this morning and will not be available until later this afternoon."

"I'm sorry, Ms. Lythe, for our abruptness," I began, "but this is an extremely urgent matter, and it simply cannot wait. Can you check with Mrs. Laughlin to see if she can squeeze us in?"

"I'll see what I can do," Ms Lythe replied.

"Thank you," I replied. "We both appreciate your understanding."

Ms. Lythe disappeared, her long skirt swirling like a leaf caught in the wind. Jenny and I remained standing, alert and ready to take on whatever challenge might confront us.

Despite our exuding confidence, my stomach churned like butterflies were flitting about. But before I could let the anxiety consume me, I reminded myself that I was strong and that I wasn't alone. I had Jenny to back me up; she was as fierce as they came. My train of thought was broken by the sudden clicking of heels on the hardwood floor. Ms. Lythe was making her way back to the front desk, her facial expression giving no clue what Mrs. Laughlin's response to our impromptu meeting request might be. Jenny and I exchanged nervous glances, then caught Ms. Lythe's gaze as she approached us.

"Mrs. Laughlin says she can squeeze you in right now, but you must make it quick."

"Done," I replied. "Thank you, Ms. Lythe."

Ms. Lythe nodded at Jenny and me as we approached Mrs. Laughlin's office. Mrs. Laughlin sat at her desk, stone-faced, staring at her computer monitor. Her eyes darted about as if she were in deep thought. It felt awkward to interrupt her, but I knew this was a now-or-never type of scenario. Jenny cleared her throat to divert her attention from the computer monitor. Mrs. Laughlin looked up from the thin veil of light that illuminated her face.

"Oh, yes. Ms. Lundgren and Ms. Forester. What can I do for you? Ms. Lythe mentioned that it was an urgent matter."

"Yeah, it is." Jenny blurted out rather uninhibitedly. "I'm not sure if you've been made aware, Mrs. Laughlin, but Kacey and I have been implicated in something that has nothing to do with us."

"I see," Mrs. Laughlin replied smugly. "Please tell me how that might have anything to do with me?"

"It's not that it has anything to do with you directly," I replied. "It's more about how you can help us prove that we are innocent of wrongdoing."

"Uh-huh," Mrs. Laughlin replied, locking eyes with me and nodding in acknowledgment. "And how, may I ask, can I do that?"

"It's quite simple, really," Jenny replied, equally as smug. "We just need you to give us your permission to review the security camera footage from months ago when Ellie was still alive. We suspect that she stole something of ours from the locker room during our stint with wrestling during P.E."

Mrs. Laughlin laughed, her eyes penetrating Jenny and me like daggers. "Why on earth would I give the two of you access to the school's security footage over a petty theft?"

"Well, that's the thing," I started defensively. "Jenny and I had a set of matching friendship necklaces, which is what we suspect Ellie stole from the locker room."

"And what?" Mrs. Laughlin interrupted brashly. "You just thought that would warrant a request to view the camera footage?"

"No!" Jenny growled, her face twisting into something ugly. "But the fact that those very same necklaces were found in the clutch Ellie was carrying the night of the dance, hidden deep in the woods where someone fitting her description was sighted, certainly warrants that request."

"Wait a second," Mrs. Laughlin exclaimed, shock written all over her face. "Why is this the first time I've heard about this?"

"That's because the authorities are currently investigating the matter. We haven't even been questioned yet. We are only aware of the situation because Kacey's lawyer called and informed her parents."

"Well, isn't this quite the revelation?" Mrs. Laughlin replied. "However, I don't think it would be appropriate for me to allow the two of you to view the security footage without consent from the authorities. This appears to be an active investigation, and I must be professional and use my best judgment."

"Just as I thought," Jenny scoffed. "I knew you'd refuse our request. I told Kacey you'd refuse even before we got here. You've always had it out for us. Why would I expect anything else?"

"Jenny," Mrs. Laughlin called out sympathetically, "I don't know what gave you the impression that I'm out to get you, but know that is simply not true. I have no ill will toward either you or Kacey. I would assist you if I could, but when a situation turns into a police matter, it is not my place to make my own judgments and decisions. Perhaps consider talking to the authorities and asking them to request the security footage. I would gladly turn over anything that could help the two of you clear your names."

"Sure, whatever," Jenny huffed. "Thanks for nothing." Jenny stomped off, proudly displaying her annoyance like a peacock.

"Thanks, Mrs. Laughlin, for entertaining our request," I called out graciously before exiting her office. She smiled and nodded as I made my way after Jenny. I nearly had to run at a marathon pace to catch up with her, her adrenaline pumping pure caffeinated-like energy into her bloodstream.

"Jenny, could you slow down for a moment?" She continued to storm her way through the sea of students in the hallway, making every attempt to dodge and duck like a professional boxer. She rounded the corner, and I nearly lost sight of her for a moment behind a couple displaying some serious public display of affection. I sidestepped around them and saw her exiting the side doors next to the drama room. How fitting, I thought, right now, Jenny was putting on a show, and she didn't give a flying fuck who witnessed it. I continued to chase after her, exiting the building and finally seizing the opportunity to catch up when she took a brief reprieve from her tantrum under the shade of a large tree.

"I told you, Kacey," Jenny hollered. "I fucking told you. Mrs. Laughlin has no desire to help us. She's always had some sort of problem with the two of us. I'm unsure what I expected by asking her to see the security footage, but I had hoped she'd have a shred of decency and do right by us."

"Jenn," I whispered calmly, "don't you think you're overreacting just a little? I mean, she had a point about the police investigation. I don't think she can legally give us access to the footage if the authorities are trying to assemble the puzzle pieces."

"No, Kacey, that's what she wants you to believe. The authorities haven't contacted us yet to ask questions, never mind contacting her. Nothing is officially being investigated yet. All they have right now is a piece of evidence relating to Ellie's disappearance, and they're trying to figure out what to make of it before they get anyone else involved. She easily could have allowed us access to that security footage without penalty; she just didn't want to because she's a bitch."

"I never thought about it like that, Jenn, but you're probably right. We only know about the clutch because my lawyer gave us the heads up."

"You're damn right that I'm right, Kace. So what are we going to do about it then? I refuse to have this little tidbit of information and just sit idly by and do nothing. I'd like some ammo to back us up if and when the authorities contact us."

"I'm not sure, Jenn. Any ideas or suggestions?"

"I say we break into Mrs. Laughlin's office tonight after everyone is gone for the evening. The custodial staff will be on-site, but there's a volleyball game tonight, and plenty of coaches and student-athletes will be on-site, too. They shouldn't question us if we are spotted roaming about. We just have to find a way to disable the cameras on the premises so we don't get caught."

"And just how do you plan to do that?" I asked.

"Well, lucky for us, Jordan is a big tech nerd. He could hack into the security system and deactivate it. That way, we won't get caught, and Mrs Laughlin will be none the wiser."

"It's a bit risky, isn't it? What if someone sees us in Mrs. Laughlin's office?"

"We'll take all the necessary precautions. Don't panic, Kace. This is our only chance to get answers."

"I suppose you're right. Ok, let's do it."

Jenny winked at me and put her arm around my shoulder. She was trying to quell my fears. This was definitely going to be one wild evening.

CHAPTER TWENTY-SEVEN

Monday, May 27th, 2024

Jordan and I arrived home pretty late after our conversation with Mr. Mason and Clara. I decided it was best to wait until morning to fill Jenny and Chase in on the events from last night to avoid waking them. I knew all too well what it was like to be groggy at the start of a busy school day.

I arrived at school extra early, hoping to catch everyone as they arrived. Jordan and Chase rolled in first, the familiar rev of Jordan's engine rumbling as it pulled into the student parking lot. Jordan caught sight of me waiting by the stairs to the front entrance and gave me an enthusiastic wave. I smiled and waved back, tossing my hair over my shoulders like a runway model. Jordan hurriedly grabbed his backpack and rushed over to me, not even waiting for Chase to exit the vehicle.

"Hey, Kace. Have you told Jenny about our meeting at the Mason house last night?"

"No. I thought it might be too late to call, so I decided to wait until this morning. Did you say anything to Chase?"

"No. I decided to wait until I had verified whether you had spoken to Jenny. I love Chase; he's my best friend, but I know he'd blab to Jenny before you could speak to her."

"Thanks, Jordan. I appreciate that. It's best if I talk to her because I was there and know exactly how information passed on from one person to another can get skewed so easily."

Chase came running up, huffing like he had just scaled a large mountain. "What are you two whispering about over here? Is there some sort of secret that I should know about?"

"Actually," I teased, "there is. I'm just waiting for Jenny to arrive, and then I'll fill you in."

Just like magic, Jenny appeared, running towards us clumsily, lugging her backpack as though it were filled with bricks. "Utilizing your superpowers again, I see."

"What?" she said, looking confused. "Did I miss something?"

"As a matter of fact, you did," I chided playfully. "I was just telling Chase I had some news to share, but I was going to wait for you and then poof, there you were."

"Well, don't leave us in suspense," Jenny exclaimed. What is this news you speak of?"

"Some interesting revelations arose from Jordan and my visit to the Mason house last night," I began. "Mr. Mason got extremely defensive when we asked him if he had any idea what could have been responsible for the power outage and if he knew what may have left the claw marks behind in the chamber. He denied any involvement. However, he admitted to being the project manager and confessed that the DNA they were attempting to extract was from an extinct Dire Wolf."

"Typical," Jenny scoffed. "Of course, he denied any involvement. Why would he admit to anything? He thinks he runs this town. He's probably got his hand in the Mayor's pocketbook or something. All he has to do is blink, and the Mayor is throwing money at him, begging him to make the next big discovery and put this town on the map."

"Totally," I agreed. "I wouldn't be surprised, with all the money that Mr. Mason has, that he wasn't running the show in some way, shape, or form. The Mayor is essentially just a lab rat, a puppet if you will, to be pushed and pulled in whatever direction Mr. Mason wants."

"That's what money and power can do for a person," Jenny sighed.

"It's weird, though, isn't it, that he got so angry and defensive?" I asked. "He seemed calm and rational until we brought up the power outage and the claw marks inside the chamber. It felt as though he were trying to hide something. He said that your father already revealed everything there was to know."

"It's bizarre, Kace," Jenny agreed. "There's no reason for him to get defensive over a question unless he does have something to hide."

"It gets even stranger, though," I continued.

"Like how?" Jenny questioned, curiosity overcoming her.

"When Jordan and I first arrived at the Mason residence, a woman answered the door. We later found out her name was Clara. She must be their housekeeper or something.

She was sitting outside Mr. Mason's office when we talked to him. She must have overheard our conversation because she asked us to return tonight. Only, she wants us to go around to the back where the garden shed is located. It appears that she has some information that she wants to share with us, information that she doesn't want Mr. Mason to know."

"I'm intrigued," Jenny replied. "I wonder what secrets she is harbouring? This could be the key to cracking this whole investigation wide open."

"That's what I'm hoping for," I replied.

"Do you think she'd mind if Chase and I tagged along? All of us are involved in some way or another. It'd be nice to hear what she has to say."

"I'm not sure that's such a good idea, Jenn. It's not that I don't want either you or Chase there; it's just that she only invited Jordan and me, and I don't want to do anything to scare her off or make her change her mind. I hope you're not too upset with me."

"No, I get it, and you're absolutely right. I want to be involved, but I understand how Clara might get a little twitchy if too many people are around. I have an idea, though."

"Oh geez, Jenn. Do I even want to know?" I groaned.

"Thanks for your unwavering faith in me, Kace," Jenn replied sarcastically. "Anyhoo, I thought Jordan could try to find a non-obvious way to livestream your conversation with Clara so that Chase and I can get in on the action. We are involved in one way or another, and it would be nice to actually be a part of the investigation, considering we're a team and all."

"That is a pretty good idea," I replied. "Jordan, what do you think? Can we make it happen?"

"Yeah, I think I can pull it off without being noticed," he replied confidently. Just have to place the camera somewhere where it won't be seen and position it in just the right spot."

"Thank you so much, you guys," Jenn exclaimed, thrilled that we entertained her suggestion. "I'm super excited to see what information Clara might divulge."

The warning bell for the start of the school day interrupted our thoughts, and the four of us sauntered off to our classes. Concentrating on the lessons for the day would be challenging, with my mind preoccupied with daydreams of what was yet to come. I sighed and prayed that time would be on my side today and the day would roll on like a rowboat floating aimlessly in the ocean. My prayers were answered because before I knew it, the dismissal bell rang, sending waves of students bustling through the halls, backpacks and bookbags slinging about like loaded weapons. I spotted Jenny elbowing through the crowded hall, desperately attempting to use her best ninja moves to navigate the sea of people. She was completely dishevelled when she reached me; her hair was messy, sweat dripping down her forehead, and her clothing crumpled.

"Geez," she cried, "It's a rat race here. You'd think the bloody pope was here giving a motivational speech or something. Where is everyone off to in such a hurry?"

"No idea," I replied. "But I bet it's nowhere near as exciting as what we've got in store for tonight."

"Right?" Jenny agreed. "I'm honestly so anxious to hear what Clara has to say. I'd be lying if I said I wasn't a bit nervous. My father has given me all he knows, but I suspect Mr. Mason has knowingly withheld some pertinent information."

"There's no doubt he's been withholding information," I replied. "Clara made it quite clear that she has something pivotal to share."

"I guess we'd better find the boys to figure out how we're going to set up this live-streaming business, huh?" Jenny inquired.

"I suppose," I replied. "I know Jordan mentioned having to rush home right after school to help his father with a few things, so I'll call him as soon as I get home."

"Sounds good," Jenny agreed. "You'll keep me in the loop, won't you, Kace?"

"Of course. Have I ever steered you wrong, Jenn?"

"No, Kace. You've been the best friend a person could ever hope for," she replied, grinning from ear to ear. "I'll talk to you soon. I will head home and give Chase the play-by-play for tonight's rendezvous. I'll catch you later, okay?" Jenny turned away, dramatically flinging her hair and gliding off seamlessly into the golden glow of the afternoon sun.

I slung my backpack over my shoulder and made my way home. My mind swirled with thoughts of Mr. Mason and the secrets that Clara might reveal. It was a mystery as to what information she might harbour, and admittedly, I was anxious to find out. However, I was ready to solve the mystery of the glowing amber eyes and finally get the closure we deserved. The whole town was ready to put this chapter behind us.

CHAPTER TWENTY-EIGHT

Tuesday, May 24th, 2022: 7:30 PM

Jenny and I sat quietly in the school's east parking lot, the building's shadow looming ominously over us from the shifting rays of the western sun. Jordan was supposed to text me when we had the all-clear to enter the building and make our move. You know the saying, "A watched pot never boils." That's certainly how it felt at that moment. I stared at my phone intensely, anxiously waiting for Jordan to text. After what felt like an eternity, Okay: I know I'm exaggerating, the familiar ding gloriously erupted from my phone, giving us the all-clear to enter the building and commence our secret mission. Jenny pounced into position, a leopard readying itself to stalk its prey, and began to usher herself eloquently toward the east entrance doors. I, not as eager to pursue this endeavour, lumbered awkwardly like a newborn elephant, hesitating at every opportunity.

"What gives?" Jenny questioned, as though she were a professional interrogator.

"Nothing," I replied, displaying my best poker face.

"Kace, if you haven't figured out by now that you can't pull the wool over my eyes, I just don't know what to say. Even your best poker face can't fool me."

I glanced over at Jenny, squinting my eyes to mimic a glare. "Who said I'm giving you a poker face?"

"Seriously?" Jenny chuckled. "Kacey, I've known you for what? 12 years now? If you were really upset with me, your nose would have that cute little wrinkle, and you'd certainly not be getting sassy with me. You're more the silent type when you're angry."

"Okay, Okay...busted," I blurted out. "I'm still a bit nervous about this. I know Jordan disabled the security cameras, but my gut still has butterflies."

"I get it, Kace. I really do. But just remember, it's our asses on the line here. We'll be directly implicated here if the authorities use this evidence. I don't know about you, but I want to avoid being on the wrong side of the law."

"I'm definitely in agreement with you, Jenny. I just can't help but worry that something will go awry. You know me, always full of doubt and worry."

"Yeah, Kace, I know you. But I also know that you've come a long way in conquering your anxiety. We've got this, okay? No worries. Jordan has ensured that there's no way anyone can trace the missing security footage to us."

"You're right, Jenn. You always are. I'll just shake it off. Jordan has got us. I trust him."

"Good. Then let's get a move on, okay?"

Jenny made her way to the East parking lot entrance, confidence evident in every stride. I trailed slightly behind, trying to mimic Jenny's enthusiasm. Jenny pushed open the door, an incessant creak echoing down the chambers of the long, dark corridor. The distant sound of cheers from the basketball tournament reverberated throughout the hallway. I glanced up at the security camera, half expecting to see the familiar red light flashing, indicating that a recording was in progress, but it was dark. Jordan must have been successful in his mission to hack into the camera software. Not that I doubted the truthfulness of his earlier text; however, my paranoia would not allow me to be at ease until I witnessed it for myself. I sighed with relief and followed Jenny past the first six rows of lockers.

We were stealthy, much like secret agents on a fantastical mission to save humanity from the threatening claws of a looming darkness, a malevolent force that whispered fear into the hearts of all who dared to resist. Okay, it's a bit dramatic and over the top, but in my mind, that's exactly how it felt. When we finally reached the last row of lockers, Jenny quickly darted across the hall and to the right, the serene glass windows of the school's office gently refracting what little light penetrated from the rays of the evening sun. The names of the office staff and school administration etched ever so carefully into the glass pane loomed like sharp, poisonous daggers, ready to trap us in their suffocating grip.

"You ready?" Jenny asked, her voice skillfully oozing with anticipation.

"Ye ye yeah," I stuttered. "No time like the present, right?"

"Right," Jenny replied.

Jenny pushed the door to the front office slowly, trying to avoid any creaking that might signal our presence. We tiptoed past the front desk before hanging a sharp right down the corridor leading to Mrs. Laughlin's office. Once inside, Jenny and I scanned the room with laser-like precision, trying to pinpoint the location of the security camera logs. We had no idea what we were looking for, but we assumed video files would be stored digitally, just like files on the cloud on our personal devices.

"The files must be on her computer," I whispered to Jenny. "I don't imagine anyone keeps hard copies of video footage or data in this day and age."

"Absolutely," Jenny agreed. "Now we just need to figure out how to access her computer. Any clues as to what her login and password might be?"

I stared silently at Jenny for what seemed like an eternity, my blank expression giving no clue what the mysterious login might be. Suddenly, an idea came to me like a light bulb lit up. "Mrs. Laughlin has a cat, right?"

"Yeah," Jenny replied. "It's the cat in the photo here on her desk. That cat is like a child to her. Gives a whole new definition to the term crazy cat lady."

"Do you remember its name?" I asked.

"Oh, something that starts with an H, I believe. Harry, no, um, Harley, no, that's not it. Harvey, yeah, that's it. Okay, so let's log in with her email and try Harvey as the password."

I took control and sat myself down at Mrs. Laughlin's desk, an unusual action for me. Typically, Jenny would be the one to seize control of a situation; however, on this evening, at this very moment, a wave of confidence washed over me. Perhaps it was my trust in Jordan and his promise to do everything he could to prevent us from getting caught. Regardless of the reasoning behind my sudden burst of confidence, it was a nice feeling to have faith in my ability to remain calm and in control. "OK, so her email is Laughlin@FRSD.Com, password Harvey." I typed each letter and symbol with slow and steady precision, taking care not to miss anything. When I hit the submit button, Mrs. Laughlin's computer lit up like a burst of light from a parked vehicle's headlight. "Voila," I squealed rather suddenly and somewhat loudly.

"Kacey, shhhhh. What's come over you?" Jenny laughed.

"I'm sorry," I chuckled. "I'm just so damn proud of myself for figuring this out."

"As you should be, girl. But don't forget we are trying to remain stealthy and not get caught in the act here."

"I know, I know. I promise there won't be any more outbursts."

"Okay, then, Ms. Smarty Pants. Where do we begin our search?" Jenny winked at me.

"Well, I suppose we start looking at her files and documents folder," I mused.

"Oh, you suppose, hey?" Jenny chided playfully. "Okay, then. Well, let's get started. No time to waste."

I swivelled Mrs. Laughlin's chair and elegantly glided my fingers over the keyboard, typing with such speed and precision that I surprised myself. Where did this newfound confidence come from? I would never in a million years have guessed that I would be the one to hack into Mrs. Laughlin's personal school computer. After several minutes of fumbling through file after file, I finally stumbled upon one file aptly named "Security Footage."

"Hey, Jenn. I think I found something," I muttered

excitedly. "Take a look at this. It's got all sorts of video clips sorted by month, day, and year. That footage from the locker room has just got to be in here somewhere."

"Keep looking," Jenn replied, eagerness emanating from her voice. "I want to get out of here before the tournaments wrap up for the evening."

"I'm going as fast as possible, Jenn," I snapped. "Just give me a bit more time, okay?"

"Well, okay then, grumpy ass," Jenny pouted. "Remind me to never get on your bad side."

"I'm sorry, Jenn. I'm so stressed already, and your rushing me isn't helping. Just give me a couple more minutes. I'm already on the files labelled March 2022. The file we're looking for should be right here." I looked up from the screen and turned toward Jenny.

"What?" Jenny exclaimed. "Did you find the file?"

"Yeah, I think I did." My eyes widened as I stared at the computer screen, the cursor hovering over the little triangular play symbol.

"What are you waiting for?" Jenny scolded. "Press play, already. I want to see exactly who is responsible for stealing those necklaces."

My finger quivered nervously as I eyed the keyboard, hesitating to press the enter button. I drew a deep breath, exhaled and pushed the enter button with authority. The screen lit up with images of various locations throughout the school. Jenny and I perused the various smaller squares depicting different camera locations throughout the school. My eyes were finally drawn to the lower left corner of the screen. Several rows of lockers with benches in between beckoned to me as though the secrets they held would fulfill my mission.

"That's it," I exclaimed quietly, my finger commanding attention as it pointed at the image in the bottom left corner.

Jenny gazed intently at the small square, almost as if expecting it to magically spew its secrets. Her hands trembled ever so slightly as she reached toward the keyboard.

"Let me," Jenny whispered. "Let me push play."

"Okay," I responded, puzzled by her sudden change in demeanor.

Jenny inched forward slowly, extending her index finger, and, after a brief pause, gently pushed the button. It was the first time I had ever seen Jenny hesitate to do anything. We both stared at the screen, waiting in anticipation. A large number of images from different months flashed onto the screen. I scanned the months from top to bottom.

"Right there," I whispered as I pointed to March. "Click on it; see if the dates pop up."

Jenny clicked on the tab for March, and 31 different video files appeared. "What day was that again?" Jenny asked. "The day the necklaces disappeared."

"Thursday, March 24th, I believe."

"Alright," Jenny muttered as she scrolled three-quarters of the way down the page. "Here's the file." Without any further hesitation, Jenny's finger pounced like a cat stalking its prey onto the play button. The sound of excited voices filled the room.

"That footage is from the first period," I said. "We didn't have P.E. until after lunch. We'll have to scroll through several hours of video footage."

"It's a good thing we can fast forward then," Jenny replied. "Let me just scroll through the first little bit." Jenny pulled the play bar forward before abruptly pausing at 1:03 pm. Her eyes widened as big as saucers, and her body tensed.

"What is it, Jenny?"

"I'm not sure what I'm looking at here," she muttered, confusion written across her face. "It's not possible. How? How can this even be real?"

"What?" I exclaimed, my voice now cracking with sheer panic.

"Kacey, it's us. The camera shows you and me taking the necklaces from the lockers."

"No, that's impossible," I squealed. "It's gotta be some kind of AI bullshit. You and I both know we never left the gym during P.E."

"No, we didn't," Jenny seethed. "So, what do we do now? Do we tell somebody that we broke into Mrs. Laughlin's office? Either way, we're going to be in deep shit, but I think the tampered video evidence is going to incriminate us and land us in even deeper trouble."

"I will talk to my mom and see what she says. Maybe she'll call Mr. Grieves to see what options we have."

"Sounds like a plan," Jenny agreed. "I wonder what the penalty will be for breaking into Mrs. Laughlin's office."

"It's nowhere near as bad as what will happen if we stay mum on this whole hacked footage stuff," I said. "Okay, let's download this footage onto our thumb drive and get out of here."

Jenny inserted the thumb drive into the USB slot and hit download. The numbers crept up faster than expected, and before we knew it, we were meandering down the hall and out the same doors we came in from.

"I'll let you know what my mom and Mr. Grieves say," I shouted as Jenny and I parted ways.

"I'm holding you to it," Jenny shouted back.

CHAPTER TWENTY-NINE

Monday, May 27th, 2024: 7:45 PM

Jordan arrived at my house a few hours after dinner, attempting to prepare me for the evening ahead. I was nervous, of course, but anxious, too. This information could provide the pinnacle moment where we could finally put all the puzzle pieces together and put this mess behind us once and for all.

"How are you feeling about tonight, Kace?" Jordan asked with concern.

"I'm nervous, of course, but I just want to end this long, overdrawn chapter of our lives," I replied with a sigh. "It's been on and off again for two years, and I'm just ready to move on."

"I get that," Jordan replied empathetically. "I think we all are, heck, the whole town even."

"So, what must we do to get this footage on camera?" I asked.

"Well, first, I've got to tape this wire to you underneath your jacket or hoodie. This will capture the audio," Jordan explained. "Then I need to figure out an inconspicuous spot for the camera. Somewhere where it won't easily be seen. It runs completely through Bluetooth so I can connect it wirelessly through my phone."

"Perhaps I could wear this headband," I suggested. "It has some small decorative stones attached to it. Maybe we could find a way to make the camera blend in with the other decorative pieces."

"Fabulous idea, Kace. Clara won't suspect a thing."

"Thanks, Jordan," I replied, hugging him tightly.

I handed Jordan my headband, and he scrutinized it, his hands gliding over it and his eyes staring intensely. "I think if I place it right here in the middle between the two green gems, it won't look out of place," he muttered. He placed the small black camera in the center of the green gems and took a black twist tie to attach it securely. "There. That looks good. What do you think, Kace?"

"Seamless," I replied. "Jordan, you're a rockstar."

"I try," Jordan chuckled. "Now, what do you say? Should we send a link to Jenny and Chase to see if they can see and hear the camera feed?"

"Yes, definitely," I giggled. "I know Jenny is sitting in her room staring holes into her phone. I guess we should be nice and end the torture."

Jordan laughed. "I can only imagine she's driving Chase crazy."

"Without a doubt," I agreed as I scooped up my phone and dialled Jenny's number. After a few swift rings, Jenny called out.

"Hello," she said, desperately trying to disguise the anticipation in her voice.

"Hey Jenn, it's Kacey," I promptly replied.

"Well, no shit, Sherlock," Jenny teased. "So what's up? Did you guys get an audio-video feed set up for Chase and me?"

"We sure did," I replied. Jordan has a wire ready to tape up under my hoodie, and the brilliant person I am suggested we attach the camera to a headband. We're all set and ready to go. We just need to send you guys the link so you can download the camera app to watch what Clara has to say."

"Well, don't keep us waiting, for goodness' sake, send it," Jenny commanded.

"Alright, alright," I replied, exasperated. I copied the link and sent a text to Jenny. Within moments, I heard the notification from her phone, ding excitedly.

"Got it," she squealed with delight. "So, will you let Chase and me know when it's time to tune in or what?"

"Yeah. I'll get Jordan to text you right away."

"Great. Chase and I will be waiting."

"Alright, Jenn, I'm going to go. Jordan has to set everything up before we take off to meet Clara. We'll let you know when we're ready to go live. Talk to you later."

"Okay, Kace. Good luck."

"Thanks, Jenn."

Jordan and I continued preparing for our excursion to meet with Clara. He carefully attached the audio wires to the front of my shirt, taking care not to have any loose wires dangling from underneath my oversized hoodie. He then slipped the headband over my head with delicate hands. His hand gently brushed my hair aside, sending tingles up my spine. "No," I scolded myself. "No time for such thoughts." I grabbed Jordan's hand and yanked him with authority toward the front door. "Time to get going," I huffed, anxiety brimming out of my voice.

"Whoa... Kace. Relax a bit," Jordan exclaimed. "Everything is going to be just fine. I highly doubt Clara is going to pat us down."

"Oh, I know. It's just a feeling I can't seem to shake. What if Mr. Mason catches us talking to Clara? What is he going to think? What is he going to do?"

"Don't worry, Kace. I'm sure Clara knows what she is doing. She wouldn't have set this meeting up in this particular place or at this time if she thought there was any risk of getting caught. She's got as much to lose as we do. I'm sure Mr. Mason would fire her if he knew she was sharing secrets with us."

"You're right, Jordan. Clara has a lot to lose. There's no way she'd risk losing this job. She must get paid a lot working for the Masons."

"Alright then, are you ready to head off?" Jordan asked.

"Yeah, I think so," I replied, trying to sound convincing.

"Okay then, let's get going," Jordan commanded, sounding confident as hell. "It's already 8:30. We don't want to keep Clara waiting."

We made our way to Jordan's car, the breeze blowing ever so slightly, causing the leaves in the trees to rustle. A thin fog created a misty veil, almost like the universe set us up for an eerily eventful evening. The weather definitely matched the mood. I was nervous, but Jordan's gentle coaching built my confidence and convinced me that this plan would reveal crucial evidence to close this chapter of our lives. Jordan graciously opened the car door, caressing my shoulder with finesse as I carefully climbed into the passenger seat. I looked up at him, smiling with my eyes. After all these years, I still struggle to comprehend how I, Kacey Lundgren, got so lucky to land a guy as thoughtful and caring as Jordan. Jordan closed the door gently behind me and climbed into the driver's seat, placing his keys into the ignition and revving the engine aggressively three times. I looked up at him with a look of disbelief.

"What?" he laughed. "Have you never seen a male with testosterone on full display before?"

"Umm, yeah, I have," I scoffed. "Just not exactly your typical MO." I had to laugh at myself. I tried so hard not to show my approval of Jordan's sudden fit of masculinity, but I failed miserably.

"Well, make a mental picture in your mind," he teased. "You're likely not going to see this Jordan again anytime soon."

I pouted, then burst into a fit of laughter. Jordan smiled and laughed along with me.

"Well, I suppose I achieved my goal, then," he winked.

"And exactly what goal was that?" I chided.

"To get you to relax and feel at ease."

My face suddenly contorted with a look of surprise. Boy, was Jordan ever good at the art of distraction? Was there nothing he couldn't do? He always knew exactly what I needed and how to execute his plan.

"I suppose we'd better head off then," Jordan exclaimed. "Wouldn't want to keep Clara waiting."

We pulled out of my driveway, turning left, the reflection of the taillights casting an eerie red glow on the pavement. I breathed a sigh of relief, knowing that whatever details revealed themselves tonight, I could handle it with Jordan by my side. My knight. My hero. The radio hummed a familiar tune as we continued to drive down the treed boulevard, the moonlight peeking through the trees casting ominous shadows that seemingly came alive as we passed. I imagined they were ghosts from past town residents, waiting to reveal all the secrets they harboured for the past two years as they quietly observed the rest of us aimlessly wandering like zombies from a post-apocalyptic movie. Oh, the things they would see and the things they could say. It wasn't long before I was suddenly jerked from my daydream by brakes squealing.

"Kace… we're here," Jordan's voice whispered.

"Already? That was fast. Jordan, were you practicing your NASCAR skills again?" I teased.

"As a matter of fact, I was," Jordan replied sarcastically. "But in all seriousness, though, you were in some sort of a daze or something. You didn't say two words the whole drive here."

"I was just in the middle of a daydream about ghosts and post-apocalyptic zombies," I replied, laughing at the absurdity of it all.

"Oh, well, if that's all…" Jordan paused.

I followed Jordan's gaze. His eyes were fixated on a dim flickering light emanating from the north side of the Mason's home. We both gazed at one another.

"Clara," we whispered in unison.

I motioned to Jordan, indicating that we should exit the

vehicle and investigate the source of the light. I was sure it was Clara, but I didn't want to take any chances—no point in getting ourselves implicated in further drama. We climbed out of the vehicle slowly, taking caution not to draw any attention to ourselves. I gently closed the door to avoid making any unnecessary noise. Jordan tiptoed to me, grasping my arm with firm yet gentle hands.

"You ready?" he asked, gazing at me with piercing eyes.

"As ready as I'll ever be," I replied, somewhat hesitantly.

The two of us made our way along the front walkway of the Mason home, darting quickly over to the house's north side to investigate the mysterious light's source. The light was partially obscured by a large bush that pressed against the back of the Masons' home.

"Clara?" I whispered. Just then, a figure cloaked in a dark, hooded petticoat emerged from the obscurity of the bush.

"Ms. Lundgren, Mr. Bally, I'm so glad you could make it. Let's not waste any time. I don't want Mr. Mason to become suspicious if he cannot reach me for an extended period. Follow me quickly."

Jordan and I followed closely behind Clara as she led us around to the backside of the house and to a rather large shed. It was so large it resembled one of those tiny houses I had seen on several home makeover shows.

"In here," she motioned as she slowly turned the doorknob.

Jordan and I followed Clara into the darkness, shadows dancing like ballerinas as the moonlight beamed through the opening of the window's blinds. It projected an ominous feeling, almost as though we were the unsuspecting victims of a horror movie. I shivered, and it wasn't even the slightest bit cold. I could feel my stomach churning, a hard lump forming in my throat.

"Please, sit down." Clara motioned to a slip-covered loveseat in the back left corner of the shed. "This will be quite the revelation, so I'd suggest making yourselves comfortable."

Jordan and I exchanged nervous glances, unsure where this tale would lead. I nodded to him inconspicuously, signalling it was time to start the live stream. I quickly texted Jenny while Jordan reached into his pocket, pressing the record button on his streaming app. We were officially live. The two of us made ourselves comfortable on the loveseat and readied ourselves for the story that was about to unravel.

"Where do I start?" Clara sighed.

"At the beginning, I suppose," I replied. "The night of the Spring Fling Dance."

"Right, right," Clara sputtered nervously. "The Spring Fling Dance. Okay then… Um, that was the night the town's residents first reported the amber eyes."

"Yes, it was," I replied. "And the same night that Ellie disappeared."

"Right, when Ellie disappeared," Clara replied, sounding frightened. "That was also the night of the power outage at the scientific research center. I remember Mr. Mason came home late that evening, just after 9:00 pm, and he was talking to someone on the phone about what had happened. I couldn't hear everything he was saying, but I definitely heard the fear in his voice. He was worried about the consequences if news got out about the claw marks in the DNA extraction chamber. He seemed particularly concerned about the report of the amber eyes in the forest."

"Did you know who he was talking to?" I pried. "Did he mention anything about Ellie?"

"As a matter of fact, he did bring up Ellie's name, or at least he referenced her by saying his daughter," Clara replied. "All I could make out was that he wanted whoever he spoke to to take Ellie to a safe place. He said he would see her later that evening to sort things out, whatever that means."

"Holy Toledo," I cried out in shock. "Clara, does this mean that Ellie is alive? That she didn't mysteriously vanish all those years ago?"

"I'm unsure, Ms. Lundgren. All I know is that the timeframe of Mr. Mason's phone call lines up with when the three of you were ejected from the dance and with the last confirmed sighting of Ellie by your neighbours, the Grays."

"How did you know about the Gray's sighting of Ellie?" I asked, surprised. "I only told my mother, the lady on the missing persons hotline, and my lawyer, Mr. Grieves."

"Whoever Mr. Mason was speaking to must have informed him of the Grays sighting. They must have overheard the Grays phone call to the authorities to report the sighting of the woman fitting Ellie's description and the scream that followed," Clara explained. "I was dusting in the hallway when he received the call and overheard the conversation."

I was stunned. The Grays heard the screams, but they had no way of knowing it was connected to Ellie's disappearance. She hadn't been reported as missing yet. Who was this mystery caller and how did they know it was Ellie who was in trouble?

"Have there been any other strange conversations or mentions of Ellie or the incident at the research center?" I asked, fazed by what I had just learned.

"I did overhear Mr. Mason tell Mrs. Mason that he had important business to attend to and that she shouldn't wait up for him. This was still the same night of the dance and Ellie's disappearance. If I remember correctly, he approached Mrs. Mason minutes after his conversation with the mystery caller."

"Hmmm… interesting," I muttered. "I wonder what Mr. Mason is trying to hide?"

"I'm not entirely sure," Clara hesitated, "Perhaps my mind is playing tricks on me, but I swear that sometimes, late at night, I hear strange noises from within the hallway walls across from the kitchen. It's almost as though something is beckoning me to take notice."

"What sort of noises," Jordan and I called out in unison, extremely anxious to hear Clara's response.

"Like random thumps and bumps. Occasionally, and I know how this sounds, I hear someone singing softly."

"Whoah, what now?" I exclaimed. "Singing? As in a human voice?"

"Exactly," Clara responded. "Like the faint voice of a young woman."

"That's really bizarre and frankly sort of frightening," I replied, scratching my head in bewilderment. "Why on earth would noises be emanating from behind the walls?"

Clara gazed at me, her pupils dilating and her upper lip quivering. "I admit that I hesitated to divulge one fact to the two of you."

"Please, Clara," I pleaded. "What is it?"

"It wasn't just singing I heard coming from behind the walls. I also heard growling. It was like some sort of wild creature was trapped within their confines."

Jordan and I exchanged nervous glances. No, it couldn't be, could it? Was Mr. Mason covering up both Ellie's disappearance and the sudden arrival of the glowing amber eyes?

"Clara, we appreciate our invitation to come here tonight," I said graciously. I can't imagine how risky this was for you. Before Jordan and I head home, is there anything else we should know? Anything at all?"

"Nothing I can think of, Ms. Lundgren. I hope this information helps you and your friends put this whole thing behind you. I cannot imagine how this has impacted your lives."

"Thank you again, Clara," I replied, grateful for these newfound revelations. "You have helped more than you'll ever know."

"Goodnight," Clara said, bowing her head slightly.

"Goodnight," Jordan and I replied, turning away and heading back to our vehicle.

As soon as we were safely in the vehicle and out of range of being heard, I whispered to Jordan. "What do we make of all this?"

"Honestly, Kace, I'm more confused than ever. We'd better meet with Jenny and Chase and see what their take on this is."

"Agreed," I replied. "I know it's late, but I think we should meet up with them tonight. I don't think Jenny will take kindly to waiting after hearing this revelation live."

"Well then," Jordan replied, "let's go." Jordan started the car and drove swiftly into the darkness as my mind raced to make sense of everything we had just heard.

CHAPTER THIRTY

Tuesday, May 24th, 2022: 8:45 PM

When I arrived home, I immediately set out to find my mother. She was cleaning up the dinner dishes in the kitchen, humming an old tune from her childhood. At first, she didn't hear me, but my impromptu throat-clearing signalled my presence. She spun around, hair fanning out behind her.

"Oh. Kacey. I didn't hear you. How long have you been standing there?"

"Actually, I just got home," I replied.

"Great," my mother said. "Can you help me dry and put away the dishes?"

"Sure, Mom," I agreed. This gave me the perfect opportunity to bring up Jenny and my discovery on the security footage from the school. We stood side by side for a short while, working together, her washing and me drying. After a few minutes of skillful dish drying, I turned to my mother, hoping to capture her attention. As she washed the dish in her hand, she turned to me to hand it over for my skillful drying methods and captured my gaze.

"What is it, honey?" my mother asked, her voice full of concern.

"Mom, I need to tell you something important. Something that Jenny and I discovered tonight. You'll probably be upset with me, but I can't keep this to myself."

Instead of the usual eye roll and the "Oh, Kacey, what have you done now?" look, her voice was soft and caring, her eyes intense with worry. "You can confide in me anytime, Kacey. You never have to worry that I'll dismiss you."

"I know, Mom. It's just that what Jenny and I discovered wasn't exactly found legally, so to speak."

I could see my mother's muscles tense and her lips pursed ever so slightly, but she maintained her composure. "That's alright, Kacey. Whatever you and Jenny have gotten mixed up in, we can figure it out together. I'm sure Mr. Grieves would happily help us with counsel and advice."

"Thanks, Mom. That means a lot," I replied with relief. "So here's the thing. Jenny and I were desperate to clear our names and erase any affiliation with this whole necklace in the clutch situation. With Jordan's help, we decided that the best way to do that was to sneak into Mrs. Laughlin's office and get our hands on the security footage from the day they went missing."

My mother stood in place, unusually still and quiet, her gaze meeting mine with such intensity that I shivered. "Kacey…" she hesitated briefly, "I can understand why you and Jenny did what you did, but I wish you had come to me first."

My eyes widened, and I gulped nervously. "Mom, I'm so sorry. I didn't think things through. I was worried you would have tried to talk me out of it. Jenny and I were desperate to erase any connection to the missing necklaces and Ellie's clutch. We needed to prove our innocence."

"I don't blame you for that, Kacey, I really don't. I can't imagine how much stress you and Jenny have been experiencing. It must be exhausting. My next question is whether the two of you found anything in that footage that would prove your and Jenny's innocence."

"Well…" I hesitated, my voice full of reluctance. "That's the thing. The video showed Jenny and me taking the necklaces out of the locker. But it's not real," I cried, angry and confused.

"Wait, what!" my mother exclaimed. "How is that even possible?"

"I have no idea, Mom," I sobbed, tears streaming down my face. "The only thing Jenny and I could think of was some sort of AI manipulation. Technology has come a long way, and it's the only semi-logical explanation we could come up with."

My mother stood in deafening silence for several minutes before turning to me. She gently touched my arm and whispered, "We will figure this out, Kacey, I promise. Give me some time to discuss the matter with Mr. Grieves. In the meantime, I need you and Jenny to promise to keep this to yourselves. Don't whisper a word to anyone, you hear me?"

"Yes, Mom. I hear you."

"Good. Now, why don't you take some time to relax?

You've been through enough tonight."

"Thanks, Mom, for being so understanding." I nimbly went up the stairs and into my room, shutting the door behind me. I exhaled deeply, releasing some of the tension that had built up in my neck and shoulders. That secret out in the open was a relief, and my mother's support was even bigger. My thoughts were soon interrupted by the persistent ringing of my phone.

"Hello," I answered, somewhat dazed from being jarred back into reality.

"So… you gonna fill me in on what your mom said?"

"Geeze, Jenny," I scoffed. "I barely had time to finish talking with her. Impatient much?"

"Really, Kace? Impatient is my middle name, if you haven't realized by now."

"Oh, believe me, I know," I replied sarcastically.

"Well, anyway, what did she say? Did she say she was going to talk to Mr. Grieves?"

"She said she was going to contact him, yes," I replied. "But, she also mentioned that it was crucial that we don't tell anyone about what we found on the security footage."

"Yeah, okay, no big deal. But we should tell Jordan and Chase, right? They've been a part of this too since the beginning."

"Of course. We know we can trust them," I replied. "Besides, I don't think Jordan would be too happy to have gone through all the trouble of disabling the security cameras and not benefit from the fruits of his labour."

"Well, no, duh, Sherlock," Jenny teased. "If it weren't for him, I don't think we'd even have gotten into Mrs.

Laughlin's office undetected, not that it matters now, I suppose."

"Yeah…" I hesitated briefly. "Well, Jenn, I will call Jordan and fill him in on my conversation with my mom. I imagine you'll want to get Chase caught up on the events of the evening."

"I suppose I'd better," she agreed. "I'll catch you tomorrow, Kace. Have a good evening. Try to get some rest, and don't fret too much. Okay?"

"I'll try my best," I promised. I hung up with Jenny and immediately dialled Jordan's number. I knew he'd be curious about the results of our security footage heist. The phone rang for a millisecond before his strong, masculine voice reverberated in my ear.

"Kacey, how'd it go tonight? Did you and Jenny find what you were looking for?"

"Hey, Jordan. We certainly found something, just not what we expected."

"What do you mean?" Jordan asked, puzzled.

I sighed loudly, taking in a deep breath. "Where do I even begin?" I muttered.

"At the beginning," Jordan replied sympathetically.

As I began rehashing the twisted tale of mine and Jenny's discovery, I could visualize Jordan's face contorted with expressions of shock and confusion. His voice rapidly turned into rage.

"That's not possible," Jordan hollered. "I know for certain that neither you nor Jenny is capable of devising such an outlandish plan. Not that I don't think you both are intelligent enough to come up with the idea; it's just I know your hearts are too pure for something so sinister. And don't even get me started on this AI crap. Who would even think of putting together such a fake piece of garbage like that? How twisted must they be to pin something like this on two innocent bystanders?"

Admittedly, I was taken aback by Jordan's sudden outburst. It was rare for him to react with such blind rage. I'm sure that had a lot to do with his desire and ability to ease my anxiety, which was unpredictable at the best of times. While his sudden outburst shook me, it was a stark reminder that his love for me wasn't just a phase or a simple high school crush. It was the real deal.

"Honestly, Jordan, I'm at a loss for words. All I know is that it's undeniable that somebody is trying to cover something up and pin it all on Jenny and me. Why? Who knows. Maybe they think they've got more to lose than we do."

"I really don't give two shits what they think they have to lose," Jordan replied gruffly. "Defamation is a crime. I sure hope whoever did this to the two of you rots in hell."

"My mom will talk to Mr.Grieves to see what he thinks our options are. The bad news is we obtained that security footage illegally, so even if we can prove that it was altered, it's doubtful we'll be able to use it as evidence to prove our innocence."

"Did your mom tell you that?" Jordan asked?

"No," I replied, disappointed in the prospect of losing any leverage we may have had.

"I just realized on my own that you can't commit a crime and use it as a defence against another crime." Jordan was silent for several moments. His silence concerned me, particularly after his previous outburst of anger.

"I'm so sorry you're going through this, Kace. I guess we'll just have to have faith that Mr. Grieves is as good a lawyer as he claims to be."

"I suppose," I replied, shaking my head in defeat. "Anyhow," I began, "I'm going to attempt to get some sleep. I'll talk to you later. Love you," I whispered.

"I love you, too, Kace. Goodnight."

CHAPTER THIRTY-ONE

Monday, May 27th, 2024: 10:00 PM

Jordan and I arrived at Jenny's place and swiftly approached her front door. Before our arrival, I texted to alert Jenny that we were almost there. When we pulled into the driveway, we saw the light on in Jenny's bedroom window and two silhouettes moving around frantically.

"Chase must already be here," I exclaimed, happy for the opportunity to sit down together and discuss all of Clara's revelations. Jordan nodded in agreement. A few moments later, Jenny flung open the door.

"Holy shit, Kace. Chase and I heard the whole thing. What the hell is happening?"

"I don't know what to say, Jenn," I sighed, exasperated. "I'm still awestruck. What on earth could be lurking behind the walls of the Mason mansion? Doesn't it seem just a little ironic that Clara started hearing odd noises shortly after the night of the dance? And don't even get me started on how Ellie mysteriously vanished that night, and those weird amber eyes made their grand debut. I don't know, guys, but I'm beginning to think that Mr. Mason knows much more than he's letting on. I think he knows exactly what happened at the scientific research centre and the whereabouts of Ellie."

"The puzzle pieces are seemingly coming together, aren't they?" Jenny asked, looking at Jordan, Chase, and me questioningly.

"I suppose they are," I replied, not entirely convinced by my own words. "I have to be honest, though, even though some things make more sense, I'm always left with more questions. Every time we gain some tidbit of information, another mystery arises."

"Tell me about it," Jenny scoffed. "So what do you all want to do? Should we have another debrief? Compare notes and review the next steps and strategies."

"Probably be a good idea," Chase chimed in. "I don't know about you guys, but I feel overwhelmed by all the revelations lately."

"You're not the only one, Chase," I sighed with exhaustion. "Things just keep getting crazier."

"So, when do you guys want to debrief?" Jenny asked.

"What about now?" I replied. "We're all here anyhow."

"I guess this is as good a time as any," Jordan agreed.

We all made our way up the stairs to Jenny's room, taking care not to make a commotion to disturb her parents' slumber. Jenny opened the door to her room slowly, making a great effort to hush the squeaking noise her door was so famously known for. She swiftly ushered us inside, shutting the door behind us. I sat in my usual spot, the lazy chair opposite Jenny's bed, while Chase and Jordan made themselves comfortable on the window bench. Jenny flopped onto her bed, flat on her stomach and feet in the air behind her.

"Well," I began. "We now know Mr. Mason was working the night of the power outage along with your dad," I motioned to Jenny. "We also know that the DNA sample of the Dire Wolf disappeared during this time frame and left strange claw marks in its place."

"Yeah, and we also know that nobody reported anything to the authorities regarding the strange occurrence at the research center," Jenny chimed in, anxious to get her two cents in.

"Exactly," I agreed. "Even stranger is that Ellie goes missing that very night, and suddenly, there are multiple reports of those eerie amber-coloured eyes. My neighbours saw a young woman fitting Ellie's description in the forested area across town, the same area where her clutch was later found with our necklaces inside. Stranger yet, Mr. Mason doesn't report Ellie missing until the next morning. Why?"

"Then, of course, there's all of the information Clara just revealed," I replied. "Who was Mr. Mason talking to that night? Why was he so concerned about Ellie? Did he already know that something would happen before anyone else did?"

"Yeah, that seems suspicious," Jenny agreed. It's as if he knew something would happen to Ellie if she didn't get to safety. But, if he did have an inclination that something bad could happen, why did he not report her missing right away?"

"And we're back to that question again," I sighed. "That

seems to be the key to solving this puzzle. What does Mr. Mason know? Why was he worried about Ellie? Oh, and let's not forget that Clara reported the sudden manifestation of the strange noises within the mansion walls. What on earth could be making those noises?"

Jordan, quiet from the moment we started our debrief, suddenly became animated. "I say we make it our mission to find out exactly what is lurking behind those walls."

"Hell yeah," Jenny squealed, delighted to be in on the action again instead of sitting on the sidelines. "And I say we go and do it tonight. It's late, and everyone's likely asleep."

"Exactly how do you propose we do that?" I questioned, looking Jordan straight into his gorgeous eyes.

"I am the tech wizard," Jordan declared, full of confidence. I hacked the school security cameras a few years back. I can hack the Mason's security system, too. Just give me an hour or so to work on it."

"Do you even know what type of security system they have?" I asked.

"As a matter of fact, I do," he quipped. "I'm a pretty observant guy, you know," he winked.

"Well then, Mr. Tech Wizard, get to it," I laughed.

"Jenny," Jordan called out, "can I use your laptop?"

"Have at it, Tech Boy," Jenny teased.

Jordan swiftly planted himself at Jenny's desk, swivelling the computer chair as if it were a merry-go-round, the clickety-clack of his fingers on the keyboard reminiscent of an old typewriter. I always admired Jordan most when he was in super nerd mode. Not that I meant that in a spiteful way, no, but instead, he was at his most sexy when he was showing off his tech skills. I watched in amazement as his fingers glided effortlessly over the keyboard and clicked on the mouse simultaneously. I honestly didn't know what I'd ever do without him. My thoughts were soon interrupted by the calling of my name.

"Kacey! Hey, Kacey?"

"Huh? What was that you said?" I called out, startled.

"I've got it all sorted out," Jordan replied. "The Masons use an Albright monitoring system with alarm and video surveillance. All I've got to do is hack into the Albright servers, and I'm in."

"Oh, is that all?" I teased playfully. Jordan, utterly oblivious to my witty remarks, continued.

"I don't understand why someone with the financial prowess of Mr. Mason would employ such a subpar company to supply his home's security needs. It's not that I'm bagging on Albright or anything like that; they're just fine for basic everyday needs. It's just their system is so basic and easy to hack into. You'd think someone with that much community status would want to protect his interests more than the average person."

I rolled my eyes and laughed at Jordan. "Are you done yet?" I asked sarcastically.

"Yeah, sorry," Jordan apologized. "Guess I went off on a bit of a tangent there."

"And that's why I love you," I replied, giving Jordan a quick peck on the cheek.

"Get a room," Jenny hollered from across the room.

Jordan and I laughed as we turned toward Jenny

and Chase and flipped her the bird in unison. Jenny returned our greeting with jubilation and continued her conversation with Chase. Jordan swiftly turned back to the computer, flipping between one page and the next. He continuously wrote down multiple strings of random numbers on a strawberry-scented paper on Jenny's desk. The scent reminded me of my favourite childhood toy, a strawberry shortcake figurine my mother passed down when I was young. "What are all these numbers for?" I asked, genuinely curious.

"These are what we call literals," Jordan explained. "Basically, it's the sequencing of numbers that creates a code that people in IT need to be able to read and interpret. They essentially communicate and store vital information about a company."

"I see," I replied, pretending to understand more than I was letting on. "So, will these codes tell you how to hack into the Mason's security system?"

"Essentially, yes," Jordan replied. He continued typing, his fingers flying over the keys effortlessly. "I just need to change this one thing and… voila! I'm in," he exclaimed excitedly.

Jenny sprinted over, bouncing around like a baby bunny. "Jordan, you're a genius," she cried out. She wrapped her arms around his neck, squeezing him with the most aggressive bear hug I'd ever seen. "Kacey, you're so lucky to have this super nerd stud in your life."

Chase glanced over, his eyebrows arched in surprise. "And what am I? Swiss cheese," he pouted, chastising Jenny.

"Oh, Chase," Jenny teased. "You know you're the only man for me." Chase smiled, seemingly satisfied with Jenny's declaration of love.

"So we're ready to break into the Mason's house?" I asked.

"Yeah," Jordan replied. "We can hop in the car and go right now."

"Don't we need some supplies or something? A flashlight, perhaps?" I asked.

"It would probably be a good idea," Jordan agreed. "Jenny? You got any flashlights?"

"Yeah, I do. I just need to grab them from the garage. Anything else we should grab while I'm in there?"

"Maybe a multi-tool or something, just in case we need to pry open a lock or something," Jordan replied.

"Alright. I'll check for that and grab it along with the flashlights," Jenny replied, scurrying into the garage at lightning speed.

Jordan turned to me, a look of concern on his face. "You ready to solve this mystery?"

"As ready as I'll ever be," I sighed, my stomach churning. Jordan grabbed my hand, giving it a gentle squeeze. This was going to be quite the night.

CHAPTER THIRTY-TWO

Wednesday, May 25th, 2022: 7:05 AM

The night passed quickly, much to my amazement. I was certain that after all of the stress from the previous evening, my mind would be too wound up to get any decent sleep. Yet when I opened my eyes, a stream of sunlight greeted me with its bright and warm embrace. The last time I could recall the time on my alarm clock, the glowing green numbers read '1:18 AM', so I must have passed out and slept right through the night. I felt so warm and peaceful under the comfort of my blanket that I made every excuse to stay huddled up underneath the covers for just a few moments longer. After hitting snooze for the fifth time, I finally coaxed myself out of bed, lumbering clumsily into the bathroom. I turned the faucet on and began my morning routine, first washing my face, followed by the minty fresh burst of my toothpaste. A few moments later, I heard a furious knock on the bathroom door. It was my mother.

"Kacey! Are you in there?" she called out.

"Yeah, Mom. Give me a second. I just want to finish getting dressed." I could hear my mother pacing as she waited outside. My mother typically only paced when there was something significant she needed to tell me. I hurriedly threw on my comfortable jeans and light hoodie and hastily exited the bathroom.

"Thank goodness, Kacey. I was about to hyperventilate out here," my mother huffed. "What took you so long?"

"Geeze, Mom. It was only like ten minutes."

"Okay, well, never mind that," my mother continued. "Mr. Grieves called. He wants to meet with the two of us right away."

"But I've got school," I sighed.

"School can wait, Kacey," my mother grumbled loudly under her breath. "This is important. Don't you want to hear what Mr. Grieves has to say about your and Jenny's situation?"

"Of course I do," I replied, exasperated. "But I'd prefer that Jenny, Jordan, and Chase could be there too. They are all part of this."

"Of course they are, dear," my mother replied sympathetically, patting me on the shoulder. "But in this particular instance, only you and Jenny were implicated in the video footage. And besides, it was just the two of you who broke into Mrs. Laughlin's office to obtain the footage in the first place, correct?"

"Technically, yes," I replied. "But Jordan hacked into the school security cameras to ensure we were clear from being caught."

"Oh, I see," my mother replied, somewhat surprised. "Well, there's no use in dragging him into this particular situation, especially since you and Jenny have admitted to having the security footage you obtained from Mrs. Laughlin. The two of you will only defend your position on how and why you obtained that footage. Jordan does not appear in the supposed altered footage and, therefore, would have no motive or reason to have been involved in breaking into the school to retrieve it. I don't see why we should bring his name into this mess."

"I suppose you're right," I admitted. I didn't want to drag Jordan's name through the mud. It wasn't as though he was the one who had to prove that the footage of Jenny and me stealing our necklaces was a farce. It wasn't Jordan, who was implicated in Ellie's disappearance due to the necklaces being found in her clutch. He was only involved because he was trying to help protect me, his girlfriend.

"Well then," my mother continued, "why don't you call Jenny or text to see if she wants to go with us to see Mr. Grieves? I imagine she'd have some insight into this whole scenario, too, and I'm sure Mr. Grieves would love to hear her side of the story."

"Yeah, okay," I agreed. I quickly retrieved my phone from my pocket and dialled Jenny's number. I put the phone on speaker and set it on my bedside table. It rang a few times as I sat anxiously, twisting my hands, willing Jenny to pick up.

"Kacey?" Jenny answered, yawning obnoxiously. "What on earth?"

I interrupted before she could complete her question. "Jenny, my mom heard from Mr. Grieves about our situation last night. He wants my mom and me to come in this morning for a meeting."

"Wow, that was fast," Jenny replied. "Do you know what exactly he wants to discuss?"

"No, my mom didn't say anything. I'm not sure she even knows what he will say."

"So, what about school then?" Jenny asked.

"Well, I'm not going. My mom said this was more important. She asked me if you wanted to participate in the discussion. She felt that since both of us are implicated by the discovery of the necklaces in Ellie's clutch and since we both are falsely shown on the video stealing the necklaces, you might have some insight into what happened or have questions about our next move."

"Absolutely, I want to come," Jenny responded authoritatively. "I'd better talk to my parents first and tell them I won't attend school today."

"Yeah, for sure," I replied. "Just call me back as soon as you talk to them. My mom wants to get going as soon as possible."

"Yeah, okay," Jenny answered. She hung up, and I went downstairs to join my mother in the kitchen. My mother looked up from her cup of coffee and met my eyes.

"So, will Jenny be joining us?" she asked.

"Yes, she just has to ask her parents first. She said she'd call me back right away."

"Well, that's good then," my mother replied. "In the meantime, why don't you grab a quick bite to eat. Can't start the day on an empty stomach now, can we?"

"I'll try," I promised. "I'm feeling a bit nervous, though, and my stomach is twisted up in knots."

"That's understandable, honey. Just try. Even a piece of

toast or something small."

I made my way toward the fridge and grabbed a ripe banana from the bowl on the counter beside it. As I slowly peeled back the layers of skin, my mind danced with images of Jenny, Ellie, and me at the Spring Fling Dance. The images were so vivid that it was almost like I relived that day. I could hear the music, feel the pounding of the bass, heck, I could even smell the distinct odour of sweat as bodies swayed in unison to the beat. Suddenly, without any warning, I saw Ellie's clutch. Only it wasn't Ellie who was carrying it, it was Autumn. What the hell… I screamed silently in my head. Why would Autumn be carrying Ellie's clutch? The scene continued playing in my head. Autumn unzipped the clutch and held it out to Ellie. The two of them huddled closely in a dark corner of the room, seemingly unaware that a pair of eyes inconspicuously watched their every move. The following image that flashed before me made me gasp out loud.

"What is it, honey?" my mother called out, concerned by my sudden outburst.

"I…I…I think I know how our necklaces got into Ellie's clutch," I stammered.

"What?" my mother gasped. "Why wouldn't you say something sooner? Why would you and Jenny put yourselves in such a precarious situation? Why go through all this trouble if you already had all the answers?"

"That's the thing, Mom," I replied defensively. "I just had a flashback from the night of the dance, and out of nowhere, I witnessed Autumn and Ellie planting the necklaces in the clutch."

"So you don't have any solid evidence?" my mother asked

hesitantly.

"No," I replied, disappointed in that sudden revelation. "I suppose that's not enough to prove our innocence, right?"

"That's a question best left for Mr. Grieves," my mother replied, confident and convincing. "By the way, what on earth is taking Jenny so long to call back?"

Right on cue, my phone rang, and Jenny's name popped up on my screen. I pushed accept and greeted Jenny with an overzealous "Hello!"

"Hey, Buttercup," Jenny greeted. "My parents agreed that speaking with Mr. Grieves might be a good idea. So, I'm coming with you, okay?"

"Uh, yeah, okay," I replied hastily. "Jenny, I've got something huge to tell you."

"Do tell," Jenny replied.

"I'll tell you all about it on the way to Mr. Grieves' office, okay?"

"Uhm, sure," Jenny replied worriedly. "Should I be nervous?"

"I'm not sure yet," I replied honestly. "Time will tell. I'll see you in a few minutes, OK?"

"Okay, see you soon," Jenny replied.

I hung up the phone and motioned to my mother, who swiftly approached the front door, pulling on her light spring jacket and flinging her purse over her shoulder. As we made our way to the car, I couldn't help but shudder. What on earth would come of this new piece of the puzzle? Only time will tell.

CHAPTER THIRTY-THREE

Monday, May 27th, 2024, 11:34 PM

The four of us arrived at the Mason home; a dark, ominous figure looming in the shadows of the night. It took Jordan next to no time to get there because traffic was virtually non-existent at that time of night. Although I was sitting up front with Jordan, I could hear the hurried breaths of Jenny and Chase in the car's back seat, their anticipation growing with each passing moment. I, too, noticed my heart racing and my breaths becoming more laboured. Damn, anxiety again! Well, this time, I wouldn't let it get the best of me. The four of us had made great strides in solving this mystery, and it was beginning to feel like this might be the turning point.

"Alright, guys," Jordan said, "I'm going to park here just out of sight of the cameras. That way, there'll be no chance of someone hearing or witnessing us exiting the vehicle. Before we get out and start this investigation, let me just hack into the security cameras and put them offline."

Everyone quietly nodded their heads and waited for further instructions. I gazed lovingly at Jordan. How lucky was I to have a man who cared so much about me that he'd move mountains to ensure I felt safe and protected? But then, a sudden realization hit me. Jordan would do anything for me, even if it resulted in him implicating himself. I didn't want that for Jordan. This wasn't his mess; it was mine and Jenny's.

"Jordan," I whispered, "are you sure you want to do this? I mean, this is all about Jenny and me. I'd hate to see you and Chase get caught up in our mess."

"Kacey, come on now. We've been together for how long? Of course, I'm sure about helping you. Besides, I've helped you several times with this situation, at least twice. I'm not going to suddenly bail on you now."

I grinned sheepishly at Jordan. I could feel the corners of my mouth tightening in embarrassment.

"I know," I replied, ashamed to have insinuated that he would bail on me. "I just don't want to see you go down for something that has nothing to do with you."

"Why don't you let me worry about that?" Jordan replied.

I smiled again, only this time it wasn't in embarrassment but appreciation. "Thanks, Jordan. I honestly don't know what I'd ever do without you."

Jordan smiled back, his eyes meeting mine in an intense gaze. "No need to thank me, Kace. That's what good boyfriends are supposed to do. What do you say the four of us get this show on the road?"

I nodded in agreement, and Jordan grabbed his laptop from his backpack and went to work typing in all sorts of codes and number sequences that I was too inexperienced to understand. The clackety-clack of his fingers on the keyboard almost put me into a trance. It wasn't until I felt something poking me in the shoulder that I snapped out of it.

"Hey, loser," I heard whispering from behind. "We're ready to go in now."

I nearly jumped out of my skin, startled out of my trance like a deer caught in the headlights. I turned around and saw Jenny staring at me questioningly.

"Did you hear me?" Jenny joked, laughing hysterically.

"Yeah, sorry," I apologized. "I was uhm... daydreaming."

"I can only imagine what," Jenny winked. "Anyhow, let's get this show on the road. I'm more than ready to put this all behind us."

The four of us exited the vehicle quietly, like thieves in the night. Jordan and Chase led the way, holding the flashlights and scanning the yard in a zigzag pattern, avoiding any obstacles that could create unnecessary noise or alert us to our presence. We made our way around to the side of the house and to the spot where Jordan and I had met with Clara. Jordan had observed that the lock on the side door that Clara had retreated to, after our meeting, was old and worn. He suspected we could easily jiggle it open and make our way in. For such a well-to-do family, I thought it strange that they had never bothered to replace it with a more secure deadbolt. We made our way up the stairs, and Jordan reached his hand out to jiggle the knob. It rattled slightly, but there was no sign of it being left open.

"You got that multi-tool?" he asked, facing Chase. Chase reached into his pocket and presented Jordan with the shiny metal tool.

"Right here, man," Chase replied.

Jordan grasped it tightly, taking care not to drop it through the cracks of the wooden staircase. He carefully inserted the knife from the multi-tool into the key lock, jiggling left and right. Jordan, stealthy as a leopard stalking its prey, was so quiet and agile that if I hadn't witnessed him picking the lock, I would have never known someone was attempting to break in. The lock slightly popped within moments, and Jordan cautiously propped the door open. He motioned us to follow him as he tiptoed timidly through the doorway. Jenny, Chase and I, quiet as mice, followed in close pursuit, taking care not to bump into each other or anything else that could create noise. We passed the kitchen before turning left down a long hallway.

"This way," Jordan whispered as he motioned for us to follow. "I think this might be where Clara was when she heard the singing and growling from within the walls."

"This is definitely it," I replied. "I specifically remember Clara saying she heard the noises in the hallway across from the kitchen."

"So, what do we do now?" Jenny asked. "Just stand around waiting for random weird noises?"

"Of course not," I scoffed. "We listen, of course, but I'd suggest we break off into pairs and search the hall and adjoining rooms for signs of a hidden passage or something."

"Like real detectives?" Jenny asked wryly.

"Yes, I suppose," I replied. "Jordan, you come with me. Jenny and Chase, you explore the room down the hall. We'll text each other if we stumble across anything."

"I don't know, Kace," Jenny giggled. Can you and Jordan

be trusted to be alone in a dark room?"

"For fuck sake, Jenny," I shot back. "This is serious. Get your head out of the gutter for once."

"Sorry, Miss Cranky Pants," Jenny huffed. "Just trying to lighten the mood a bit."

"Yeah, I know," I replied. "I'm sorry. I'm just a little on edge."

"I appreciate the apology," Jenny replied. "So what do you say we get to it, then. I, for one, am looking forward to some alone time with Chase." Jenny winked in Chase's direction, and he grinned sheepishly.

"Yeah, absolutely," I agreed. "Jordan and I will start checking out this room here. You two go explore the room next door, okay?"

We parted ways, and Jordan and I hurriedly entered the room before us. It was quite a large room filled with trophies, photographs and other sporting memorabilia. One photo stood out in particular, Ellie in a cheerleading uniform, standing on top of a skillfully formed pyramid. Her golden hair glistened in the sunlight, and her teeth sparkled like diamonds, typical Ellie, perfection in a pretty package. Oblivious to the photograph and my fascination with it, Jordan opened drawers, moved pictures off the wall, pulled books from shelves, and pushed random objects around. I looked at him, somewhat bewildered.

"What are you doing?" I asked.

"Well, we are supposed to be looking for some sort of secret entrance into the voids behind the walls, are we not?"

"Yeah," I replied, puzzled. "But why are you opening drawers and pulling books off the shelves?"

"Kacey! Seriously? Have you not watched any of those detective movies on TV? That's the first thing you do. You know, open drawers to look for hidden buttons, pull books off shelves in case they open some mystery door."

"That's not real," I scoffed, chastising Jordan.

"Oh really," Jordan teased. "And how would you know that? Have you ever participated in a secret hidden passage search before?"

"Well, no," I replied, somewhat embarrassed.

"Well then, don't knock it until you try it."

I followed Jordan's lead and began to grab, push and pull at nearly every object in the room. Suddenly, without warning, a loud thump echoed from within the walls. I jumped, startled by the sudden noise and fell into the crook of a large armchair.

"Kacey, are you okay?" Jordan whispered.

"My arm's a little sore, but otherwise, I'm okay," I replied. "Did you hear that noise?"

"Yeah," Jordan replied. "What the hell was that?"

"It came from over here," I replied, pointing to the wall behind the armchair. "It was so loud that I felt the wall vibrate from underneath my hand."

"That must be the same thumping noise Clara mentioned hearing," Jordan pondered.

"Did you notice anything unusual about the wall in that area, Kace?"

"Not really," I replied as I lifted myself from the chair and continued to explore the wall with my hands. No sooner had the words escaped my mouth than I suddenly felt a strange indent on the edge of a large picture frame.

"Jordan," I called softly. "Over here." Jordan stumbled over, making every attempt to avoid colliding with something and creating unnecessary noise. I motioned, pointing at the wall and the large picture frame.

"What are you pointing at?" he asked, now curious about what I had found.

"Give me your hand," I demanded. Jordan held his hand out to me, and I embraced it gently, pulling it to the edge of the wall and the picture frame. "See right here; there's some sort of an indent sticking out from beneath the frame. I know that walls have dips and dents sometimes, but this one seems quite prominent."

Jordan glided his hand over and around the edge of the picture frame and the wall, carefully examining the area. He looked up and down the picture frame, checking every inch of the wall surrounding it. "You're right, Kace; there's something here. You wanna help me take this picture down? I suspect there's something hidden underneath it."

I approached the picture frame, grasping one bottom corner while Jordan clutched the other side tightly. We lifted in unison, gently easing the picture up and off its hook before placing it down gently onto the floor. Jordan inspected the wall more closely, using his hands as a guide to note any further abnormalities. He began gently pushing various parts of the wall, but he stopped abruptly.

"What is it?" I asked.

"Kace, there's something behind this spot. The wall has some give and doesn't feel like a solid piece of drywall. I bet there's something hidden back here."

"Should we text Jenny and Chase?" I asked.

"Not yet," Jordan responded. "I want to ensure that there's

something worthy of investigation before interrupting their search."

"Makes sense," I replied. "So, what's our next move then?"

"I still have the multi-tool. I will use the knife to cut open a portion of the wall in that area. Then we can check out what's behind it. If it's anything interesting, we'll text Jenny and Chase."

"Alright, Jordan. I'll let you get to it then," I replied. I watched Jordan insert the knife into the wall and feverishly start cutting away strips of drywall. It wasn't an easy task. The knife on the multi-tool wasn't precisely the most excellent cutting tool, and what should have been an effortless task was quite arduous. Not to mention, Jordan was making every effort to keep the noise level down, so he sawed away slowly and steadily.

"I think I see something," Jordan whispered, squinting into the black void he had just cut into the wall. "Do you have a flashlight, Kace?"

I reached into the left pocket of my jacket and pulled out a compact flashlight. I handed it to Jordan, who wasted no time grabbing it and inserting its light into the crevice he had just cut. He reached his hand into the crevice slowly, and before I knew it, he was yanking out what appeared to be some sort of quick-start remote, similar to the ones used in automobiles.

"What is that?" I asked curiously.

"A remote of some sort," Jordan replied. "I'm not sure for what, but I'll bet it has nothing to do with the vehicles or the garage door." Jordan stared, puzzled. I could see his brows furrow deeply as his mind raced to find an answer to this newfound discovery. Then, as though a lightbulb lit up in his head, he suddenly straightened his body and raised his eyes to meet mine. "I think I might have an idea as to what this remote could be."

"Really?" I responded, meeting Jordan's eyes questioningly. "What is it then?"

"My guess is it's a remote to open some sort of hidden chamber door," he responded confidently. "Why else would a remote like this be hidden with so much effort?"

"That could be it," I agreed. "Especially considering what Clara mentioned about the sounds within the walls. There's some sort of hidden room or something back here. We even heard some of the noises ourselves."

"Yeah, true," Jordan agreed. "There's definitely something or someone hidden back there."

"Maybe we should text Jenny and Chase now; let them know what we found," I suggested.

"That sounds like a good plan," Jordan agreed. Give them a text now, and we'll set off together in search of the mystery object that this remote belongs to."

I yanked my phone from the front pocket of my pants and hastily dialled Jenny's number. A call would be quicker than texting a bunch of words. With barely a ring, Jenny was ready with sticky fingers, waiting for my call.

"Did you guys find something?" she whispered excitedly.

"Yeah, we did, actually," I responded hesitantly. "We just don't know what it is yet."

"What do you mean?" Jenny asked, sounding confused.

"Why don't you and Chase join us in the room? We'll just show you," I suggested.

"Yeah, sure, okay," Jenny agreed as she hung up the

phone.

Within minutes, Jenny and Chase arrived in the room, their eyes scanning mine and Jordan's eyes for clues. I waved them over, excited to show them what Jordan and I had discovered.

"So, what did you two find?" Jenny asked impatiently. "Inquiring minds want to know."

Jordan held up the remote, clasping the attached keychain in a vice-like grip. Both Jenny and Chase squinted, trying to get a better look at the object in the darkened room.

"What is that?" Jenny asked, confused.

"Some sort of remote starter," Jordan replied. "It was hidden in the wall behind this large picture frame." He pointed at the picture frame, still leaning up against the wall.

"Kacey was feeling around the wall and noticed an anomaly from behind the frame. We decided to pull the frame off the wall and investigate the anomaly further."

"And…?" Jenny replied, hanging on in anticipation of Jordan's every word.

"And we cut open the wall," Jordan continued. "That's where we found this remote."

Jenny's eyes widened with excitement as she glanced over at Chase, who appeared equally enthralled by this discovery.

"So what's the plan, then?" Jenny asked, staring directly at Jordan.

"We work together to try and find out what this remote opens," Jordan replied. "My first instinct is that it opens a secret passageway or chamber. Considering the reports that Clara has given us, it is quite obvious that something is lurking behind the walls. Just before we discovered this mystery remote, Kacey and I heard loud thumps coming from within their confines."

"Are you serious?" Jenny gasped. "What the hell are we waiting for, then? Let's get this show on the road. I'm ready to finally put this shit behind us."

The four of us moved out of the room and back into the hallway. Jenny and Chase examined one side while Jordan and I focused on the other. Jordan randomly pressed the remote button, hoping it would give us a hint or clue, a noise, anything to reveal its purpose. As we neared the end of the narrow hallway, Jordan suddenly stopped dead in his tracks.

"Do you guys hear that?" he asked, whispering.

We all craned our necks. desperately trying to hear whatever it was that Jordan was hearing. At first, I heard nothing. Then, after a few seconds, I heard the faint sound of a motor.

"I hear it," I whispered. "It's sort of a low hum, like the sound a refrigerator would make."

"Quiet," Jenny commanded in a hushed tone. "I'm trying to hear it, too." She stuck her head out and cocked it to one side, cupping her ear. Within seconds, Jenny's face contorted into a state of confusion. "I hear it," she exclaimed. "I just don't know what it could be."

Jordan continued down the short distance to the end of the hall, pressing the button on the remote and placing his ear flush to the wall. His body, relaxed and poised, suddenly went rigid. His eyes met mine as he scanned the hallway, looking for Jenny and Chase.

"Whatever this remote opens, it's right behind here,"

Jordan exclaimed. "I can hear it and feel the vibrations against my ear."

"So, what's our next move?" I asked.

"We cut it open, just like in the other room," Jordan replied. "Did anyone think of bringing a box cutter? I don't think the multi-tool will suffice this time."

"But how do we hide our tracks?" I asked. "I'm pretty sure we don't want to leave behind evidence of our snooping."

"Good point, Kace," Jordan agreed. "There must be some way to open the wall without destroying the drywall. If something is back there, I'm sure the Masons aren't repairing holes daily. Hand me a flashlight, will you?"

I passed Jordan the flashlight, and he grasped it tightly, shining the silvery beam toward the wall. His eyes scanned the wall, and he used his hands to feel around, pressing and prodding with precision.

"Right here," he exclaimed. "There's a small niche in the drywall." Jordan continued to maneuver his hand around the niche. Just then, a loud click echoed through the hall. "It's a handle of some sort," he said. He pulled the handle and then pushed the wall inward. There was a creaking noise as the wall suddenly inched forward.

"Whoa…" Jenny exclaimed excitedly. "What do you think it is?"

"I don't know," Jordan replied, "but we're certainly going to find out."

Jordan shined the flashlight into the large crevice. It was large enough for him to slide through and fit in behind the wall.

"I see something," Jordan whispered, peering into the

darkness. He motioned for Jenny, Chase, and me to follow him into the darkness of the crevice.

We entered the void behind the wall and followed the flashlight beam. Behind the wall was a corridor, much like the hallway we had just exited. Just a few feet away, I could see the shimmer of something metallic sparkling in the thin beam of the flashlight.

"What is that?" I asked, meeting Jordan's eyes.

"It's what we've been looking for," Jordan replied. He pressed the button on the remote, and suddenly, the metallic object started to make that same humming noise we had heard earlier. Then, without warning, it lit up and shifted to the right, much like a pocket door.

"I guess that's our secret passage?" I remarked, both shocked and amazed.

"It sure is," Jordan replied, smiling with satisfaction. "It sure is."

CHAPTER THIRTY-FOUR

Wednesday, May 25th, 2022: 7:55 AM

My mother pulled up to Jenny's house and parked the car, giving two swift and polite honks to signal our arrival. I saw Jenny's face peer out the front living room window, and she gave me a witty smile and waved. Within minutes, she rushed out the front door, slinging her backpack over her shoulder and munching on a strawberry toaster pastry. She flung open the car door without hesitation, tossing her backpack recklessly into the back seat.

"Good morning, Mrs. Lundgren," Jenny greeted, mumbling, her mouth full of pastry.

"Good morning, Jenny," my mother replied. "Are the two of you ready to fill Mr. Grieves in on your discovery?"

"What discovery are we talking about exactly?" Jenny asked. "I know about the altered security footage stuff, but Kacey told me there was something more she needed to tell me."

"Oh…" my mother hesitated. "Kacey hasn't told you yet?"

"Told me what?" Jenny replied, staring me directly in the eyes.

"Well, that's what I was going to tell you on the way to see Mr. Grieves," I replied defensively. "Just before you called me back to let me know that you were coming with us to see Mr. Grieves, I had a flashback from the night of the dance."

"Oh really?" Jenny replied, her eyes lighting up with curiosity. "So what exactly did this flashback entail?"

"Well," I began, "it's related to how our necklaces ended up in Ellie's clutch."

"Really!" Jenny exclaimed, her eyes widening as her interest piqued. "Well, don't leave me hanging. Fill me in on this mysterious flashback of yours."

"I was just eating a banana when suddenly it was as if I had been transported back in time. It all felt so real, as if I were reliving the night of the dance all over again. I could feel the bass, hear the music, and even smell the familiar smells from that night. I was enjoying the dance when my eyes suddenly averted to the room's dark corner. I could see both Autumn and Ellie huddling closely together. It was obvious that they were up to something. It wasn't long before I witnessed the most shocking thing, the one thing that could clear our names of this whole mess."

"Well, what was it?" Jenny cried out. "Don't keep me in suspense."

"I saw Autumn carrying Ellie's clutch," I exclaimed.

"Yeah, so what?" Jenny replied. "We know that Ellie had the clutch at the dance. Maybe she asked Autumn to hold it for her or something."

"Well, that's the thing," I replied. "It's not just that she was carrying the clutch. I witnessed her and Ellie planting our missing necklaces into the clutch."

Jenny's jaw dropped, her eyes meeting mine with a look that questioned my sanity. I didn't blame her, really. It was such a random flashback that there was no rhyme or reason behind why I suddenly had these images dancing around. It felt like my subconscious had made every attempt to make me forget what I had seen.

"What!" Jenny yelled. "What did you just say?"

"I saw…"

"I…I… I know what you saw," Jenny stammered, interrupting me. "Why now? Why would this memory just suddenly reveal itself now?"

"I don't know," I replied, shaking my head. "I just don't know."

"So, how do we prove that what you saw actually happened?" Jenny asked.

"Well, that's what we're going to talk to Mr. Grieves about," my mother interjected. "I'm sure there must be security footage from the night of the dance, too. You secured that falsified footage of the two of you removing the necklaces from your gym locker, right? So, it would stand to reason that there would be footage showing what you remember witnessing Kacey."

"That would make sense," I agreed. "Hopefully, that footage isn't doctored as well."

"We'll worry about that once we get the footage," my mother replied. "In the meantime, let's focus on updating

Mr. Grieves on the recent events regarding this case."

We drove the rest of the way in silence, Jenny and I exchanging worried glances occasionally. Despite having vivid memories of what I had witnessed the night of the dance, I couldn't help but worry that this security footage may have also been altered. It was clear that somebody had gone to great lengths to implicate Jenny and me in Ellie's disappearance by falsifying the locker room footage. Why wouldn't they have gone to equal lengths to cover this up, too? My thoughts were interrupted by the sound of the car door slamming.

"We're here," Jenny said, shaking my shoulder gently to get my attention.

I snapped back to reality, realizing it was time to control my fears and emotions. It was time to see what, if anything, Mr. Grieves could do to get Jenny and me out of this mess.

Jenny and I followed my mother's lead up the front steps and through the rotating door leading into the foyer of Mr. Grieves' office. The front desk loomed in front, almost threateningly, its curved ridges and dark corners beckoning to me like a tree branch swaying in the wind. My stomach churned nervously, and I couldn't help but fear the worst. I was almost sure that Mr. Grieves would bombard us with evil tidings. Only time will tell.

"Okay, girls, sit down while I go check in with the receptionist," my mother said, motioning to the row of chairs lined up flat against the wall.

My mother marched to the front desk, feigning her best confident walk. She waited patiently for the receptionist to finish her phone conversation before interjecting herself into a conversation.

"Good morning," my mother greeted the receptionist. "Mr. Grieves should be expecting us. My name is Mrs. Lundgren, and this is my daughter Kacey and her friend Jenny Forester."

"Oh yes, Mrs. Lundgren," the receptionist replied, staring at her appointment book. "Right this way, please." She stood up from her chair, walked around the desk, and across the room. She turned back to look at us, motioning with her hand to follow her. We followed her down the narrow hallway and entered the first room on the right. Sitting at his desk with a pile of papers stacked high, Mr. Grieves glanced up at us, his wire-rimmed glasses on the edge of his nose.

"Good morning, everyone," he said, organizing the stack of papers into a neat pile.

"Please excuse the mess. I've been pulling some late nights at the office and haven't had much time to housekeep. I understand that Kacey and Jenny have some information for me regarding Ellie's clutch and your missing necklaces."

"Yes, we do, Mr. Grieves, sir," I replied.

"No need to call me sir," Mr. Grieves replied. "Mr. Grieves will suffice."

"So, Mr. Grieves," I began, "Jenny and I discovered some altered security footage from the school gym locker room. It showed that we were the ones who stole our necklaces from our lockers. But the thing is, we didn't do that. We believe that someone was trying to frame us, you know, get us in trouble."

"And what would the motive be for someone to do such a thing?" Mr. Grieves asked.

"I'm not sure," I replied. "But I don't think the footage

was altered until after Ellie went missing. I suspect whoever stole the necklaces was trying to avoid being blamed for Ellie's disappearance and backtracked after the fact."

"I see," Mr. Grieves replied. "So are you implying that whoever stole the necklaces and altered the security footage might be responsible for Ellie's disappearance?"

"To be honest, Mr. Grieves, I don't think the whole necklace thing is even related to Ellie's disappearance. It's not exactly news that neither Jenny nor I got along with Ellie. I suspect that Ellie was trying to set us up by making it seem like we planted our necklaces in her clutch to get us into some sort of trouble. It would make sense."

"I see," Mr. Grieves responded. "Do you have anybody who could verify that this feud the three of you seemingly had with one another extended above and beyond the incident at the dance?"

"Mrs. Laughlin could confirm," Jenny chimed in. "She's the one who kicked the three of us out of the dance. We've been to her office multiple times for various altercations."

"I'll have to contact Mrs. Laughlin then and get some perspective on your association with Ellie," Mr. Grieves replied. "Now, I understand that the two of you obtained this alleged security footage illegally. Is this right?"

"Yes," I stammered, embarrassed. "Trust me, it's not like we wanted to commit a crime by breaking into the school or anything. We were just scared, you know? I've never been accused or implicated in any crime before, especially involving a missing person, so naturally, I wanted to prove my innocence."

"I completely understand," Mr. Grieves sympathized. "Unfortunately, that doesn't change the fact that the footage could be considered inadmissible. I'll have to see if there is some sort of workaround for that. Your mother also tells me that you have some other information that might be relevant to your case. Is that correct?" Mr. Grieves asked, turning to face me.

"Yes," I replied, feeling somewhat nervous and scared. "I'm not sure if it will be helpful, though."

"Any bit of information, whether you think it's important or not, could be the one thing that clinches the case in your favour," Mr. Grieves replied. "Never feel as though you can't tell me something just because you think it might be stupid."

"Thanks, Mr. Grieves," I replied, relief flooding over me. "So, um, just before we were supposed to come here, I had a flashback to the night of the dance."

"Tell me a little bit about it," Mr. Grieves prompted.

"I recall witnessing Ellie and one of her close friends, Autumn, huddling closely in a dark corner of the gym. I couldn't hear what they were saying; the music was far too loud, and I was too far away. I could clearly see Autumn holding something in her hand. She clutched the object tightly to her chest, trying to conceal whatever she carried. After a few moments, I could see Ellie reaching out to grab the object. It was her clutch purse, no doubt about it. Shortly thereafter, Autumn reached into her pocket and pulled out mine and Jenny's matching necklaces. Ellie unzipped her clutch, and Autumn gently placed the necklaces inside."

"Interesting," Mr. Grieves replied. So this would suggest that the security footage you obtained was indeed falsified."

"Exactly," Jenny argued. "If we stole our necklaces, there's no way on earth I'd be giving it to Autumn or any of those bitch minions of Ellie's. Like, what would be the point of that?"

Mr. Grieves sat silently for several moments, looking back and forth from his monitor to a notebook in which he had been feverishly scribbling. His eyes remained focused and attentive. Jenny and I sat motionless, clutching one another's hands tightly. The nerves were bubbling up, but I would be lying if I didn't say that I felt some relief, having gotten all that off my chest. My mother must have been feeling the nerves, too. She sat quietly, wringing her hands and staring off into space. Mr. Grieves suddenly became animated.

"Okay, so here's what I'm going to do," he began. "I'm going to go and talk to Mrs. Laughlin; try to confirm your relationship with Ellie and her friends. I won't mention anything about the falsified footage the two of you stumbled across, but I will mention what you recalled concerning the evening of the dance. I'll request access to the security footage of the gym for that evening, and we'll see if your memories serve you correctly. Is that alright with you, Kacey?"

"Yeah, definitely," I replied, feeling even more relief.

"Okay, then, well, I think that's all I need for now," Mr. Grieves replied. "I'll reach out if I have any more questions. Otherwise, expect to hear from me within the next several days. I'll update you on any progress as soon as possible."

"Thank you, Mr. Grieves," my mother whispered calmly. She motioned for Jenny and me to stand up and exit Mr. Grieves' office. We followed her out, shuffling our feet on the patterned carpet. When we went outside, my mother asked if we were hungry.

"I could go for a bite," I replied. "How about you, Jenny? You have anything better to do for the rest of the day?"

"Not a thing," Jenny replied sarcastically. "And I'm absolutely famished, by the way. Thanks for the invite, Mrs. Lundgren."

"Anytime Jenny. Anytime," my mother replied, smiling.

CHAPTER THIRTY-FIVE

Tuesday, May 28th, 2024: 12:13 AM

Jordan crept first into the darkness, shining the flashlight into the black void. He scanned from right to left, taking care to observe all of his surroundings. Jenny, Chase and I followed in close pursuit, taking equal care to observe what was around us. The light from the flashlight pooled like a pond glistening in the sun at the end of the dark corridor, only revealing slivers of objects in the distance. The walls were eerily bare, only adorned with a few rusted nails and shreds of what appeared to be some old, weathered and torn fabric. It only added to the eerie feeling, and I wondered if someone was indeed being held captive back here and how they could survive living day in and day out in such bleak conditions. Jordan continued to creep forward slowly and cautiously, and after a few moments, his flashlight caught a glimpse of something on the wall. I paused dead in my tracks and tapped him on the shoulder.

"Kacey! What is it?" he whispered.

I pointed to the wall, now enveloped in the flashlight's glow. I couldn't get the words out; my voice had suddenly abandoned me. Jordan leaned in the direction I was pointing, squinting in an attempt to see what I was noticing. His hands reached forward, and he pressed his fingers to the wall, carefully tracing the indentations. His eyes widened as a sudden realization hit him.

"I think these are claw marks," he announced. "Didn't they find claw marks inside the DNA extraction chamber at the scientific research centre on the night of the dance?"

"They sure did," Jenny replied confidently. "My father told me all about what happened that night, and claw marks were definitely present."

"Hmmm… interesting," Jordan replied. "So what are claw marks doing here inside the walls? Didn't Clara mention hearing some kind of growling from back here?"

"She absolutely did," I confirmed.

"And what about the sighting of the amber eyes in the forested area on the night of the dance and the attack on Jenny at the diner a few weeks back?" Jordan asked. "Didn't you say it looked like some kind of wolf-like creature that attacked you, Jenny?"

"It did," Jenny agreed. "I couldn't make out exactly what it was, but it certainly had features you would expect to see on a wolf."

"So again, I'm left puzzled by how and why these claw marks are on the wall," Jordan said. "What is going on?"

"I really don't know, but it's definitely strange," I answered. "We should keep looking around and see what else we find."

"Agreed," Jordan replied. "I think I see another door just

up ahead."

He shined his flashlight slightly to the right, and sure enough, there was a white-coloured steel door. I thought it was strange that the door was white, considering everything else was dark and bleak. What made this door so special that it deserved to get slapped with a fresh coat of paint? Jordan inched closer to the door, taking his time not to make any loud or abrupt noises. Who knew what lurked behind it? I certainly didn't want to alert anyone about our presence if I could help it. The door had a deadbolt-style latch, but not the kind you would expect to see in a private residence. No, this latch was heavy-duty. It was obviously meant to keep something in or keep others out, maybe both, for all I knew. What need would there be for such a high-security feature, I thought to myself? Jordan drew the flashlight closer, and out of the corner of my eye, I caught a glimpse of something pink on the ground in front of the door. I stooped over to pick up the mystery object.

"What is that?" Jenny asked, whispering as quietly as she could muster.

"It's a hair elastic," I replied, staring at the object in my hand. "What is a hair elastic doing here?"

"I don't know," Jenny replied, equally as puzzled. "Maybe it belongs to Ellie. I mean, she lived here. Maybe it somehow got inadvertently brought in here and was left and long forgotten."

"I mean, that does make sense," I agreed. "But it has been two years, though, since Ellie vanished. Do you think remnants of Ellie are still scattered about this place?"

"I mean, it's possible," Jenny replied. "Especially back here behind the walls. I'm pretty sure nobody's coming back here to clean regularly. We definitely know that Clara isn't. She's the one who alerted us to the noises emanating from back here. I'm sure she has no idea this room even exists."

"I can't argue with that," I replied

"Just another strange occurrence," Jordan quipped. "Something is afoot, and it's not good."

I stared at Jordan, waiting for a signal or some sort of communication directing us on what to do next. Do we attempt to break into this mystery room? Do we confront Mr. Mason with our discovery? I had no clue what to do and certainly did not know what was going through Jordan's mind. I shifted my gaze to Jenny and Chase, who looked equally unsure of our next move. I looked back over at Jordan questioningly. He gave me a quick smile and nodded at me. I knew exactly what he was thinking.

"I think I can maneuver this lock and break our way in," Jordan explained. "I just need to figure out the best way to accomplish that task. I still have the multi-tool, but did anybody think of bringing a screwdriver or something with more substance?"

Chase spoke up for the first time in quite some time. "I did think to grab this," he replied, holding a small kitchen torch.

"Why on earth did you grab that?" Jenny asked sarcastically. "My parents use that for baking."

"I don't know," Chase replied. "I just thought that it might be helpful."

"Helpful for what?" Jenny giggled. "You gonna bake someone to death?"

"You're a genius, Chase," Jordan chimed in. "That might

help make the metal just pliable enough so that I can pop off the bolt latch with the multi-tool."

Chase glared over at Jenny, seemingly pumped by the ego stroke Jordan had just given him and burst out laughing. She returned the favour by giving him a dead stare and then laughed. I couldn't help but smile at their escapades. It was refreshing to see a young couple still so in sync with one another after all the years that had passed. Jordan and I, too, still moved to the beat of the same drum, so our whole friend group was quite the anomaly.

Chase retrieved the kitchen torch from his backpack and passed it to Jordan, who grabbed it with such enthusiasm that I feared he would accidentally press the button and set himself on fire. Jordan then plucked the multi-tool from his pocket and began strategizing how to maneuver the torch and the multi-tool simultaneously to disengage the latch and bolt.

"Hey, Kace," Jordan called out. "Could you hold the flashlight for me? Just point it here, right on the latch and bolt. I just need to ensure that I won't burn off any appendages or anything."

I smiled at Jordan and retrieved the flashlight, shining its luminescence onto the latch and bolt as he instructed.

"You'd better not burn off any appendages," I replied playfully. "Don't wanna be married to a man who doesn't know how to care for himself properly."

Jordan suddenly stopped dead in his tracks, turning to face me, his expression as serious as I'd ever seen it. "What did you say?" he asked.

Stunned, I replied, "I didn't want to marry a man who didn't know how to care for himself properly."

"You want to marry me?" Jordan asked.

"Uhmmm…" I stammered. "I never really thought about it before, to be honest. It kind of just came out. So yeah, I guess subconsciously I do."

Jordan grinned, his smile growing larger with each passing second. "Gee, Kace," Jordan replied, "I knew you loved me, but I didn't know you loved me that much. Do you really wanna marry me? Me, the trainwreck?"

"You're not a trainwreck, Jordan," I replied. "Far from it, in fact. You're my superhero. My super hot nerd, man. And yes, I do want to marry you. I couldn't imagine my life being married to anybody else."

"Well, guess what, Kace? I want to marry you, too," Jordan replied.

I leaned forward, kissing Jordan on the cheek. He grabbed my face, turned it toward his, and kissed me passionately.

"Hmmm… Hmmmm…" Jenny cleared her throat, trying to get our attention. "You two know we're still here, right?" She motioned to Chase, who was standing behind her.

"Oh yeah, sorry," Jordan apologized. "Okay, just shine the flashlight here," Jordan motioned.

I held the flashlight steady, providing enough light so Jordan could see what he was doing. He pressed the button on the torch, the bluish-orange flame flickering steadily as he held it up against the metal latch. Conversely, he angled the multi-tool to fit the flat part of the knife under the latch and pulled it up gently.

"Is it doing anything?" I asked

"I think so," Jordan replied. "I can feel a little give as I pull up on the latch."

Jordan continued to direct the flame onto the latch, slowly heating it up and continuously applying more pressure with the knife. After several more minutes of the same song and dance, the latch finally snapped off, crashing to the ground.

"Well, holy hell," Jenny exclaimed. "You did it. Way to go, superhero. So what do we do now? Do we just go in?"

"Yeah, we do," Jordan replied. "But we should prepare ourselves for what we might find on the other side. There's no telling what is back there and what this deadbolt is meant to keep in."

"So what do you propose we do?" Jenny asked.

"I guess we should make our way in slowly and quietly so as to not alert anyone or anything to our presence. Maybe we should hold onto the torch and the multi-tool just in case we need to defend ourselves," Jordan replied. "I'll lead the way since I've got the flashlight and the multi-tool. Kace, you hold onto the torch, okay?" I nodded my head in agreement.

Jordan pushed the white steel door slowly, careful not to make excessive noise. He shone the flashlight into the room, scanning every inch. The room was quite large, stretching further back than light from the flashlight could reach. We continued to inch forward cautiously while Jordan scanned the room with the flashlight. A glimpse of something white caught my eye as Jordan's flashlight made its way to the centre of the room. A bed with white sheets!

"Jordan," I whispered excitedly. "Could you move the flashlight back over that way?" I asked, pointing to the center of the back wall. "I see something."

Jordan moved the flashlight back to the centre of the room. Up against the back wall was a poster-style bed with white sheets. I stood staring, perplexed by what I was seeing. What on earth was a bed doing back here? Did Mr. Grieves kidnap someone? Was he holding them hostage? Just then, I caught a glimpse of something moving on the right side of the bed. I jumped, startled by the sudden motion.

"Kacey, what's the matter?" Jordan asked, perplexed by my sudden jolt.

The words escaped me; they were stuck just like a lump in my throat. I pointed shakily in the direction of what had just startled me, and Jordan's gaze followed the direction of my finger.

"What the fuck," he yelled out loud.

Jenny and Chase, focused on the same place Jordan and I had been fixated on, gasped out loud.

"There's no fucking way," Jenny exclaimed, her face contorted in shock. "It can't be, can it?"

"It's…it's…Ellie," I gasped.

CHAPTER THIRTY-SIX

Monday, May 30th, 2022: 3:45 PM

Several days had passed since our meeting with Mr. Grieves. The weekend had come and gone; truthfully, it was a blur. It was challenging to convince my mind not to fixate on the events at Mr. Grieves' office but rather take some time to relax. In those rare moments when I could push aside those anxious thoughts, I spent much of my time dabbling in arts and crafts or reading. On the other hand, Jenny was energetic and eager to be on the move. She made several attempts to get me out of the house and go for a hike, but my anxiety wasn't having it. She eventually got the message and stopped calling, but admittedly, I felt bad. I never did like saying no to Jenny, but some days, you just have to have the courage to speak up for yourself and do what's best for your mental health.

On Monday morning, I was rested enough to function and get some work done at school. Even though I initially found it challenging to get my mind in study mode, it didn't take long for that to change. I was blessed to have a critical project assigned during my first block of the day, and it kept me quite busy and occupied my mind instead of all the other nonsense that swirled around. When I returned home from school, my mood had lifted somewhat, and I felt relaxed and hungry. I entered the kitchen, searching for a snack to tide me over until dinner. My mother was there, sitting at the kitchen table, her laptop open, perusing what appeared to be something of great importance. Her eyes lifted from the screen and met mine.

"Oh, hey, Kacey," she said. "I didn't hear you come in. Come and sit down for a moment. I have some news from Mr. Grieves that I'd like to share with you."

My eyes widened in anticipation, not knowing what to expect. I was hopeful that Mr. Grieves would gain access to the security footage from the night of the dance, yet a part of me still clung to the fear that something would go awry. I wanted all of this to be over, and the best way to accomplish that was to prove that my flashback was a reality and not just a figment of my imagination.

"Did he say anything about the video footage from the dance?" I asked excitedly.

"He did, yes," my mother replied. "Do you want me to share the news now, or would you like to call Jenny first and have her come and join us?"

"I can call her later and fill her in," I replied. "I don't think my body can wait any longer than absolutely necessary."

"Fair enough," my mother replied. "So, anyway, Mr. Grieves called this afternoon and let me know that he was able to talk with Mrs. Laughlin about getting access to that security footage from the dance. She was very accommodating despite knowing that she legally didn't have to turn over anything without a warrant from the police. She told him she would go through the security footage and turn over the appropriate footage as soon as she could pinpoint which disc it was stored on. Apparently, they transfer the footage onto CDs from the cloud every two weeks. His impression was that Mrs. Laughlin's main focus was to aid in the solving of Ellie's disappearance and any involvement her students may have had in the whole scenario."

"Well, that's good news, I guess," I replied, feeling skeptical about Mrs. Laughlin's willingness to prove our innocence.

"I know that both you and Jenny have had issues with Mrs. Laughlin in the past, but I sincerely believe that she has everyone's best interest at heart," my mother replied, trying her best to convince me that her words held some truth.

"I suppose," I agreed reluctantly. "Did Mr. Grieves mention anything about the relationship between Ellie, Jenny and me? Like, did Mrs. Laughlin confirm that we weren't exactly close and had some pretty severe conflict?"

"Yes, Mr. Grieves also had that discussion," my mother confirmed. "Mrs. Laughlin had no shortage of stories detailing the antics that the three of you were involved in."

"I bet," I replied, rolling my eyes. "The number of times Ellie came after us for absolutely no reason was absurd."

"Well, that's all in the past now," my mother sympathized. "No need to rehash it and get yourself worked up."

"You're right," I agreed. "Anyhow, do you mind if I go upstairs to my room? I want to call Jenny and update her on what Mr. Grieves accomplished this afternoon."

"Of course, honey. I'll call you when it's time for dinner. Sound good?"

"Yeah, Mom. Thanks for helping Jenny and me with this whole mess. I'm unsure if I could have handled all of this alone."

"No need to thank me, honey," my mother laughed. "I'm your Mom. It's sort of my job, you know?"

I smiled warmly at my mother as I walked up the stairs and into my room. I felt some relief knowing that Mr. Grieves had confirmed our relationship woes with Ellie. Even though I didn't fully trust Mrs. Laughlin, I had enough confidence to admit that she wouldn't set out to purposefully make Jenny or me look guilty. Once comfortable, I pulled my phone out of my pocket and called Jenny. I had no idea what to expect next; that would all depend on what Mr. Grieves found in the security footage from the dance. I could only hope that the footage would confirm my suspicions and get Jenny and me off the hook for the necklaces found in Ellie's clutch. Jenny soon picked up my call, and I began filling her in on the news Mr. Grieves had shared earlier. We both agreed that Mrs. Laughlin wouldn't intentionally withhold any information that could be pertinent to solving Ellie's disappearance. We also trusted Mr. Grieves and his judgment and felt it was best to put aside our personal feelings about Mrs. Laughlin and let him do his job. After several more minutes of back-and-forth conversation, I heard my mother hollering for me from the bottom of the stairs.

"Hey, Mom, is dinner ready?" I hollered back.

"No," my mother replied. "But Mr. Grieves just called.

He said that he just picked up the security footage from Mrs. Laughlin. He asked if we wanted to meet at his office to view it together."

"Right now?" I asked.

"As soon as you're ready," she replied.

"Yeah, absolutely. Can Jenny come too? She's as much a part of this as I am."

"Of course," my mother replied. "Why don't you give her a call?"

"I'm actually on the phone with her right now. Jenny, you wanna go see what's on that security footage?"

"You don't even have to ask. Of course, I want to go," Jenny exclaimed. "Text me when you arrive, and I'll meet you outside."

My mother exited the front door and started the car while waiting for me to gather my belongings. I moved swiftly. I didn't want to hold anybody up; truth be told, I was genuinely curious about what the video footage would show and what Mr. Grieves' recommendations would be. Jenny and I should finally have the evidence to move on from this drama. We should finally be cleansed of any implication in this entire mess.

We pulled up to Jenny's house within minutes, and it was no secret that Jenny was just as anxious as I was to view the video. She smiled and waved and then, in typical Jenny fashion, began to chew my ear off about what the video would reveal and whether Mr. Grieves would have a plan of action. I entertained her chatter the entire ride, knowing that I would certainly get an earful later about not being a supportive friend if I didn't.

After what seemed like the longest drive in history,

primarily due to Jenny's incessant talking, we arrived at Mr. Grieves' office. I was both nervous and excited. I was sure that what I had envisioned was the truth and that Mr. Grieves could clear our names of any wrongdoing. Jenny squeezed my hand as we walked up the stairs and into the front lobby. The same receptionist sat at her perch, typing away on the keyboard, doing what I could only assume was of paramount importance. She did not even lift her head to look in our direction or even acknowledge us with a "How can I help you?" It took the sound of my mother clearing her throat to divert her attention away from her monitor.

"Oh, hello," she said. "My apologies. I was so engrossed in my work that I hadn't noticed the three of you walking in. I assume you are here to see Mr. Grieves again?"

"Yes, we are," my mother replied. "In fact, he should be expecting us. Can we show ourselves in?"

"Absolutely," the receptionist replied. "You know the way, right?"

"We do, yes. Thank you," my mother replied.

Jenny and I followed my mother to Mr. Grieves' office. Although I was excited to confirm what I already believed to be true, I couldn't help but feel some anxiety. On the other hand, Jenny was overly pumped up and came across as confident and fearless. When we arrived at Mr. Grieves' office, he was already waiting at the door for us. He motioned for us to follow him into his office, directing us to have a seat.

"So, I assume your mother has filled you both in on why I have asked you to stop by this afternoon?" he asked.

"Yes, sir," I replied. "Jenny and I are eager to see the video and hopefully put all this behind us."

"I haven't had the opportunity to watch it yet," Mr. Grieves stated. "I thought maybe we could all watch it together and then discuss any outcomes immediately. No sense in waiting for another opportunity to meet up again at a later date."

Jenny and I nodded our heads in agreement.

"Well then, I'll press play if you're ready."

The video footage began to play. I first noticed Jenny, Chase, Jordan, and me dancing on the dance floor. We were all smiling and clearly enjoying our evening. Little did we know then that things would drastically change over the next hour or two. We continued to observe the events from the video. After several more songs and embarrassing footage of the four of us busting out our best dance moves, I caught a glimpse of something white and flowy emerging from the top right frame of the screen. It was Ellie, and she was accompanied by Autumn. My body began to stiffen, and I leaned forward in my seat. I continued to watch, anticipating each moment to unfold as I remembered. The next thing I observed confirmed my suspicions. On camera, as plain as day, Autumn passed the clutch to Ellie, who unzipped it and held it open. Autumn reached into the pocket of her shawl, and Jenny's necklace and mine were in her hands. She swiftly and gingerly placed them into the clutch, and Ellie, quickly observing her surroundings to make sure nobody had seen them, zipped the clutch back up and held it tightly against her body.

"So," Jenny began. "Those bitches did set us up. What the actual fuck!"

Still in shock, I sat motionless, unable to say a word. I already suspected that my flashbacks were actual, real-life memories, but just seeing them replay on the screen for all to see filled me with so much emotion. Was this really over? Did we just prove that we were innocent and not involved in Ellie's disappearance? I gazed over at Mr. Grieves, waiting for some sort of confirmation.

"Well," Mr. Grieves started. "The video footage certainly confirms your claims. Autumn was indeed responsible for placing the necklaces into Ellie's clutch. I believe this will be enough to remove you and Jenny from any suspicion related to Ellie's disappearance."

"Mr. Grieves," I began. "I want to thank you for helping us obtain this footage. I don't think things would have gone in our favour without it. I still don't believe the whole necklace thing is related to Ellie's disappearance, though. I'm pretty sure Autumn was not involved in that entire mess. I'm still sure it was a ploy to get Jenny and me in trouble. It's pretty clear that Ellie didn't think very highly of us and would have done just about anything to make our lives miserable, including making claims that we were trying to frame her for theft. As for the altered footage of us stealing the necklaces, I suspect Autumn was responsible for that. She's pretty good with tech, and I imagine that after Ellie vanished, she feared she could be pinned for her disappearance if the footage of her stealing the necklaces ever came to light."

"That all sounds reasonable and quite frankly plausible," Mr. Grieves agreed. "I'll have to contact Autumn and get her side of the story. Knowing what we now know about how the necklaces ended up in Ellie's clutch, it shouldn't be hard to pinpoint whether Autumn's version of the story matches up with the evidence."

"When can we expect to hear from you, Mr. Grieves?" my mother asked.

"I can't say for certain," Mr. Grieves responded. "I intend to contact Autumn immediately; however, I cannot guarantee when she will be available to meet. No worries, though. I won't leave you all hanging. I'll contact you as soon as I have something to report."

"Thank you, Mr. Grieves," my mother replied, ushering Jenny and me out of his office and back outside to our car.

Jenny and I exchanged satisfied grins, knowing that this was the beginning of a new chapter for us, a chapter without suspicion related to Ellie's disappearance. I breathed a sigh of relief and felt the built-up tension immediately release from my body. Now, we just have to wait to hear Autumn's version of the story.

CHAPTER THIRTY-SEVEN

Tuesday, May 28th, 2024: 12:42 AM

"Ellie?" I called out. "Ellie, is that you?"

The figure moved swiftly into a corner of the room, desperately trying to conceal its face. There was an urgency to the movement, and saying it made me uncomfortable was nothing short of an understatement. I continued staring, fixated on this thin, pale, lean figure before me, crouching awkwardly in the corner. The figure's hair was gold-like spun straw and hung in curls surrounding the shoulders. I was so confident it was Ellie that I couldn't resist moving closer to get a better look. The closer I got, however, the more erratic the figure became. It was clear that our presence was causing a lot of undue stress. I reached out slowly, not making any sudden or abrupt movements. I gently pulled the silken gold hair away from the figure's face and leaned in for a better look. Sure enough, it was Ellie. There was no mistaking that golden hair or the piercing blue eyes. She was frail, and her eyes had sunken in, but there was no mistaking her for anyone else.

"Ellie," I called out gently. "What are you doing here? Everyone thought you were dead. You've been missing for two years."

"No, no, no…. You mustn't," she cried out.

"Mustn't what?" I asked.

Ellie turned to stare at the four of us for the first time, her eyes wide with panic. Jenny stared incredulously at the sight before her. It was the first time I had ever witnessed her rendered speechless. The boys, equally shocked, stood there in silence, their mouths agape.

"Mustn't what?" I repeated, making an attempt to coax Ellie to reveal more.

"You must leave. You shouldn't be here," Ellie whispered, seemingly frightened.

"Why, Ellie? Why shouldn't we be here?" I asked.

"It will come," she muttered, almost unintelligible. "It will come."

Jenny, Jordan, Chase and I all exchanged puzzled glances. What was this "IT" that Ellie was referring to? Why was she so terrified of whatever this "IT" was? I had no idea, and it was obvious nobody else had any clue. We all stared at one another questioningly as though we expected one or the other to have an answer.

"Ellie," I began. "What do you mean IT will come? What is IT?"

"Im… I'm… I'm not supposed to tell," she stuttered.

"Why Ellie? Why can't you tell us?" I coaxed gently.

"Because he said not to," she replied. "He said not to tell anyone."

"Who said not to tell anyone?" I asked.

"My father," Ellie replied.

A look of astonishment washed across my face. I knew that Mr. Mason had been hiding something intentionally; that much was clear, but I never suspected that he would be guilty of hiding his daughter, a daughter no less, who was missing and presumed dead.

"Your father's been hiding you here for two years?" I asked. "Do you know why?"

"He says that I'm dangerous," Ellie whispered.

I looked at Jordan, Jenny, and Chase, and a look of confusion washed over me. Dangerous? Ellie? How on earth could anyone ever think this small and frail human could be dangerous? She looked so weak that I had doubts that she could even stand, never mind cause any physical harm to anyone. I continued to press Ellie for more information.

"Why would he think that you're dangerous, Ellie?" I asked.

"Because of the experiment," she replied.

Jenny and I glanced at one another, the confusion deepening. This was all so strange and yet so fascinating. I couldn't help but continue with my questions. What else would Ellie reveal?

"What experiment, Ellie? What did your father do?" I asked.

"The research center," she replied. "He made a mistake."

"A mistake?" I asked. "What kind of mistake?"

"He messed up the DNA."

"The Dire Wolf DNA? Is that what you're talking about, Ellie?" I asked.

She nodded her head up and down. "Ye…yes…" she stammered.

I glanced back at Jenny, Jordan and Chase again, looking for confirmation that they had just heard the conversation unfolding. They all seemed as stunned as I was.

"Jordan," I called out. "What should we do? We can't just leave her in here. She needs to go to the hospital and get some medical attention. Just look at her. She's a mess."

"I agree," Jordan replied. "We just have to figure out how to get her out of here without alerting anyone."

I still had no idea how being locked away in here and how she could be considered dangerous were connected to the Dire Wolf DNA situation at the research center, but I knew we would have to worry about sorting that out later. For now, the most important thing to do was to get her out of here. I gazed over at Jenny and Chase, looking for suggestions on accomplishing this task.

"I suppose we just put her arms over our shoulders and escort her out," Jenny suggested. "Hopefully, she won't collapse. She doesn't look all that strong."

Jordan and Chase approached Ellie cautiously, taking care not to startle or stress her out further than she already was. They each grabbed an arm, slung it over their shoulders, and gently lifted her to her feet.

"Jenny, Kacey," Jordan called out. "Could the two of you lead the way with the flashlights?"

Jenny and I took the lead, gripping the flashlights we had brought and aiming the beams of light back in the direction we had come from. Jordan, Chase and Ellie followed in close pursuit. We had only meandered our way a short distance when the sudden sound of a growl echoed through the chamber. Both stunned and scared, Jenny and I suddenly reversed our position, looking back at Jordan, Chase, and Ellie. The light emitted from the flashlight revealed the most frightening thing I had ever witnessed. There, standing between Jordan and Chase, was what I could only describe as a hybrid wolf/human-like creature. I let out a shrill scream and dropped my flashlight onto the dark stone floor. Jordan and Chase looked over at Ellie and instead caught sight of what was now standing between them. Their faces contorted from bewilderment to fear as they suddenly realized Ellie had transformed into something frightening and unimaginable. They both dropped the creature to the floor, running ahead and grabbing mine and Jenny's arms as they passed.

"Holy shit," Jordan and Chase screamed in unison. "Run!"

The four of us ran as fast as we could, desperately trying to cling to our only flashlight. Behind us, we could hear the snarls and growls of the creature. We didn't dare look back; we just kept running, doing our best to locate the entrance to the sliding white steel door. Jenny and I squeezed through first, followed by Jordan and Chase, who miraculously did not bowl us over. Jordan desperately fished in his pocket, looking for the remote to close the steel door behind us and prevent the creature from escaping. In his haste, he dropped it.

"Shit, shit, shit," he cursed. "Jenny, shine the flashlight down here, quick."

Jenny aimed her flashlight down to the floor, and Jordan retrieved the remote in one hurried motion, pressing the button with such force that the plastic snapped and the remote crumbled apart in his hands. Luckily, the door edged its way shut and entirely concealed the monster within its chamber walls. We all breathed a sigh of relief.

"Well, that was fun," Jordan said, trying to laugh off the moment to quell our nerves.

If looks could kill, Jordan would have keeled over dead. My eyes, daggers of steel, penetrated his soul, daring him to let loose one more joke.

"Sorry, Kace," he apologized. "Just trying to lighten the mood a bit."

"Well, don't," I snapped. Jordan, his eyes full of hurt, stared over at me, making me feel guilty for getting upset with him in the first place. I glanced at Jenny and then at Chase, who seemed shocked by my sudden outburst. "I'm sorry," I apologized. "I'm just really stressed and still confused about everything that happened."

"I think we all are, Kace," Jenny sympathized. "Why don't we all go home and get some sleep. We can discuss this in the morning. I'm sure there'll be lots to discuss, especially how we'll approach Mr. Mason with our newfound discovery."

I reluctantly agreed. We were all tired, and there was no way we could collect our thoughts and have a rational conversation in this state. It would be best to wrap this up for the night and wait until morning. The four of us quietly and cautiously climbed out from the hole in the wall, quietly closing the makeshift door behind us. We returned out the side door by the kitchen and into Jordan's car. We drove home in silence, dropping Chase off first, then Jenny. When we arrived at my house, Jordan didn't say a word. He leaned over and gave me a quick kiss on the cheek, waited for me to exit the vehicle and then drove away. It was going to be a long night.

CHAPTER THIRTY-EIGHT

Wednesday, June 1st, 2022: 3:05 PM

A few days had passed since our meeting with Mr. Grieves, and it was honestly the most refreshing two days I could fathom in my most recent memory. My worries faded into the back of my mind, and it almost felt as if life had returned to its natural rhythm. Jenny was her usual chipper self, but she had an air of relaxation about herself that went above and beyond the norm. The school day flew by, and I felt just as calm and relaxed. Before I knew it, the dismissal bell rang, and it was time to head home. Jenny came bouncing down the hallway, greeting me at my locker.

"What's up, girlfriend?" she greeted me.

"Nothing much," I replied. "Things are calm and relaxed. I honestly feel great. This is the best I've felt in about two years."

"Tell me about it," Jenny replied. "I almost forgot what it was like not to have a dark cloud hanging over me. Speaking of which, has Mr. Grieves spoken to Autumn yet?"

"Not that I'm aware of," I replied. "My mother usually texts me when there's an update, but she hasn't yet. I'm going to assume there's nothing new to report."

"You'll let me know when there is some news, right?" Jenny asked.

"Of course, silly. I'd never leave you hanging. I'm not that cruel."

"Great. Well then, I'm going to head off to work now," Jenny said. "Text me anytime. My boss is pretty understanding and won't mind if I take a moment to reply."

"Will do," I replied, smiling.

Jenny and I parted ways, and I swiftly made my way home. I was anxious to talk to my mother, but equally anxious to grab a snack. My stomach was unforgiving and doing a fantastic imitation of a rabid dog. When I entered the front door, I saw that my mother was on the phone. She glanced in my direction and motioned for me to wait a few moments before I could leave her sight. I planted myself down on the couch, observing my mother's body language for any signs of context from her conversation. But, surprisingly, there were none. She was as stealthy as they come on this particular day. I continued to wait, twirling the ends of my hair with my fingers and anxiously licking my lips. I could feel my calm demeanour fading despite my attempts to disallow my anxious thoughts to take over. A few more minutes passed before my mother ended her call. She approached me slowly, almost anticipating the rise in my anxiety.

"Kacey, that was Mr. Grieves on the phone," my mother started. "He had an update concerning the video footage of

Autumn and Ellie."

I stared at my mother with curious eyes, waiting for her to continue.

"He mentioned that he was able to arrange a meeting with Autumn just before the end of the school day. He and Mrs. Laughlin met in her office to review the video footage together with Autumn."

Without speaking a word, my eyes remained locked on my mother's, and I hung on to her every word for more information.

"They pointed out that Autumn and Ellie were engaging in suspicious behaviour by huddling together in a dark corner and that Autumn made some attempt to conceal the fact that she had the clutch when she passed it off to Ellie."

"And what did she have to say about that?" I asked.

"She was very open and honest about the fact that she did have the clutch on her person," my mother replied. "She did not attempt to deny it."

"Well, that's not surprising," I huffed. "It's not like she could disguise being caught red-handed in the video."

"Mr. Grieves did mention that he had made certain to let Autumn know that any images from the video could be used as evidence against her in court if she concealed any details. Maybe that scared her a little bit," my mother suggested.

"Perhaps," I agreed. "I still have a difficult time accepting that Autumn would just admit to everything so openly. There has to be more to the story."

"There is, actually," my mother continued.

I stared my mother dead in the eyes, waiting for her to

continue.

"Autumn claimed that Ellie was the one who stole the necklaces from your locker that day in the gym. She insists that Ellie was persistent about needing to frame you and Jenny for theft. She said it was as though Ellie were possessed, and nothing else was more important than getting the two of you in trouble with Mrs Laughlin. Do you know why she might have been so keen on setting the two of you up?"

"No, no idea at all," I replied. "Did Autumn say anything else?"

"Well, Mr. Grieves did ask her about the falsified footage of you and Jenny," my mother replied.

"He did? And? What did she say?"

"She admits to using AI to change the video to show that you and Jenny were responsible for stealing the necklaces."

"But why?" I asked. "What would she have to gain by doing that? She and Ellie were already close. It's not like she had to kiss her ass to get in her good graces."

"Well, that's the strange part," my mother replied. "According to Mr. Grieves, Ellie was blackmailing Autumn. According to Autumn, Ellie threatened to blame her if she refused to alter the footage and set the two of you up."

"What!" I exclaimed. "But why? I thought Autumn was Ellie's best friend. I'd never do something like that to Jenny."

"And we're back to that question again," my mother replied. "Why was Ellie so upset with the two of you? What motive did she have for wanting to set you and Jenny up for theft?"

"I'm going to have to ask Jenny that question," I replied. "I really can't think of any reason off the top of my head that would warrant that kind of response from Ellie. I'm not naive or anything; I know we didn't exactly get along, but I can't think of anything that could elicit that kind of extreme response. Did Mr. Grieves forward the video footage and a transcript of Autumn's response to the authorities?" I asked.

"He did," my mother replied. "They have now removed you and Jenny from the suspect list in Ellie's disappearance. However, it now seems Autumn has been added to the suspect list."

"Makes sense, I suppose. Even though Ellie blackmailed Autumn and had her do all of these awful things to Jenny and me, I still don't think Autumn is capable of physically harming anyone. I still think it's all a coincidence, the timing of it all, I mean. I think Ellie's disappearance is related to the incident in the forested area across the other side of town."

"The amber eyes sighting?" my mother asked.

"Yes," I replied. Jenny and I saw the emergency vehicles flying in that direction while on our way home from the dance. We heard the report from Mr. and Mrs. Grays relating to the sighting of a woman fitting Ellie's description on that night in that part of town. And, of course, the news footage the next morning, the reports of a woman's scream and the amber eyes sighting. It's evident that Ellie's disappearance had nothing to do with either Jenny, me, or Autumn."

"Are you going to call Jenny and fill her in on all of this?" my mother asked.

"Yeah, I'm going to text her if it's okay with you."

"Absolutely, honey. Let me know if you have any more questions. Perhaps Mr. Grieves or I could help."

"I will. Thanks, Mom," I replied as I turned to go to my room.

As soon as I entered my room, I shut the door and grabbed my phone from my front pocket. I wasted no time texting Jenny all of the details. She was somewhat shocked, needless to say, but not completely surprised. We both knew that somebody had framed us and after my flashback the other day, we both felt confident that Autumn would be the culprit. While Mr. Grieves proved my premonition correct and gave us some closure, Jenny insisted we get together with Jordan and Chase to discuss these new findings. I agreed, and immediately after texting with Jenny, I phoned Jordan, who immediately made his way to my place. He arrived in under fifteen minutes, and after hearing the familiar vroom of his car engine, I raced outside to meet him.

"So what's the big emergency?" Jordan asked.

"Do you mind if I wait until we're together at Jenny's place to fill you in?" I asked. "This is just one of those things we should all be together to discuss."

"Of course," he replied, kissing me softly.

We made our way to the front door of my house to wait for Jenny to get home from work. Once she got home, Jordan and I hastily made our way outside to his car so that we could meet up at her place to discuss the news that Mr. Grieves had shared. I could not believe this could finally be over once and for all. No more worries of being implicated in Ellie's disappearance, no more lawyers, no more police investigations, no more worries about episodes of bullying from Ellie or her minions. Jenny and I might finally be able to live peacefully and enjoy our high school years. Little did I know that two years later, the investigation would once again rear its ugly head, and chaos would ensue.

CHAPTER THIRTY-NINE

Wednesday, May 29th, 2024

I was so exhausted from the previous night's events that I slept straight through the night, not waking up once, which was unusual for me. There was so much information to process, yet my brain was too exhausted to make sense of it all. Jenny's suggestion to sleep it off and leave all the discussion for the following day was the correct decision.

Upon waking up, I discovered that Jenny had arranged for us to get a ride to school with her father. I was super appreciative as taking the bus after our rendezvous the night before wasn't what I considered to be a good time. School would be another challenge I wasn't prepared to take on. Still, it was one of the few places where Jenny, Chase, Jordan, and I had the opportunity to gather together and discuss our discovery. By the time the morning classes had passed, I was eager to sit outside and have lunch together under the shade of the birch trees. This conversation needed to happen, and I couldn't wait any longer.

The lunch bell rang, signalling the end of our second class, and I raced outside to the birch trees, waiting for everyone else to arrive. Jenny and I had texted Jordan and Chase our plans earlier that morning so they knew exactly where we would be. It wasn't long before Jenny and Chase arrived, hand in hand, followed closely by Jordan, who stumbled clumsily attempting to balance a lunch tray and his backpack.

"Hey guys," he mumbled, his mouth full of sandwich. "What's up?"

"Well, I was hoping to rehash the events from last night," I replied. "Hence why Jenny and I texted you and Chase asking to meet us here at lunch."

"Well then," Jordan began. "I'll just set my tray down, and we can begin whenever you're ready."

"What I really want to know is what do we do about Ellie?" I asked. "Obviously, she's alive, but she's also not exactly…uhm, entirely human."

"That's an understatement," Jenny scoffed. "So, do we just go to the Mason house and demand we speak to Mr. Mason?"

"That would be a start," Jordan agreed. "We may need to approach this from a different angle, though. I'm unsure if four teenagers bombarding him with facts and demanding an explanation will convince him to come clean."

"So then, what should we do?" Jenny asked.

"The truth?" Jordan asked, staring Jenny straight in the eyes.

"Yeah," she replied. "Don't sugarcoat it. Literally, tell me what we should do instead."

"The best bet is to go to the authorities. They'll know how to handle it, and we'll keep our noses clean. We are just about at the tail end of this two-year saga, and I'd prefer not to get ourselves tangled up in it any further," Jordan replied.

"That makes sense, I suppose," Jenny agreed. "I'm definitely over all of the drama of the past couple of years, but I have to admit, a part of me likes the adrenaline rush of the chase. A small part of me is going to miss it."

"I totally get that," I agreed. "But I will say, I'm not going to miss all of the anxiety that goes along with it."

"Agreed," Jordan, Jenny and Chase replied in unison.

"When do you guys want to go talk to the authorities?" Jordan asked.

"Does today after school work for you all?" I asked, glancing at Jordan, Jenny and Chase one at a time.

"It works for me," Jenny replied. "Chase? How about you?"

"I'm good to go after school," he replied.

"Jordan?" Jenny asked.

"I'm down for whenever you guys decide."

"Okay, it's set then," I answered. "I'll meet you all back here at the end of the day, and we'll report this to the authorities together."

Everyone gave a nod of approval and continued to enjoy their lunch. Jordan put his arm around my shoulder, pulling me in for a hug. I reciprocated the act of affection by giving him a quick peck on the cheek. I expected Jenny to seize the opportunity to tease the two of us about our public display of affection, but instead, she leaned into

Chase, who welcomed the invitation with open arms. I smiled at Jordan lovingly and then shifted my gaze to the sky, welcoming the sight of the fluffy white clouds and the warmth of the sunshine on my face. Things were slowly starting to feel normal once again.

The end of the school day rapidly approached, and soon, it was time to leave for the day. As planned, we all met by the birch trees, and I couldn't have been more excited to report our discovery to the authorities. Even though Jenny and I had been cleared of any involvement in Ellie's disappearance years ago, it would be nice to close this chapter in our town's history. I hoped the police investigation would uncover the same horrors we had discovered. Although I didn't necessarily want Mr. Mason to end up in prison, the fact was that he had hidden his daughter for two years and lied to the authorities about her going missing. This made it very clear that he was not the loving father he had made himself out to be. There was also the question of what he did to Ellie. She obviously was experimented on as she seemingly took on the persona of an extinct wolf/human hybrid-type creature. What type of person would use his own daughter as the subject for such a horrific experiment?

The four of us arrived at the police station in record time, and it was clear that we were all ready to give our statements about what we had seen and how we had made the discovery in the first place. I harboured some guilt about having to out Clara; however, she was the one who alerted us to the possibility of something being hidden behind the walls. Besides, we knew it was necessary to alert the authorities to Ellie's whereabouts. Jordan held open the door to the police precinct, and we all stumbled in like a bunch of drunks.

We were quite elated to finally have solved the mystery of Ellie's disappearance and be able to put it all behind us. When we approached the front desk, the officer looked at us questioningly and appeared confused at the sight of four teenagers walking in with smiles plastered across their faces.

"Can I help you?" she asked?

"Yes," Jordan answered. "We would like to talk to the lead investigator in the Ellie Mason case."

"Ah yes, that would be Officer Tarik," she replied. "It's been a couple of years since we've had any updates on the case. Do you have new information?" she asked.

"Yes, ma'am, we do," Jordan answered.

"Oh, really," the officer replied, her eyebrows arching in curiosity. "Well, right this way then."

We followed her to a large room with a desk and several leather-backed chairs. She motioned for us to sit before returning to the entrance door. She turned to look at us before exiting the room.

"I'll let Officer Tarik know you are here to see him. What were your names again?"

"My name is Jordan, and this is Kacey, my girlfriend," Jordan replied, motioning to me. "This here is Jenny, and next to her is Chase."

"Kacey and Jenny?" the secretary pondered for a moment. "You were the two young ladies whose necklaces were found in the clutch, weren't you?"

"Uhm… yes, that was us," I replied hesitantly.

"Interesting," she mumbled as she exited the room, closing the door behind her.

"What does she mean by interesting," Jenny asked,

sounding annoyed. "Is she trying to imply that we're up to something?"

"Who knows, and who cares," I replied, annoyed. "We were cleared of any wrongdoing two years ago."

"Very true," Jenny agreed. "It's not like we can get blamed for this disaster of a situation. We didn't lie about Ellie's disappearance, and we certainly didn't lock her up for the past two years."

"Amen to that, sister," I replied, breathing a sigh of relief.

A few moments later, Officer Tarik entered the room, his clean, crisp uniform hugging his upper body, alluding to the possibility of a hidden six-pack underneath. He scanned each of us individually, meeting our eyes as if he were looking for any sign of nervousness. He strutted confidently to his desk, pulling out his chair a few inches before having a seat.

"So, I understand that the four of you have some new information you'd like to share regarding the missing Mason girl's case."

"Yes, sir," Jordan replied, trying to exude confidence.

"Well then, who wants to fill me in?" Officer Tarik asked.

The four of us looked around at one another, waiting to see if someone would be the first to volunteer. Jordan rose to the occasion, which truly wasn't a surprise. He was the group's rock, and I knew that Jenny and Chase appreciated his assertiveness in these situations.

"Well, Officer," Jordan began, "my girlfriend and her friend Jenny were the two ladies implicated in Ellie's disappearance when their necklaces were somehow found in the clutch she was carrying the night of the dance. They were cleared of that accusation once Autumn admitted to using AI to falsify the video footage of the necklaces being stolen from the gym locker room."

"Yes, I'm fully aware of all that," Officer Tarik replied. "What does that have to do with your visit today?"

"Well, despite all that," Jordan continued, "we were dragged back into the drama only a few short weeks ago when confronted by some sort of creature up at the local waterfall."

"Creature?" Officer Tarik asked, confused. "You mean the one with the amber eyes everyone reported seeing the night Ellie disappeared?"

"Yes, that creature," Jordan replied. "That same creature attacked my friend Jenny here at Shelby's Diner a few weeks later."

"Why am I only hearing about this now?" Officer Tarik asked. "Why wouldn't you have reported the incident?"

"Well, that's the thing, Officer," Jordan explained. "Jenny's father works at the scientific research center in town here, and he informed us that there was some sort of a blackout on the night of Ellie's disappearance. He claims that during the blackout, the sample he was working on mysteriously vanished from the chamber where the DNA was extracted. All that was left was some strange claw marks on the walls. Coincidently, that was also the night the amber eyes were first reported. While visiting Jenny at the hospital after our first encounter at the waterfall, he asked my girlfriend, Kacey, to keep quiet about what happened. We assumed we should also stay hushed regarding what happened at the diner."

"I see," Officer Tarik replied. "I'm having difficulty understanding why Mr. Forester would ask you not to report the incident to the authorities. Was he purposely trying to hide something about Ellie's disappearance?"

"We don't think so, Officer," Jordan explained. "Mr. Forester claimed that he was worried that he might be accused of covering up Ellie's disappearance like you just implied."

"Fair," Officer Tarik answered. "He still should have reported it, but I can understand his concern. So, how does that bring us to today? I still don't see the connection between these incidents and your reason for coming in today."

"Well, that's the thing, Officer," Jordan replied. "We haven't been able to shake the feeling that something is afoot since the amber eyes reappeared. Why, after nearly two years, have they suddenly come back?"

"That's a good question," Officer Tarik agreed. "This is the first sighting I've been made aware of in the two years since Ellie's disappearance. Strange that they have suddenly reappeared now."

"The four of us just couldn't let it go, you know?" Jordan continued. "Especially with all of the drama with the necklaces and Ellie's clutch, the original sighting of the amber eyes on the night of Ellie's disappearance. We just had to know what prompted this sudden reappearance."

"And did you come to any conclusions?" Officer Tarik asked.

"Actually," Jordan began. "We think we've solved the mystery of the amber eyes and Ellie's disappearance."

Officer Tarik stared at the four of us, his eyes wide with shock and wonder. He hesitated briefly, almost as if contemplating what he wanted to say, before turning back to Jordan.

"What makes you believe you know what happened to the Mason Girl?" he asked Jordan.

"After talking to her father about the incident at the research center on the night of the dance, Jenny filled us in on the newfound information. As a group, we decided that Kacey and I would talk to Mr. Mason since he was the project manager for the DNA research that Jenny's father was working on. It was confirmed that he was also present that night when the power outage occurred. We thought he might have more information about what happened to the DNA sample and what could have left the claw marks inside the extraction chamber."

"And?" Officer Tarik probed. "Did he?"

"He didn't really say anything, but he sure was upset that we would imply that he had anything to do with what happened at the research center. When we brought up the idea of finding some closure regarding Ellie's disappearance, he claimed he had made peace with it long ago."

"That is strange," Officer Tarik pondered. "So what did the two of you do then? Did you just leave?"

"We did, yes," Jordan replied. "But before we could reach the front door, the Mason's housekeeper, Clara, stopped us. She asked if we could return the following evening. She claimed to have some information that might help us figure out what happened at the power plant and perhaps the source of the amber eyes."

"Go on then," Officer Tarik prompted, grabbing the arms of his seat and leaning forward, his eyes widening.

"When we returned, we decided to livestream the conversation to Jenny and Chase. We didn't want to scare Clara away by bringing extra bodies with us, but we also knew that Jenny and Chase should have the opportunity to hear all the details. Anyhow, Clara told us that upon Mr. Mason's return from the scientific research center, he made a phone call to someone, Clara didn't know who, but she mentioned that he sounded scared about the events at the research center getting leaked to the public and was concerned about the consequences if it did get out. She also mentioned some concern when the news came out about the reports of the amber eye sightings."

"Interesting," Officer Tarik mumbled. "Did Clara mention anything about Ms. Mason or the amber eyes?"

"She did, actually, which intrigued us the most," Jordan responded. "Clara said he asked the person on the other end of the phone to take Ellie to a safe place. This happened just after Jenny, Kacey and Ellie were kicked out of the dance. Our first thought was that Ellie might still be alive and Mr. Mason knew of her whereabouts."

"I must admit, all of this sounds intriguing," Officer Tarik replied. "But if Mr. Mason really knew of Ellie's whereabouts, why would he not say something? Why would he lead the entire town into believing she had gone missing? It's been two long years now. Why would he be harbouring such a huge secret?"

"That's what we wanted to know," Jordan replied.

"Did Clara overhear anything else that might lead us to believe that Ellie was still alive," Officer Tarik asked?

"That's the strange part, sir," Jordan replied. "Clara overheard Mr. Mason telling Mrs. Mason he had business to attend to just moments after hanging up the phone. He told her he would be late and that she shouldn't wait up for him. We suspected it was about where he asked the person on the phone to take Ellie."

"Did you have any evidence to prove that theory?" Officer Tarik asked.

"Nothing specific," Jordan replied. "It was just a theory at that point until Clara revealed one last bombshell."

"Oh! And what was that?" Officer Tarik asked, raising an eyebrow.

"Well, she claimed to have heard strange noises from within the walls," Jordan explained. "She mentioned hearing both growling and soft singing."

"Really!" Officer Tarik exclaimed, more curious now than ever. "And did you confirm these mystery noises for yourselves?"

"As a matter of fact, we did," Jordan replied.

"And exactly how did you all manage to do that?" Officer Tarik asked.

I looked up at Jordan hesitantly. We all knew that breaking into the Mason home was against the law, but I wasn't sure what consequences we would face if we admitted it here and now at the police station. He stared me straight in the eyes, reassuring me that everything would be okay. I fully trusted Jordan's judgment and nodded back approvingly.

"Well, sir, we broke into the Mason home. We needed to find out if Clara's reports were true, and we knew that Mr. Mason would never let us back into his home."

"Hmmm…" Officer Tarik took a moment to think before responding further. "And what did you find?"

"We found Ellie, sir," Jordan replied.

Officer Tarik's jaw dropped. His eyes swept over the four

of us as if he were trying to decipher all of what we had just told him was actually true. "What did you just say?" he asked.

"We found Ellie," Jordan repeated. "And the source of the amber eyes."

"I don't understand," Officer Tarik replied. "You found Ellie and the mystery creature?"

"Yes," Jordan explained. "They are one and the same."

Officer Tarik sat in stunned silence as though he was contemplating how to respond to such a critical piece of information. His eyes scanned each of us meticulously, searching for any hint that we were trying to pull one over on him. After several moments of awkward silence, he got up from his chair and left his office abruptly. The four of us exchanged nervous glances, unable to decipher what was happening.

"What's going on?" I asked, both worried and confused.

"I'm not sure," Jordan replied, equally as concerned.

"Should we wait for him to come back?" I asked.

"He didn't say we could leave," Jordan replied. "My best guess is that he wants us to stay."

"How long should we wait before we leave or say anything to the officer at the front desk?" Jenny chimed in.

"Maybe ten minutes," Jordan replied.

We continued to wait, barely saying two words to one another. We all were terrified as to Officer Tarik's whereabouts. When he finally came to his office, it was as though a pin had dropped; the silence was deafening.

"So," Officer Tarik began. "I spoke with our Chief of Police and filled him in on what you told me today.

Unfortunately, we cannot get a warrant to search and enter the Mason home on the word of four teenagers alone. You will have to provide me with some evidence to prove your claims, and I will then submit that evidence to the Chief for approval."

Jordan thought for a moment and suddenly became animated.

"When Kacey and I met with Clara, we specifically went without Jenny or Chase. We were worried that too many people might discourage Clara from disclosing any information. Jenny and Chase, however, wanted to be a part of what was going on, so we live-streamed the audio feed to them. We recorded that entire conversation. We can give you access to the files."

"Please send me the files," Officer Tarik replied. Do you have access to them right now?"

"Yes, I do," Jordan replied. "They're right here on my phone. Just give me a minute or two, and I'll send them to you. Where should I send them?"

"Send them to my email, tarik@FRPD.com."

Jordan pulled his phone from his pocket and began to scroll through his files, his eyes focused and intense. I watched him with fascination as the blue light from the screen reflected in his pupils, causing them to dilate periodically. Suddenly, he shifted his gaze to Officer Tarik.

"Found it, sir," he said. Jordan's finger quickly moved over the send button at the bottom of his screen while Officer Tarik anxiously awaited it in his inbox. A familiar ding rang out, indicating that the email had been received. Officer Tarik, like lightning, was suddenly hovering over his keyboard, his attention laser-focused on his monitor.

"All right, I've got it," Officer Tarik replied. "You can all be on your way now. I'll be in touch with any updates on our next moves as soon as I've reviewed the audio."

The four of us nodded, acknowledging Officer Tarik's request. Jordan got up from his seat first, and we followed closely behind.

"I wonder what Officer Tarik will think once he hears the audio," I asked.

"I guess we'll know soon enough," Jordan sighed, trying to sound optimistic.

This was one of the first times I recalled Jordan showing signs of pessimism. It actually worried me that he was doubtful and unsure about the outcome of our visit with Officer Tarik. I did my best to maintain my composure and not show how anxious I felt. For once, it was my job to maintain a sense of hope. It was up to me to hold it together for us all.

CHAPTER FORTY

Wednesday, June 1st, 2022: 3:55 PM

Jordan and I were greeted by the sight of Jenny and Chase perched on the front stoop, basking in the warmth of the afternoon sun. Jenny waved at us enthusiastically.

"So, I guess we better fill the boys in on the day's events," Jenny suggested.

"I suppose," I replied.

"Enough of the banter, you two," Jordan huffed, his voice increasingly anxious. "Get on with it already."

"Alright, alright," Jenny exclaimed. "Reel it in Jordan. We'll get to it in just a minute."

Jordan, obviously frustrated, let out a loud sigh. Jenny shot an annoyed glance in his direction. Jordan reciprocated the stare, ensuring that Jenny was fully aware of his displeasure.

"So," I began, "Mr. Grieves had a chat with Jenny, me, and my mother about the situation with Ellie and the whole thing regarding the clutch. He contacted Mrs. Laughlin and asked if he could access the video footage from the dance. Mrs. Laughlin obliged, and upon inspection of the footage, Mr. Grieves confirmed that Autumn had the clutch in her possession that evening. At one point in the footage, Autumn and Ellie were observed huddling in a corner, which obviously was suspicious. Mr. Grieves and Mrs. Laughlin could ascertain that Autumn had passed the clutch off to Ellie."

Jordan and Chase stared wide-eyed, hanging on to my every word.

"There's more," I continued. "After viewing the video footage, they arranged to meet with Autumn to confront her about what they observed in the video. They allowed her to view the video and carefully observed her reaction. Autumn didn't take long to admit that she had the clutch in her possession. She then revealed that Ellie was the one who had stolen our necklaces from the gym locker. She claims that Ellie had devised an elaborate plan to frame us and make us appear that we were the ones who were trying to actually frame her for the theft of our necklaces. Ellie, apparently, was so focused on her hate for us that she went to great lengths to make us look bad."

"There's no way," Jordan exclaimed. "Why on earth would Autumn do something like that? I know Ellie had her and the others wrapped around her little finger, but to put herself in such a precarious position just to please her is plain ridiculous."

"I guess when you're desperate to fit in and be on the right side of the popularity train, you'll do just about anything," I replied.

"So I guess this means the two of you are officially off

the suspect list in connection with Ellie's disappearance?" Jordan asked.

"Yes, Mr. Grieves confirmed we are both in the clear. He forwarded the video footage and Autumn's confession to the authorities."

"And Autumn?" Jordan asked. "What's going to happen to her?"

"I'm not sure," I replied. "Mr. Grieves did say that she was likely going to be a suspect in Ellie's disappearance, but I don't really know much else."

"I'm just relieved that you and Jenny can move on with your lives now," Jordan exclaimed. "It'll be nice to feel a sense of normalcy again."

I nodded my head in agreement. It had been a long and stressful several months, and I had almost forgotten what it felt like to live freely without worries. I sometimes questioned if I deserved it, but then I reminded myself I was worthy of happiness. Hell, I was more than worthy. Jenny was more than worthy. Jordan and Chase were more than deserving. I glanced at Jenny and Chase, who melted into each other, almost as though they were celebrating their newfound freedom. Her smile lit up the room, and Chase's body relaxed as he held onto her with all his might.

"So," Jordan began, "What do we do now?"

"Well," Jenny piped up, "I'm not sure about you guys, but I think we deserve to have some fun." She looked back and forth at us, scanning our eyes for approval.

"I agree," I replied. "Any ideas, Jordan? What should we do? Movie? Dinner? Mini-golf? Escape room? You pick."

"Wait," Jenny objected. "Why does he get to pick?"

"Okay, fine, Jenny," I replied. "What would you like to do?"

"Nah, it's fine," Jenny teased ."Jordan can pick. I was trying to grind your gears a bit."

I laughed out loud at Jenny's attempt to be humorous. Boy, was it ever nice to feel normal once again. It was honestly refreshing. Little did I know that the drama surrounding Ellie's disappearance would again rear its ugly head, just not for a couple of years in the future.

CHAPTER FORTY-ONE

Friday, May 31st, 2024: 5:07 PM

It had been two whole days since our meeting with Officer Tarik, and to say that we were enveloped with anxiety would have been an understatement. I did everything I could to keep busy, attending all of my classes, engrossing myself in extracurricular activities, and even volunteering for the bake sale at school. Despite my best efforts, my mind still refused to let go of all the ifs and buts of the situation. What if the authorities didn't believe our story? What if they didn't investigate and Ellie remained trapped within the walls? I had to find a way to escape the doom and gloom that had taken over my life. Jenny was the cure to my ailment, as always. Her relaxed and carefree nature made it easy to forget life's worries, even if just for a moment.

"Hey, Buttercup," she chirped happily from the other end of the phone. "What's going on? Any news since we left school at the end of the day?"

"No, nothing yet," I sighed. My mind is swirling with these doom-and-gloom scenarios, and I struggle to remain optimistic."

"I feel that one hundred percent," Jenny agreed. "Believe it or not, Kace, despite my brilliant outward appearance and the air of confidence in my voice, I'm struggling too. We've been through a lot, and I'd think it foolish to believe that we all aren't struggling in some way or another."

"I know," I replied. "You know me, Jenn. I just let my anxiety take over, and once that happens, my mind goes to these dark places."

"Now you stop it," Jenny interrupted assertively. "You've come a long way, Kace. I've seen you step up despite your anxiety and conquer fears you never would have dreamed of conquering. And, despite all of the drama we've been through over the past couple of years, you've managed to maintain a sense of calm and peace regarding your relationships. That takes a huge amount of effort and commitment. Don't sell yourself short."

I was utterly stunned by Jenny's sudden declaration of achievement on my behalf. My eyes began to water, and despite my best efforts, the tears rolled gracefully down my cheeks. I took a deep breath, trying to regain my composure before responding. My silence must have triggered something within her because she suddenly began to console me from the other end of the phone.

"You okay?" Jenny whispered softly. "It's okay to be emotional. We're all humans, after all, and I'd never judge a person for displaying their emotions openly."

"Yeah, I'm good," I replied, wiping a tear from my eye. "I'm just really touched by what you said. It's not often I get someone singing my praises. I suppose I'm just not used to it."

"Well, get used to it," Jenny commanded. "You've been front and center for this entire roller coaster ride. Truthfully, I don't know what I would have done without you."

I smiled and then let out an abrupt giggle. I couldn't help but be amused by Jenny's commanding tone.

"What's so funny?" Jenny asked.

"Nothing," I replied. "I'm just amused by your assertiveness."

"Well, I'm glad I could make you laugh and lighten up the mood, even if just for a minute or two," Jenny replied.

"You always know how to turn a frown upside down," I replied.

Our conversation was interrupted by footsteps thundering their way up the stairs and toward my room. A loud and abrupt knock reverberated throughout the room.

"Hey, Jenny. Hold on a second. Someone's knocking on my bedroom door."

I quickly pounced to my feet, tossing my phone recklessly onto the bed. My mother stood on the other side of the door, her face stone cold and serious.

"Hey mom," I greeted hesitantly. "What's going on?"

"Kacey?" she asked. "Why is Officer Tarik calling to speak with you?"

I quickly ran over to the bed, picking up my phone. "Jenny, I'll have to call you back."

My mother gazed at me intensely, waiting for me to return my attention to the question.

"Uhm, yeah, Mom. Sorry, I was just going to tell you about that," I muttered. "Jenny, Jordan, Chase and I decided to reinvestigate Ellie's missing persons case."

"What?" my mother exclaimed, surprised by this sudden revelation. "Why? Why would you want to reopen that can of worms?"

"Well," I began. "It's a long story."

"I've got all the time in the world," my mother replied gruffly. "Start talking."

I explained the meeting details with Officer Tarik to my mother, who listened intently to my every word. She nodded her head in acknowledgement several times but never once interrupted me. I was half expecting her to lash out in anger or frustration, but she never once gave a glimpse of what she was thinking. That's one thing that always scared me about my mother; her facial expressions never revealed her inner thoughts or feelings. She could have been planning my murder, and I'd never have been the wiser. After I finished rehashing all of the finer details of our meeting with Officer Tarik, she turned to me and hugged me tight.

"Kacey, you should have told me all of this. I had no idea that you and your friends had seen the amber eyes again or that Jenny had been injured, not once, but twice. And the whole connection to Ellie and the Mason family. Why wouldn't you come to me? Why put yourselves through all of this again?"

"To be honest, Mom," I began hesitantly. "Other than the reappearance of the amber eyes, we had no inclination that there was a connection to Ellie's disappearance, at first, anyway. It wasn't until Jenny conversed with her father about the events from the night of the dance that some suspicious information came to light."

"What events?" my mother pried. "You mean the reports of a young woman screaming and the Grays reporting seeing a young woman fitting Ellie's description on the edge of town by the wooded area?"

"No," I replied. "Like how there was a power outage at the scientific research center and how Mr. Forester found the DNA sample he was working on had vanished."

"What!" my mother exclaimed, shocked by my revelation.

"That's not all, Mom," I continued.

"There's more?" she questioned, her voice increasingly high-pitched.

"The DNA sample was that of an extinct Dire Wolf," I continued. "And when the power came back, not only was the DNA sample missing but there were claw marks on the steel walls inside the extraction chamber."

My mother's eyes grew wide, and her body language indicated she was having difficulty contemplating the scenario I was describing.

"Not only that, Mom, but Mr. Forester had also reported hearing growling from within the chamber just before the power was restored."

"So what you're telling me is that all of this occurred the same evening of the dance—the same evening that the amber eyes were first reported—the same evening Ellie disappeared?" my mother asked.

"Yes," I replied. "Everything coincides with the events of that evening. That's why we decided to reinvestigate the case after our encounter at the waterfall. When Jenny ended up in the hospital, I ran into Mr. Forester. He was adamant that Jordan, Chase, Jenny, or me not report the incident to the authorities."

"Well, that's a bit strange," my mother replied questioningly. "Why would he ask that you not report the incident? Wouldn't he want the town folk to know that something was lurking and that extra precaution may be necessary while the authorities investigate the matter?"

"That's exactly what I thought," I replied. "That's why I suggested that Jenny speak to her father once she was released from the hospital."

"And how did that go?" my mother asked.

"It took a bit of time for Jenny to build up her courage to ask him, but when she did, he explained everything that had happened at the research centre and told her that the only reason he thought the incident at the waterfall was best left quiet was because he was concerned about being implicated in something by the authorities. He was worried they would assume he was involved in Ellie's disappearance, especially since whatever chased us at the waterfall had the same amber-coloured eyes as the ones that first appeared that night."

"I suppose that makes sense," my mother pondered. "I'm just struggling to understand how Mr. Forester thought it was a good idea to not bring any attention to the incident at the scientific research center. I know you had mentioned that he was scared of being implicated in Ellie's disappearance, but there had to be somebody who could have verified his whereabouts that night? There must have been other employees who had seen him, or perhaps security footage with a time stamp showing the events of the evening as they unfolded."

"You're absolutely right, Mom. Mr. Forester was not thinking straight. It's not as though he made the connection between the events at the research center and Ellie's disappearance. As a matter of fact, he wouldn't have even known about Ellie's disappearance until the following morning."

"That is true," my mother replied. "Not a single person in town knew what had happened that evening until the following morning. But still, you'd think he'd mention it after the fact, you know, in case it could lead to information that could help solve Ellie's disappearance."

"So, did Officer Tarik say what he wanted?" I asked.

"No. He wouldn't disclose any information to me; however, if everything you've told me is true, I'm going to assume he's got some information about what you and your friends discovered at the Mason house."

"Did he want me to call him back?" I asked.

"He didn't say. But I will assume he called you for a reason, and it wasn't just to exchange pleasantries."

"I suppose you're right," I exclaimed. "Do you mind if I go call him back now?"

"No, not all. Go do whatever it is you need to do."

"Thank you, Mom." As I walked away, I felt my mother's hand gently tap my shoulder.

"Kacey, don't hesitate to contact me if you need anything. I'm your mother. I'll always have your back, no matter what."

I turned to face my mother and smiled warmly as I walked up the stairs and to my room. I was nervous about what Officer Tarik might say, but I knew ignoring the problem wouldn't solve anything. I had to suck it up and face the music. I pulled my phone from the pocket of my jeans and slowly dialled the number on the business card that Officer Tarik had given me the other day. A few rings later, a voice emanated from the phone.

"Hi, Officer Tarik. It's Kacey."

CHAPTER FORTY-TWO

Friday, May 31st, 2024: 5:28 PM

Officer Tarik answered the phone, his voice breathless and his tone rushed and hurried, almost as if he had just run a marathon. I was taken aback as it hadn't been that long since his conversation with my mother.

"Officer Tarik here," he huffed. "How can I help you?"

"Yeah, ummm… it's Kacey Lundgren, sir. My mom had mentioned that you wanted to speak to me."

"Oh yes, Ms. Lundgren. I did call and initially wanted to follow up regarding the reports you made concerning the Mason residence. Fortunately for you, there was a break in the case in the short time between my initial phone call and now."

"Oh!" I responded, my curiosity growing. "Are you allowed to give me any details? I wouldn't ask if I didn't have a personal connection to the case."

"Actually, Ms. Lundgren, I can. I'm pleased to tell you

that Ms. Mason has been located safe and sound. After two long years, she is finally free."

"Free?" I asked.

'Yes, free," Officer Tarik replied. "It's exactly like how you reported. Ms. Mason was being held captive behind the walls of her home in some sort of makeshift shelter. As it turns out, Mr. Mason was behind her disappearance the entire time."

"Are you serious?" I cried out, both shocked and saddened by the thought of Ellie being forced to live two years of her life in isolation. What kind of a father would do that to his own child, I thought? Even when your relationship with someone is less than ideal, sympathy is still a quality I hold dear to my heart, and my heart undoubtedly hurts for Ellie. "But what about needing a warrant and all that? Did the audio footage of our conversation with Clara provide enough evidence to issue a search warrant?"

"Not quite," Officer Tarik replied. "It did give us a clear indication that we needed to meet with Clara and further question her insights into the happenings within the home over the past two years. Her testimony gave us enough evidence to produce a warrant and thoroughly search the home."

"And what about the creature?" I asked. "We witnessed Ellie transforming into a wolf-like creature with amber eyes? You know, the same amber eyes that everyone reported on the night of her disappearance. The same amber eyes that we saw up at the waterfall a few months back. Did Mr. Mason give an explanation for that?"

"Not yet, however, we took him into police custody, and we will be interrogating him soon."

"What about Ellie?" I asked. "If you haven't been able to confirm with Mr. Mason the connection between her and the creature, then where is she being kept? I can't imagine it would be safe or wise to allow her to wander freely as she desires."

"Ellie is currently safe in an undisclosed location. We will be conducting an interview with her in addition to Mr. Mason."

"Okay then," I replied. "Will you please keep me posted with any news or updates?"

"I will, Kacey. And I won't need to interview you any further. We have all the information we need for now."

"Thank you, Officer Tarik. Is it alright if I fill in Jenny, Jordan, and Chase on the most recent events?"

"Yes," Officer Tarik replied. "All of you played an integral part in helping find Ellie. I have no issues with you sharing the details of our conversation with them."

"Thank you, Officer Tarik. Have a great evening."

"You too, Ms. Lundgren."

No sooner had I hung up with Officer Tarik than I was dialling Jenny's number. I could hardly fathom that this two-year mystery could finally come to a close. It wasn't long before I heard a slight clicking on the other end of the phone.

"Hey, Jenny," I called out. "Officer Tarik called. He's got some news about Ellie and what we discovered at the Mason house."

"Oh, really?" Jenny asked, her voice oozing with curiosity? "What did he have to say?"

"Apparently, our audio file from the conversation with

Clara prompted the authorities to question Clara further about the happenings within the Mason home. Her testimony allowed the authorities to issue a search warrant."

"Oooohhh…interesting. So, what happened? Did they find Ellie?"

"Oh yeah. They found her alright," I replied. "They took her to a secure location; I guess they want to make sure she's safe and that the public isn't in danger until they can get a statement from Mr. Mason."

"Makes sense," Jenny replied. "Have they asked Ellie about how she ended up behind the walls of her home and remained unnoticed all those years?"

"Officer Tarik didn't say. All he would tell me was that she was somewhere secure. He did tell me that he would keep me posted on any new information that came to light. He did say that since we were so closely connected to the case, he could keep us in the loop and that it wouldn't be a conflict of interest."

"Well, that's something, I guess," Jenny retorted. "I wonder what Mr. Mason will have to say for himself? How is he going to explain what happened at the research centre? How will he explain the timing of Ellie's disappearance in conjunction with the dance and the appearance of the amber eyes? I have so many questions."

"I think we all do," I agreed. "I'm not sure how long it's going to take to hear back from Officer Tarik, but I think we should fill Jordan and Chase in on the news in the meantime."

"I suppose we should," Jenny replied. "You want to call Jordan, and I'll call Chase, or do you think we should all get together and discuss this in person?"

"This sort of feels like an in-person type of conversation, don't you think?"

"Yeah, it really does," Jenny agreed.

Jenny and I swiftly broke away from our conversation, anxious to fill the boys in on the current situation with Ellie. My fingers feverishly dialled Jordan's number. The phone rang several times in succession, which was strange because Jordan usually had his phone glued to his hand. I was just about to hang up when he answered, his voice breathless.

"Hey, Kacey. What's up?"

"I was just about to ask you the same thing," I replied suspiciously. "Anything you want to tell me?"

"I was just getting ready to head over to your place. I've got some news I wanted to share with you."

"Oh really," I replied, my eyebrows arching. "Exactly what type of news?"

"News about Ellie and what we discovered the other night."

I grew silent for several seconds, but it felt more like minutes. My mind swirled with all of the information I had discussed with Jenny and Officer Tarik. How did Jordan know anything about Ellie's situation? Officer Tarik had never mentioned calling Jordan. In fact, he gave me permission to fill Jordan in on the details of our discussion.

"So, did Officer Tarik call you?" I asked.

"No, actually. I ran into him at the coffee shop about 15 minutes ago. He told me all about how our audio file led to a search warrant, how Ellie was found safe, the whole thing."

So that's why Officer Tarik sounded tired and out of breath when I returned his call, I thought. He must have been out running errands before making a pit stop at the coffee shop.

"Well then, I guess I don't need to fill you in on the details of my discussion with Officer Tarik," I replied. Sounds like he filled you in on everything already."

"Yeah, I guess he did," Jordan replied. "He also told me that he would interrogate Mr. Mason tonight. He said he wanted to get the whole story sorted out as soon as possible to get Ellie out of isolation and back home with the rest of her family."

"Really!" I exclaimed, surprised by this admission. "Officer Tarik never mentioned anything to me about interrogating Mr. Mason tonight. I wonder why he decided to inform you of his plans, not me?"

"He did receive a call while we discussed the case, and he seemed rather flustered. I don't know who he was speaking to, but whoever it was must have had something significant to say because that's when he blurted out that he had to leave right away so he could go and talk to Mr. Mason."

"Strange," I replied. "And all he would say is that he wanted to interrogate him right away so Ellie could go home as soon as possible?"

"Yeah, exactly," Jordan replied. "I asked him why he had to rush off so fast, and that's all the information he would give me. I'm pretty sure there's more to it, but he didn't seem eager to continue our conversation. He just grabbed his coffee and rushed out the door."

Jordan's account of his interaction with Officer Tarik gave me something to ponder. Perhaps there was more to this story than we were aware of, but there was only one way to find out.

"Hey Jordan? I know you were on your way to my place. Do you want to come pick me up? Then we'll go get Jenny and Chase. I think there's somewhere we should be."

"Sure. I'll be there in about ten minutes."

I hung up the phone and made my way to the front porch. As I sat on the stoop waiting for Jordan to arrive, my mind manifested every wild scenario possible. What was Mr. Mason hiding? Whatever it was, it had to be really big if Officer Tarik took off in such a hurry. I was anxious to find out. Jordan suddenly pulled up, and I hurriedly climbed into the passenger seat, anxious to get some answers.

CHAPTER FORTY-THREE

May 31st, 2024: 6:25 PM

After making a pitstop to pick up Jenny and Chase, I finally let Jordan in on the location of our mystery destination. He appeared rather surprised and hesitant to go to the police station. Jenny, as per usual, was full speed ahead, ready to take on anything. Just as we approached the police station, Jordan slowed down, looking for the perfect spot to park his vehicle. Once he found the ideal place, he slowly pulled in and shut off the engine. He hesitated briefly before glancing over at me, his eyes searching for any clue as to why we were there.

"Jordan, I know what you're thinking," I began, "You're trying to figure out why I dragged you all over here to the police precinct."

"Sort of," he replied, sounding confused. "I thought we were all free and clear from this point on. What could the authorities possibly still need from us? Wasn't the audio file enough?"

"You're right, Jordan, you're absolutely right," I agreed. "There's just something that doesn't feel quite right like something is beckoning me to come here. I can't explain it. It's just a feeling I have."

"Well," Jenny interjected, "If something is beckoning you, Kace, I say we just march in there and demand to know what's going on with Mr. Mason." She looked around, first at me, then at Jordan and lastly at Chase. I nodded, and without saying another word, the four of us exited the vehicle and entered the police precinct.

I gently pushed the door to the precinct open, and it squeaked with authority, garnering the woman's attention at the reception desk. She lifted her head from her computer screen, tilting her glasses slightly down the bridge of her nose.

"Can I help you?" she chimed enthusiastically.

"Uhm…," I hesitated. "Yes, you can. I spoke with Officer Tarik earlier today regarding the case concerning Ellie Mason. I was informed that Officer Tarik may have stumbled across some information regarding Mr. Mason's involvement in the case. I was hoping that, since the audio file my friends and I submitted led to the discovery of Ellie, we could talk to him and perhaps get an update on any new developments in the case."

The woman stared at the four of us questioningly for a moment, her eyes perhaps searching for sincerity in our motives. She looked down at her computer monitor and began typing. She scanned from left to right before clicking her mouse and scanning the next page.

"What are your names?" she asked, glancing up briefly to

meet my eyes.

"My name is Kacey Lundgren," I replied. "This is Jordan, Jenny Forester, and Chase." I pointed at each of them as I recited their names.

The woman continued to type, scanning each page of text with precision. "Ah, yes," she began. "I see here that Officer Tarik contacted you earlier this afternoon. There's a notation here saying that it was no longer necessary to interview either yourself or any of your friends. May I then ask what business you have with Officer Tarik?"

"I just told you all of that," I replied, increasingly frustrated. "I'm here because my boyfriend Jordan ran into Officer Tarik at the coffee shop after the Officer and I had spoken. Jordan told me that, while there, Officer Tarik received a phone call implying that there had been a break in the case. He had to rush off in a hurry to question Mr. Mason."

"I see," the woman replied. Could you please give me a moment? I'll check to see if Officer Tarik is available to meet with you."

She scurried off down the hall toward Officer Tarik's office. I exchanged nervous glances with Jordan, Jenny, and Chase. The three of them instinctively knew my anxiety was heightened and raced over, blanketing me in a warm embrace. It was all too easy to overlook the importance of a friend support group, but at that moment, I vowed never to take it for granted again. A few moments later, the woman returned, motioning for us to follow her. We followed the woman reluctantly down the hall, our faces showing signs of exhaustion. All we wanted to do was to put this behind us once and for all. Just as we neared Officer Tarik's office, we heard loud thumping followed by an exasperated sigh.

The woman hesitated before opening the door to the office, knocking delicately three times.

"Is everything okay, Officer?" she called out with concern. "I've got Ms. Lundgren and her friends here."

"Yes, everything's good," Officer Tarik replied, his voice audible through the closed door. "You can show them in."

The woman opened the door and gently popped her head in to meet Officer Tarik's gaze. He motioned with his eyes at the row of chairs from across his desk. The four of us entered the office without a word, plunking ourselves down into the chairs. Officer Tarik was laser-focused on whatever was plastered across his computer screen. His eyes met mine briefly before he gestured with his hand.

"Just one moment," he called out. "Let me just finish up with my report." Officer Tarik continued typing furiously, his eyes squinting every so often in frustration. His brows furrowed as though he were in deep thought. After several minutes of typing, he finally acknowledged our presence. "Hey there. Sorry about that. I had some important business to take care of. I'm assuming you heard the news about Mr. Mason?"

"Well, that depends on what news you're referring to," I replied. Jordan told me he ran into you at the coffee shop sometime after our earlier call. He said you received a phone call, and you had to rush off super fast because of something to do with Mr. Mason."

"That's true," Officer Tarik replied. "I suppose that's why you're here?"

"Yes," I replied. "You did say that you could disclose information concerning the case, after all."

"Yes, I sure did," Officer Tarik replied. He drew in a deep

breath. "You might want to grab yourselves a drink and hunker down. This is going to be one hell of a story."

Jordan, Jenny, Chase and I sat still, our eyes focused on Officer Tarik.

"So, when I ran into Jordan at the coffee shop, I got a call from one of my colleagues at the department here. He said that Clara, the housekeeper, had stopped by with some information that she wanted to share. Apparently, it had something to do with Mr. Mason and Ellie's disappearance. Of course, I was intrigued. I asked my colleague to fill me in on what other information Clara had to share. He advised me to head down to the station immediately as this was better handled in person than over the phone. So, that's when I rushed out of the coffee shop and returned to the station."

Jenny, Jordan, Chase and I exchanged curious glances. What other information could Clara have regarding Ellie and Mr. Mason? When Officer Tarik and I last spoke, he spoke as though everything had been settled and there was nothing more to investigate.

"So?" I questioned. "What did Clara have to say?"

"Well, here's the thing," Officer Tarik began. "By the time I arrived back here, Clara had already given her statement and had left the station. I wasn't exactly pleased as I had wanted to speak to her myself, but circumstances didn't provide me that luxury. So, I met with my colleague who recorded the statement, and the information he shared was shocking, to say the least."

My eyes widened, and my heart thumped wildly in my chest. I could see Jordan's brows arch upward in curiosity, hanging on to every word Officer Tarik spoke. Jenny and

Chase frantically exchanged glances, then stared at Officer Tarik in anticipation, longing to know what he would reveal next.

"Clara claims that while cleaning in Mr. Mason's office, she stumbled across a document that had blown off his desk from a gust of wind from the nearby window. When she went to pick it up, something caught her eye, and she couldn't help but sneak a quick glance."

"So, what was it?" Jenny asked.

"You are all going to find this hard to believe," Officer Tarik started. "The document revealed that Mr. Mason's discovery of the Dire Wolf specimen led to a new specialized method of extracting DNA and that this new piece of equipment that Jenny's father was put in charge of was the catalyst for his latest experiment."

"That's not exactly new information," Jenny retorted. "My father told me about the new equipment and how it was designed to extract DNA from fossilized remains."

"But that's not everything," Officer Tarik interjected. "The document also showed that in addition to extracting the DNA from the Dire Wolf specimen, a human subjects DNA was also involved."

My eyes widened in shock. "A human subject?" I asked. "Who would volunteer for such an experiment? Wouldn't there be risk involved? And what exactly would a human subject have to do with extracting DNA from a Dire Wolf?" It suddenly dawned on me. Is this how Ellie managed to turn into a vicious, snarling, wolf-like creature? Is this why Mr. Mason had her locked away for all of these years? Was he actually using his own daughter as a subject for his wildly controversial experiments? I had a suspicion this is what happened, and this new information confirms it. "I don't believe there was anything voluntary about what the human specimen was subjected to," Officer Tarik continued. Our initial investigation and the subsequent conversations with Mr. Mason confirm that."

"So what you're saying is that Ellie was forced to be a part of this experiment," I replied. "That Mr. Mason used his own daughter to further his career against her will."

"Yes and no," Officer Tarik replied.

I looked at Officer Tarik, puzzled by what he had just said. "What do you mean by yes and no?" I asked. "How can it be both?"

Officer Tarik looked me straight in the eyes, his facial expression as serious as I had ever seen it. "Yes, Mr. Mason used his daughter in his experiment, but no, it wasn't Ellie he subjected to it."

Jordan, Chase, Jenny and I all exchanged confused glances.

"But…" I paused briefly, "Mr. Mason only has two children; Jason and Ellie."

"That's where you're wrong, Ms. Lundgren," Officer Tarik corrected. "After confronting Mr. Mason about the document that Clara found, it was revealed that Ellie has a twin sister."

"What?" we all gasped in unison.

"But if that's true," I began, "then where has she been all this time? How is it that nobody knew that Ellie had a twin sister? Why did Ellie never mention having a twin?"

CHAPTER FORTY-FOUR

May 31st, 2024: 6:38 PM

The four of us sat stunned, clinging to every word Officer Tarik muttered. Every so often, Jenny would glance at me, her eyes searching mine for reassurance that she wasn't imagining this entire situation.

"According to Mr. Mason, Mrs. Mason gave birth to twin girls, Ellie and Kaitlyn," Officer Tarik explained. "Mr. Mason had already long been involved in various expeditions for fossil recovery. During the early years of his expeditions, he became interested in the concept of DNA extraction and manipulation. So when he discovered that he and Mrs. Mason were expecting twins, he took that as the perfect opportunity to push his obsession with DNA manipulation into full tilt."

The four of us continued to listen intently, taking extreme caution not to miss a single syllable.

"Ellie was the firstborn and was approximately 4 minutes

older than Kaitlyn," Officer Tarik continued. "According to Mr. Mason, he paid the hospital staff quite a hefty sum of money to fake Kaitlyn's death and then leave the country. He claims he wanted to cover all of his bases by ensuring that there was no risk the hospital staff would let his secret leak. Apparently, Mrs. Mason had no idea that her infant daughter was, in fact, still alive. Mr. Mason claims to have taken Kaitlyn to an undisclosed location where she was taken care of and raised by a privately hired nanny who was also paid a large sum for her discretion."

"So Ellie never knew she had a twin sister?" I asked, perplexed. "Mr. or Mrs. Mason never thought to tell her? And what about Jason? He didn't know either?"

"As Mr. Mason explains it, he convinced his wife it would be best to never let the other children know of Kaitlyn's existence so that they wouldn't have to live through the same trauma they were forced to endure," Officer Tarik replied.

"What trauma?" I shouted. "I can understand Mrs. Mason having trauma, but Mr. Mason? He knew the entire time that his daughter was alive. He's a monster for doing that to his family. What kind of a person would willingly put his family through something so horrific?"

"I feel the same way you do, Ms. Lundgren," Officer Tarik agreed.

"So, what you're telling us is that the girl we encountered behind the walls in the Mason house wasn't Ellie at all, but rather her long lost twin Kaitlyn?"

"Exactly, Ms. Lundgren. Mr. Mason confessed that he had kept his daughter hidden all of these years for the sole purpose of his DNA research. He admits to taking extracted DNA from the Dire Wolf specimen and injecting it into his daughter."

"Does that mean that the mysterious amber eyes people reported seeing on the evening of the Spring Fling Dance belonged to Kaitlyn?" I asked. "What about the events that unfolded at the research center that night? Was the mysterious growling and the claw marks inside the extraction chamber a result of Kaitlyn attempting to break free? And how about the power outage? Was that just orchestrated by Mr. Mason to keep his secret from getting out?"

"All questions we asked Mr. Mason during the interrogation," Officer Tarik replied. "And yes, he confessed to all of it."

"Then what about Ellie?" I asked. "Where has she been for the past two years? The Grays reported seeing someone fitting her description at the edge of town close to the forested area. Others reported hearing the screams of a young woman. Then there was the clutch with our necklaces found nearby. Where is she?"

"That's the missing piece of the puzzle, isn't it?" Officer Tarik asked.

Jordan, Chase, Jenny, and I glanced at one another questioningly and then averted our gaze back to Officer Tarik, desperately searching his eyes for any shred of information.

"Sadly, Mr. Mason confirmed that Ellie has passed," Officer Tarik continued.

Our mouths dropped open in shock, and despite our questionable history with Ellie, Jenny and I quietly shed a tear.

"What…what happened?" I stammered.

"It turns out that Ellie ran into Kaitlyn, or rather the wolf-like creature version of her, on the way home from the dance. Frightened, she ran toward the wooded area to attempt to hide. According to Mr. Mason, this is where Ellie was violently attacked and eventually succumbed to her wounds."

"So Kaitlyn killed her?" I asked.

"I'm afraid so," Officer Tarik replied.

"But… what happened to her body?" Jenny asked. "She's been reported as missing for the past two years. If Mr. Mason knew about her death, why would he go on national television and pretend that she was missing?"

"We asked Mr. Mason that question too. He claims that he knew that if anyone found out about Ellie's death, there would be an investigation into the matter, and that might blow his cover in regards to his experiments with Kaitlyn. He says he couldn't risk anyone finding out about Kaitlyn's existence despite his despair over Ellie's death. So, despite his personal feelings, he played the role of the victim, leading Mrs. Mason and everyone else to believe that Ellie had mysteriously vanished on her way home from the dance."

"I wonder if this is why Mr. Mason didn't report Ellie's disappearance right away?" I asked. "He probably needed time to figure out what to do with her body and create a false cover story to protect his own interests. Did Mr. Mason mention where Ellie's body was?"

"He did," Officer Tarik replied. "He claims to have buried

her body in a shallow grave a few miles into the woods on the edge of town."

"Hey, Jordan," I called out, suddenly having flashbacks from our conversation with Clara. "Do you remember Clara mentioning that Mr. Mason had been talking to someone on the phone about taking Ellie to a safe place?"

"I vaguely remember, yeah," he replied.

"I bet he was talking about her body. It all makes sense now. He even told Mrs. Mason that he had important business to deal with and that she shouldn't wait up for him. My god, he actually covered up his daughter's murder."

"It's all true," Officer Tarik agreed. "Mr. Mason admitted to everything. We're holding him here overnight, and then he'll be transferred to a maximum security facility until his court hearing."

"What's going to happen to Kaitlyn," I asked. "She's never been integrated into society. She's never met any of her family aside from her father. She's had no real social interaction. She's probably never even had a formal education. Not to mention, she's been exposed to this Dire Wolf DNA. What measures are in place to help keep her safe and healthy?"

"For now, we're keeping her in a secured psychiatric facility," Officer Tarik responded. "She isn't restrained or anything like that, but she is separated from other patients for both their safety and hers. We have reached out to some of the finest scientists specializing in DNA research and extraction to try and find a cure for her...," Officer Tarik paused, "disease or ailment, I suppose, for lack of a better word."

"What happens if there's nothing you can do for her?" I asked. "Does she just stay in the psychiatric facility forever?"

"We haven't thought that far ahead, Ms. Lundgren, but I assure you she is being well taken care of. We have informed Mrs. Mason and the rest of the Mason family about Kaitlyn. We also had to break the unfortunate news regarding Ellie's death. Kaitlyn is in good hands, I promise."

I nodded in agreement before turning to look over at my friends, who all wore expressions of shock. I didn't know what to say or how to process this information. It was like something out of a science fiction novel. Jenny, out of the four of us, had the closest connection to this whole debacle, as her father was an employee of the scientific research center. Although we all knew he wasn't involved in the controversial experiments that Mr. Mason had subjected Kaitlyn to, it didn't ease Jenny's worries about her father's safety and job security. Like the rest of us, she was concerned about potential backlash from the community toward the employees of the research center. I hugged Jenny tightly and reassured her that we would support her in any way she or her family needed.

"So…" I began, staring Officer Tarik squarely in the eyes. "I guess this whole chapter of Fort Richfields' story is officially closed?"

"I suppose it is," Officer Tarik replied.

The four of us stood up from our seats and made our way out of Officer Tariks office. We all linked arms and huddled close together as we made our way down the hall and toward the exit of the police precinct. The mood was solemn yet strangely light. It felt like a huge weight had been lifted. Just before we exited the building, I turned to look at Officer Tarik, who looked at the four of us with a smile. I think he felt some sense of relief, too. I waved at him, and he waved back enthusiastically.

"Goodbye, Ms. Lundgren," he whispered as the four of us disappeared out of sight.

ABOUT THE AUTHOR

Crystal Tamboline is a wife and mother of one son and 4 fabulous dogs. She was born in Vancouver, British Columbia, and eventually relocated to Spruce Grove, Alberta, in 2018. She attended David Thompson High School in Vancouver, which is where her passion for writing took flight. She credits her creative writing teacher and drama teacher for instilling in her a love for writing and the creative arts.

After spending 20 years working in the retail industry, Crystal found herself contemplating a career change when her husband was offered a job in Edmonton, Alberta. The move from B.C. to Alberta provided the perfect opportunity to further her education, eventually leading to her role as an educational assistant.

Crystal now works with students, providing educational support and instilling in them the same passion for writing that her teachers instilled in her.

In her spare time, Crystal enjoys listening to music (her favourite pastime), attending concerts, reading, going on road trips, and spending time with her family and dogs.

You can reach out to Crystal at crystalbill@telus.net

www.ingramcontent.com/pod-product-compliance
Lightning Source LLC
Chambersburg PA
CBHW070841260626
47170CB00007B/2463